SOLITAIRE

by

JOY PEACH

Copyright © Joy Peach 1996

All rights reserved.

No part of this book may be reproduced by any means, nor transmitted, nor translated into a machine language, without the written permission of the publisher.

Prospero Books
46 West Street
Chichester
West Sussex
PO19 1RP

A CIP catalogue record for this book is available from the British Library.

ISBN 1 873475 95 0

Printed and bound in Great Britain.

Solitaire is a work of fiction and none of the characters are based on real people. Any similarity between one of them and any living person is purely coincidental.

Cover photography by Bill Watson.

to Chris with love.

For Walter, the very best of friends.

*And for my children,
Richard, Georgie, Will and Kate.*

With love.

*from

Joy Leach*

"As soon as I could write, I made a little book with a calico cover, and every Sunday I wrote in it any merry time or good fortune we had had in the week, and so kept them. And if times had been troublous and bitter for me, I wrote that down too and was eased."

**from Precious Bane
by Mary Webb**

Chapter One

I suppose you could say it started when I went down to Sussex on that painting weekend.

It was easy enough to get to Chichester by train, but the Conference Centre itself was way out in the country, nine or ten miles at least, with no public transport as far as I could discover. I mentioned this problem on my application form, and the Bursar phoned to suggest I should contact this Rear Admiral fellow who lived in Chichester and could probably be persuaded to give me a lift out to Donnington from the train.

"He's a delightful old boy," the Bursar told me. "One of our regulars. I've had a word with him this morning, so he'll be expecting to hear from you." He gave me the phone number and left the rest to me.

"Of course, I'll be only too pleased to run you out there," Rear Admiral Redbridge assured me when I got through to him that evening. "No trouble at all, my dear. Now which train were you thinking of coming down on?"

"There's one that gets in at five-forty-five. I thought that would be about right."

"Well, I've a better idea," he said warmly. "Why don't you get an earlier train. The one that arrives at three-forty-five would give you time to have a cup of tea with me before we set off for Donnington."

So that's what I did, and although I'm a pretty independent buddy nowadays, I had to admit it was nice to be met at the station.

"How shall I pick you out?" I'd asked him on the phone. "Will you be wearing your admiral's hat?"

"No, I'm afraid not," he chuckled. "All that paraphernalia has been in mothballs for years. I'm bearded, if that's any help. A grey beard. And tall and thin. How about yourself?"

"Oh, Lordy - I'm a bit scruffy really," I explained, suddenly realising what an incongruous companion I was for anyone of rank or distinction. "I generally wear jeans and an old dufflecoat, and I'll have my painting gear in a haversack."

"Righto! I'll be looking out for the scruffiest person on the train, then. That should be an easy assignment."

And it was, of course. He'd picked me out before I'd reached the barrier.

"Admiral Redbridge?" I'd asked, knowing full well it was him. Tall and spare and erect. A thin intellectual face with bushy eyebrows and a neat beard. A Jesus face grown grey. This was certainly the only admiral in sight.

But, "No!" he said, whisking the case out of my hand, and steering me across the road to his car. "It's Walter. Just plain Walter. Now come along, my dear. I'm sure you must be more than ready for a cup of tea."

I had sensed that he was on his own. So many widowers go to pieces, don't they. But not this one. There was a well-cared-for feeling about his little house, the end one in a modest Georgian terrace near the station. We were soon enjoying tea and scones, the firelight reflecting the friendly scene in the plump silver teapot.

"I like to try my hand at new recipes," said Walter, pressing me to another slice of his excellent walnut loaf.

It was a good course. Lots of talented and interesting people, all of them bursting with enthusiasm. Two whole glorious days to devote to painting. No domestic distractions. No Pop music or contentious teenagers to put up with. Bliss!

It was the first time I had left them on their own, but my friend Stella had promised to look in, and if anything serious happened they could always phone their father. They'd probably enjoy coping without me. It wasn't as if I was neglecting them completely. I'd left a cold chicken in the fridge, and a blackberry and apple pie, their favourite. And good heavens, they were scarcely children any longer. Claire would be sixteen after Christmas. Henry was seventeen already.

Anyway, there comes a time when you just have to do your own thing, no matter what.

I hadn't always wanted to paint. The idea had sprouted when the children were quite small. I can tell you exactly when germination took place.

I'd dived into the Art Gallery in the High Street one winter afternoon, simply to get out of the rain. I was on my way home from a particularly unpleasant visit to the dentist. I seem to have lost at least one tooth for each baby the way so many mothers do. It's a good job I stopped at four.

There was an exhibition on, I remember, of the work of the local Art Club. Probably many of the paintings were pretty mediocre, but for me they were magic. I treated myself to a catalogue, which was an act of independence in itself. I always had to account for every penny I spent, and exhibitions and fripperies of that sort were definitely not on Pete's list of priorities. But then, very few things were.

First I went round the pictures in order, checking them off against the catalogue, noticing the names of the artists and the titles they had chosen. Then after a few minutes gathering my strength on a seat opposite a particularly splendid landscape - downlands at harvest-time : I can still recall its vivid shades of brown and orange and red - I went back to the ones I had liked most and began to study them in detail.

I forgot about the younger children left with Madge-next-door, and Thomas and Charlotte who would be coming in from school to a cold empty house. I forgot about the line of nappies getting soaked in the storm, and everyone waiting for tea.

"We're closing now, Madam," the attendant called out rather grumpily, as if maybe he'd said it before and got no response. "The gallery shuts at six."

Six. Six o'clock! Quick, quick - now there would be trouble.

And there was!

From that day forward, secretly, silently at first, as if it were a shameful weakness, an addiction, I began to paint. I hadn't got much of a clue, mind, not in the early days. I'd done Art at school, of course, for what it was worth. Art with a capital A. But I'd not enjoyed it much, and I certainly hadn't shone. Just average, you know, as I am at most things.

I've wondered since whether I had to go through those years with Pete before I found my way. My labour pains, perhaps.

There would be this fellow coming to see my work one day. Not yet. Later. After all the ballyhoo and publicity that came from Jim's book, *our* book, winning all those prizes. Some kind of Art Critic he was, on one of the Sunday papers. He took photos of several of the paintings for his article, and bought one too. The 'Spring Meadow'. Sparkling with daisies. One of my favourites, but there it is, you can't hold on to all of them.

When he was leaving he propped the picture against the front door to grasp both my hands in his, and announced rather formally in his slightly foreign accent (Polish, I think it was, or one of those Mid-European states) : "There's suffering in your landscapes, and a sadness that moves me powerfully. Now that I've met you, I shall go back and visit your exhibition again." And he took his leave with a stiff little bow.

But *then*, on this dismal afternoon in the Municipal Art Gallery, there was still pain to come. The contractions were only just beginning.

The children were unusually subdued when I stumbled in, wet but elated. They'd had tea. The boys were washing up. That is, Tom was working his way through a stack of dishes as best he could with Henry at his elbow drying the cutlery with elaborate care. He'd already learned the danger of, say, dropping a spoon when Daddy was in charge of operations.

"I would appreciate it if you could manage to accomplish that very simple task quietly, Henry. *Quietly*!"

People who didn't know my husband often used to say how lucky the children were to have not merely a teacher, but a headmaster for their father. Little did they know!

"And may I ask where you have been till now?" he asked. "I think we'd better have a little chat in my study."

See what I mean? He saw us all as obstreperous ten year olds. Me and Henry, Thomas and Charlie and Claire. And all the rest of the world too. A funny bloke. I don't much care for teachers.

"Right," he said when he was seated in the only chair in the small spare bedroom which he'd requisitioned. "And what have you got to say for yourself?"

Say for myself? SAY FOR MYSELF . . . ?

Suddenly with excruciating clarity I saw the road ahead.

"I'm going to evening classes," I told him calmly. "I'm going to learn to paint."

Chapter Two

The art class I found met on Thursday evenings. I wangled £1.7.6d from the housekeeping, and made them fishcakes for Sunday lunch.

It was a drawing class luckily so that all I needed was a soft pencil. Cartridge paper was provided.

The first week I almost didn't make it. It had been a scramble getting the two little ones to bed. Kids always sense when you are wanting to rush them, and prolong things accordingly.

"No, we're *not* washing our hair tonight, Henry. No!" as he squeezed the sponge over his sister's head. And "No!" again as he stood up and slid back into the water with a great splash once he had the bath to himself.

"Look, now Claire's nightie's all wet. I'll have to find her a dry one. Come on. Out you get, or I shall pull the plug out, and you won't like that!"

Even then he sat there, braving it out defiantly till the last dreadful moment when he would be sucked down the plughole. Eventually they were tucked up, clean and sweet, side by side in her bed, waiting for a story.

"*Topsy and Tim,*" they chanted. "*Topsy and Tim.* We want *Topsy and Tim.*"

"Daddy's going to read to you tonight. For a treat. Be good children, now. He'll be through in a minute." Then putting my head round his study door, "They're all ready for you, Pete. It's time I was off."

"Ah! They'll just have to wait a little longer, I'm afraid. I must finish marking these compositions first." And with thinly disguised irritation he called: "Be quiet, you two! Be quiet till I come through."

My heart sank. They wouldn't be quiet. Of course they wouldn't. And there would be trouble and tears. And no story. Oh dear . . .

"Couldn't you just read them a quick one now, Pete? Then they'd settle down and go to sleep."

"No. I'm sorry, but this comes first. Not that I'm complaining about your class. But that doesn't mean I'm prepared to shoulder all your responsibilities on Thursday nights. I'm busy enough as it is. You know I'm not one to neglect my duty, which is rather more than you can claim, I'm afraid."

This was his way of referring to the running battle of the bed. Before we were married it had been OK. Not that I'd anything to compare it with. We didn't sleep around in those days. 'Nice girls' didn't, anyway. More's the pity. Like so many others, I thought having it off with your boyfriend more or less clinched things. You slept with him - you married him. End of life story.

I don't respond to hustling. Surreptitious couplings in hay stacks and summer fields were one thing, but the minute I found myself in that damned marriage bed it was a different matter altogether.

"You're just perverse," he wailed night after night. "You used to be so bloody sexy."

But it was no good. I could always see it written in fluorescent lights on the ceiling : IT IS YOUR DUTY AFTER ALL.

"You're not being fair to him," my mother scolded, anxious to avert the inevitable. "You've got to pretend. It means so much to a man."

"Well I can't and I won't," I bawled. "I'm sorry. I just can't stand it. The way he assumes it's his *right*. 'Come on, I'm entitled to it. I pay the bills, don't I? What more do you want, woman?' Grrrrr! It's obscene. What about the friendship thing? And cherishing, eh? What about that?"

And of course I was right. There was never any, er, hanky-panky with Walter, for example. But there were plenty of other things.

"It would be easy for us to jump into bed together," he told me once. "It's very tempting."

It was the first time he came up and took me out for a meal. I'd invited him to a party the week before, but he'd cried off.

"Forgive me," he'd written, "but I'm not much of a party man. I'm getting too old, I suppose. I generally find myself talking a lot of nonsense in a very loud voice, and desperately wishing I hadn't come. It's a sure way to start the old asthma, a party. But allow me to take you out to dinner instead. I'll leave you to book a table somewhere nice - you probably know the good places locally - and we'll have a little treat on our own. Which night would suit you? Tuesday?"

"I realise this could probably lead to a physical relationship," he told me shyly over our second cups of coffee, "but quite honestly I think we would be in danger of losing the friendship we have now. And that has come to mean a lot to me, lass."

Perhaps that was the trouble. Perhaps that was all we ever had, Pete and I. A sexual relationship that soon tarnished. Though it still worked occasionally, it's true. If we went out for a walk on our own, perhaps, and had a tumble on the downs; a bike ride into the forest from his mother's leaving the children with her for an afternoon. I could almost remember what had drawn me to him, then. When I was still a volunteer.

Yes, I was perverse. He was right.

Towards the end, when he'd at last got round to learning to drive, we bumbled off for a drink in a country pub once or twice, and had a cuddle in the backseat in a quiet lay-by on the way home. After I'd picked up the habit with someone else. Poor Pete. It was pathetic really.

Once we found an isolated Dutch barn full of hay. We made a nest on top of the stack and were just warming to our work when an irate farmer arrived with a powerful flash-lamp and a nasty looking dog,

"Get out of my hay, you filthy fornicating buggers!" he yelled. "Clear off before I set the dog onto you. You deserve to be branded, you adulterous pigs!"

Hastily collecting up our clothing, zipping ourselves together as we slid down to the ground, we tried to calm his wrath.

"We didn't mean any harm . . ."

"We are married, you know. It's not what you think."

But this only seemed to incense the old boy further. "Get the hell out of here before I do you an injury."

I never could abide the routine, the monotonous, the predictable. Maybe it's to do with my stars. In my promiscuous period, it was always the build-up I enjoyed most. The illicit phone calls, the plots, the false alibis and the red herrings.

"I'm needed down at the theatre tonight. Said I'd help to paint the scenery. Don't know how late I'll be."

Scurrying happily to my rendez-vous, no longer waiting in the wings. A speaking role at last. Life was happening to me after all!

But we're not there yet, not by a long way. First there was the art class to be faced.

I popped my head round the sittingroom door on the way out.

"Bye, lovey. Don't be late for bed."

Charlie at nine had just discovered the delights of crocheting. She was humming along to *Top of the Pops*, her head bobbing in time to the latest hit, her fingers busily manipulating the brightly coloured wools.

"Bye, Tom," to the platinum head bent studiously over the Latin Primer at the kitchen table.

In spite of everything I reached the converted primary school that now served as Further Education Centre in plenty of time. But suddenly I discovered I could not open the door and walk in. It was a long time since I had last braved the world at large.

In my head, in excruciatingly slow motion, I could see the scene as I opened the classroom door and stood there transfixed, unable to think of anything to say, unable to walk casually in and find a seat.

I shrank away from the lighted porch. There was a pottery class in one of the rooms. Through a window I could see people milling around, laughing, collecting clay from a bin, boards from a cupboard.

A guitar lesson was underway nearby. "One-and-two-and," chanted the teacher. "Let it *sing*!"

I'd retreated as far as the school gate when a car caught me in its headlights.

"Is this St Swithun's School?" the driver wound down the window to ask. "I'm looking for the art class."

"Yes. Oh, yes." And with a sudden rush of courage, "I'm looking for the art class myself."

It was easier entering the room together, and once you're in it's not so bad.

We each had a shell to draw, with its intricate spiralling and convex surfaces. Not as easy as it looked.

"Only put down what you *see*," Mr Wilkins ("But everyone calls me Eddie.") said, crouching down beside me, picking out the weaknesses in my drawing with a few bold strokes of his own. "Not what you think you should see. Start again." And he ripped the paper away from me and tossed it in the basket.

He was fierce with us, was Eddie. And intimidating until you got to know him. And he was one of the best things that happened to me. He was a strict believer in discipline. Discipline of hand and eye. Of time and effort.

"Talent's no good to anyone without discipline," was one of his favourite observations. "Self-discipline is the key to success."

Yes, I owe a lot to Eddie.

"How did you get on, then?" Pete enquired a little grudgingly when I got home. I handed him the drawing I had eventually produced.

"Not much to show for the evening, is it? A shell!"

But I knew it was a hell of a lot I'd achieved that night. The sound of the sea that I heard in my shell was the sound of a tidal wave that was to sweep us all from our moorings.

Chapter Three

"Don't worry," said Walter, driving me home one summer evening after a heavenly day walking and sketching in the Purbeck Hills. "I quite see why you went off the rails. What does surprise me is how you stuck it out so long."

We'd eaten our lunch on a headland above Swanage.

"I'm rather good at picnics," he'd told me when we were arranging the trip. "Leave everything to me."

And he'd produced a feast. Chilled watercress soup. Brown bread and pate and salad. And huge juicy peaches that we'd picked up from a roadside stall. All set out on a sparkling linen cloth, with wine, and napkins, and silver forks. Just like something by one of the French Impressionists.

Afterwards, when we'd tidied everything back into the wicker basket, Walter got out his watercolours. "I must have a go at capturing that sky," he said, settling down on a convenient outcrop of rock. "You never told me what happened in the end."

I rolled onto my tummy and stared out across the Channel criss-crossed by moon daisies and tall grasses . . .

It was after I'd gone back to work. The children were all at school by then.

I took a couple of temporary teaching posts, but the small amount of self-confidence I'd once had had gone, and the kids recognised my weakness before I was across the netball court and into the staff room. I'd never been much good, mind. And it was seventeen years since I was last in front of a class.

It's the worst thing in the world to be bad at, teaching. Your life is sheer hell.

Never mind, I thought, waiting for an interview at the local employment bureau, there are plenty of other ways of earning an honest penny.

"Can you type?" asked the young receptionist, preparing to tick things off on a questionnaire.

"No, I'm afraid not . . . "

"Can you operate a duplicating machine?"

" . . . a switchboard?"

" . . . an addressograph?"

"No. No. But I have got academic qualifications."

"They're not really going to be much use to our clients, I'm afraid. Perhaps domestic work would be more in your line." She turned to a cabinet labelled MANUAL/ UNSKILLED/ DOMESTIC and began rifling half-heartedly through some index cards.

The phone rang.

"I'm sorry. No, not at such short notice. It's a busy period for us. All our temps are working, what with holidays and that. Unless . . . hold on a minute. We may just be able to help you out."

She covered the mouthpiece and turned to ask me wearily, "You can answer the phone, I suppose? Trenchards have got a crisis on their hands. All they need is someone to man the phone for a couple of days. They'll take anyone. Think you could cope?"

"Yes. Yes, of course. I'll have a go, anyway."

Which is how I started my secretarial career. I was with the firm for the best part of a year, and they taught me all I needed to know about office work.

"A methodical mind is the most important thing in this job," Mr Grimshaw told me, after deciding he would risk taking me on for a trial period in spite of the obvious deficiencies of my education. "A methodical mind, and a working knowledge of the alphabet."

I thought he was being funny, and exhilarated by his faith in me as a trainee accounts clerk, I laughed aloud. But of course he was right. If everything is kept in strict alphabetical order your office runs as smooth as clockwork.

Yes, Trenchards were very good to me, allowing me to work flexible hours so that I got home by four o'clock. Letting me take time off if there was sickness in the family. By Christmas I could have filled in quite a few ticks on that old questionnaire as well.

"I've decided to spend Christmas with my mother this year," Pete announced the week before they broke up for the holidays. "Not that I'm particularly bothered whether I go to see her or not, but she'll expect me sometime before we start back to school. May as well get it over and done with. That way I'll have a clear week here afterwards before term begins to concentrate on my thesis."

I couldn't believe it. He wasn't much help at Christmas, and no fun at all. Most of the day he was busy working out how much more we had spent on other people than they had spent on us. A complete fiction, as I could barely scrape together enough for presents for our own children, let alone worrying about all my brothers and sisters and their offspring, while they invariably sent us super exciting family parcels which were opened with screams of delight on Christmas morning.

"Right! Will each of you tell me exactly what Kate and Tony sent you. For my list. One at a time, please. Thomas?"

Pete had an extraordinary gift for spoiling everything. But nevertheless you'd expect a father to want to share the festivities with his family, wouldn't you. Especially as he'd just had an article published in *Teachers' World* about the importance of family traditions and ceremonies to young children. Hysterical it was really!

You couldn't discuss it with him, of course. "Ah," he'd say vaguely. "Mm . . . Hm . . . " and carry on marking his fourth year compositions.

"Never mind, Mum." Tom tried to console me manfully. "He's always an old misery at Christmas. We'll be better off without him."

But it wasn't easy. I was working till mid-afternoon on the twenty-fourth, which didn't leave much time for last minute shopping. I treated myself to a taxi from the Broadway, feeling very quilty about such an indulgence, but it was Christmas.

When I staggered in with carrier bags and parcels, the house was bursting with noise and activity. The telly was on in the sittingroom where Charlie and Claire were putting the finishing touches to the tree. The boys had been along Chilcomb Lane on their bikes for holly and other greenery which they were threading through the bannisters with great glee. Lights were on all over the place, and in the kitchen the radio was playing pop music and the table was set for tea.

"Ooh! Haven't we made it pretty!" said five year old Claire with pride, as they all rushed out to help me carry the rest of the shopping in from the gate.

"What's in this knobbly parcel, Mum?"

"What a lovely lot of tangerines!"

"Ooh - *crackers*! We've never had crackers."

"Sit down, Mum. I'll put the kettle on."

"They say it might snow."

"Can we carry our plates through and have tea by the fire, Mum, while we watch Blue Peter?"

It doesn't matter whether he's here or not, I thought to myself. It's going to be a lovely Christmas.

And it was. Though when my mother rang next morning and I tried to explain to her that Pete had simply pushed off to Nottingham for a week I suddenly started bawling my eyes out. Not that I missed him, but I saw myself as she and my father must be seeing me. Abandoned. Neglected.

"How disgraceful!" My mother nearly exploded with indignation, which only made me feel more sorry for myself.

"What is he thinking about, leaving you to cope on your own! His mother could quite well have come down and spent Christmas with all of you."

But she wouldn't have done that. Afraid of the pipes freezing up. She'd never go anywhere in winter.

In the New Year I developed these awful boils. All over me. I felt an absolute mess.

"I think I must be run down," I said to the doctor, showing him my neck, my arms, my back. "I'm covered in the disgusting things. Can you give me some penicillin or something? I can't go round like this."

Dr Lewis thumbed through my notes and then came round and sat on his desk. "Now, what's the real problem, my girl?" he asked in his jovial way, pulling down my eyelids to see if I was anaemic.

"You must have something you can give me for them. A prescription? One of your magic potions?"

But he wouldn't be fobbed off. "You're not going out of my surgery until you tell me what's eating you up," he said firmly.

It was no use protesting that I had no more problems than anyone else, anyone else with a houseful of kids and a husband who saw no further than the end of his thing-y. The doctor's kindness and concern had blown the lid off my carefully preserved self-control. The protests were drowned in tears, choked by sobs.

In the end it all came out. Outside his consulting room a queue of expectant mums waited restlessly for their monthly check-ups, no doubt imagining when I finally emerged red-eyed and snivelling that I was suffering from some particularly nasty terminal disease that had taken practically an hour to diagnose.

"It's all very trivial, you see," I concluded lamely. "He doesn't beat me or anything. But he's not properly alive."

Dr Lewis sat a moment longer perched on the edge of his desk and then twirled round and tore up the prescription he had begun to write. "Penicillin won't help," he said, looking me straight in the eye. "What you need my girl is a good old-fashioned love affair. And, no - don't look so shocked. I recognise your symptoms quite well."

"Oh, come on! For heavens sake! Who the hell's going to fancy me?" Middle-aged, care-worn, plump and dowdy. "You must be joking."

But he meant it all right. "You work nowadays, don't you? Well at least you have a little money to play with. You should treat yourself to a holiday. On your own. Go on one of those package tours, to Paris or Amsterdam. It needn't cost much. They'll manage without you for once. And if you don't find anyone there, then look around at home. That will cure the boils, I promise you."

"And did it?" asked Walter, licking the tip of his paintbrush before cleaning out the ultramarine.

I'd almost forgotten he was listening as I rambled on, lying there in the sunshine.

"I'll tell you about that on the way home," I answered, suddenly confused. "Hey, you caught the clouds a treat."

"Hm! Not too bad, though I say it myself. Come on, lass - I thought we were going to have a swim?" And as we raced down to the water, "I won't let you off the hook, mind. We'll find a friendly pub and you can tell me over dinner."

Chapter Four

Ted, of course, was a swine, though it took me a long time to recognise it. Or at least to admit it to myself.

There had been so few men in my life. Real men, that is. A great deal of my time and energy had been spent adoring this fellow or that from afar. Completely idiotic, I agree, but that's how I was.

Most of my infatuations were for doctors, the family GPs. The only men I ever came into contact with. It sounds pretty corny, I know, but it wasn't corny to me at the time.

In Norfolk things ran true to form.

"You'll not find it easy to make friends down there," my sister Peggy warned me when she heard where we were going. "We hated it. And it will be a lot worse for you, with Pete being headmaster and all."

"Rubbish!" I told her scornfully. "What difference can that make? You're a right old Tory, you are. What's his position got to do with it?"

But it had a lot to do with it, as I quickly discovered.

The feudal backwater in which we found ourselves was a two tier society. Scattered thinly across the hedgeless landscape were the gentry in their manor houses and imposing villas, while in the single line of council houses that straggled around the cross-roads trying to pass itself off as a village lived the thirty-two families of farm labourers and lorry drivers.

In the old school house on the corner we were out on a limb, neither fish nor fowl.

I tried to make friends with the women on the row.

"Won't you come in for a cup of tea?" I asked Mrs Dixon, when she called round one morning to invite Charlie to her little girl's birthday party.

"Oh, no - thank you all the same. My man will be home from the sugar beet lifting at mid-day, and I has to have his dinner on the table or he do get so mad."

"Well, never mind. Perhaps you've more time in the afternoon. Before the children come out of school, say?"

"Thank you kindly, and I should like that fine. I'll come over half-past-two should I?"

Charlie was a great ice-breaker. She was just turned four when we moved to Eccleston and she found it lonely at home with me, now that Tom had started school properly. Playtimes were all right. She'd sit on the back step anxiously listening for the bell to bring the children out into the yard. Sometimes she managed to sneak in and join the eleven mixed infants in their singing class or art lesson with kind Mrs Clark, but her father got very cross about this.

"Charlotte must not be allowed to take advantage of her connection with the headmaster." His promotion was going to his head.

I was expecting Henry that winter, and pregnancy always made me so tired. When we'd had our lunch we'd sit down for *Listen with Mother*, Charlie and I, and almost invariably Mother would flop off to sleep. And that's when Charlie did her socialising. She'd cover me with a rug, and creep off to visit one of her friends in the Row.

"Your little girl's a caution, and no mistake," Don-the-Postman from Number 24 told me one morning, knocking on the back door with a parcel from Granny for Tom's sixth birthday. "My missus do say she comes a-callin' just like a little ol' lady. And there ain't nothin' she enjoys more 'n a cup a tea and a good ol' gossip. She's a rum un and no mistake!"

She certainly knew all the families and their problems.

"Mrs Mason's cat's had four kittens," she announced at tea-time. "But Mr Mason drownded them in a bucket. Said he wasn't sweating his heart out in the beet fields to feed all them varmints."

And at bed-time, "Mrs Freeman's Freddy has got to go into hospital next week. He's a proper terror, she says. If he don't like what they do to him he'll come right on home. In his night shirt and all!"

Charlie was picking up the local idiom as well as the news.

"You've been invited to Dawn Dixon's party on Saturday," I told her at lunch-time. "And her Mummy's coming over to have a natter this afternoon."

"Oh, that's nice," said my four year old daughter. "It might cheer her up a bit. She doesn't get out much. And she's worrying something terrible about her old dad over at Harling. He's on his own and nearly eighty."

Charlie had no problem making friends.

But, oh dear, when I answered the door at half-past-two it wasn't homely Mrs Dixon from Number 17, but a vision of delight in purple trouser suit, dangly ear-rings, bouffant hair-do. The lot! All done up to visit the Headmaster's wife. And I'd only meant we could share a pot of tea at the kitchen table while I finished the ironing.

Yes, they were lonely years in Eccleston. It's not really surprising that I filled my emptiness with dreams. Like a newly hatched duckling, I attached myself to the first warm-hearted creature that crossed my path. It could have been anyone - the crabby old vicar from the next hamlet, the Lord of the Manor of Wilby, the library van man, *anybody*! But luckily for me it was Dr Olaf Svenson who burst into our lives in the middle of tea a week or two after we'd moved in.

"Hello! Hello!" he called bounding into the kitchen. "Thought I'd better come and get acquainted. You're sure to be needing me before long, one or other of you." And pulling another chair up to the table he started telling us an hilarious story that he'd heard from a pig farmer up the road that morning.

" 'But them thar noses runs in 'is family, Doctor,' the chap's wife shouted from the dairy. 'That ain't nuffin' to go by.' "

He was still laughing when he left, and I was fatally hooked on this large noisy compassionate Swede who had somehow come to settle in a country practice in the backwoods of East Anglia.

I used to pray for someone to be ill. Yes, it's true. So that I could leave the children for a few minutes to cycle the half mile to the phone box and leave a message at the surgery asking Dr Olaf to call in on his way by, and take a look at Tom's spots, or listen to Charlie's chest. I was actually pleased to be pregnant, because at least I would see him once a month when he came to take my blood pressure and everything.

I guess he knew I was lonely. He took to leaving his visit to the school house on the crossroads till the end of his rounds and would come roaring in with, "A cup of tea, girl! A cup of tea! Christ, I'm dying for a cup of tea!" Soon I learnt when to expect him and had the kettle on and a good fire going, and we'd sit like old friends, discussing the news or some book he'd lent me, or just enjoying the quiet and the strong hot tea together. He was a real character, was Dr Olaf Svenson.

My friend Wyn asked me once, "Were your two youngest Doctor Olaf's babies?" I choked back a guilty cry, thinking she had cottoned on to my infatuation, but of course it was only the local way of asking if Olaf Svenson had brought them into the world.

It reminded me of that powerful story where this woman has a secret passion for a family friend and her feelings eventually become so strong that lo-and-behold! she gives birth to a baby, *his* baby. It was all in her mind. No contact between them. Certainly no sex. But still, there was the baby. (It could have been Thomas Hardy who wrote it. I can't remember. But I can remember the story.)

That's how I was getting with Dr Olaf. Mind you, it did me a bit of good spiritually.

I knew very well he was a bell ringer. He'd talked about it from time to time. But one day he mentioned that he also sang in the church choir over at Harling, some three or four miles away.

Shamelessly I decided to start cycling over to Even Song, and before long I managed to get myself invited to join the choir too. What bliss! What happiness! I could now be practically certain of seeing the good doctor at least once a week, whether or not there was sickness at home.

All the children had arrived by this time, and it took some organising to get away every Sunday evening, but I stuck to my guns, and usually left Pete supervising tea, very grumpy at being called through from school where he spent almost all his waking hours. He fancied himself as one hell of an administrator, but on reflection he could not have been that good. As far I knew, other head teachers did not put in seventy, eighty, ninety hours a week. There were only thirty children in the school.

I cycled along those dark country lanes in frost, fog, rain, snow. Nothing could divert me from Even Song. As I approached Harling I strained my ears for the sound of the church bells wafting across the fields. If they were ringing, there was a good chance that it was Dr Olaf on the end of Great Tom's rope. No births or deaths or farm accidents to deal with tonight. Then I would pedal gaily over the last mile or two, angelic voices singing in my head.

It often occurred to me as I processed up the aisle in starched gown and ridiculous blue hat, that I deserved to be struck down in my tracks by the Good Lord for using His church as a cover for my illicit fantasies. But He spared me.

The last year we were in Norfolk I professed an interest in campanology as well, and cycled far and wide between the cow parsley and the ripening corn to attend practices, and to ring at patronal festivals and feast days up and down the Brecklands. Sometimes Olaf Svenson was there with the team, but he couldn't be relied on.

This *affair* went on for years. Long after we'd moved from East Anglia we kept in touch. We still do spasmodically. He is a grand correspondent, writing long rambling letters - unusual for a man - peppered with maps and sketches, his racey humour and his tremendous zest for life. He gives me vivid descriptions of his latest voyage on his yacht, with diagrams of his route and odd little gifts he has picked up along the way : a feather from a deep Dutch duvet, a ferry ticket, a menu, a pressed flower.

Years later, after I had *taken my medicine* from Ted, we met in London, Dr Olaf and I. He booked us into a hotel, and we had dinner at a posh restaurant and a bit of a wild night together. But it was a mistake. I really wish we'd left things as they were, because of course he couldn't live up to the Dream Man I'd been in love with for so long. And it's sordid in a hotel when you've come together specifically for that.

We still write, but it's not the same.

There had been other infatuations after Dr Olaf. But they were all totally innocent until I found myself in the back of a big smart car up on Cheesefoot Head, sipping gin and tonic, while Ted breathed his philosophy of sexual freedom down my quivering neck.

Chapter Five

Yes, Ted was a swine all right, but he did me a power of good. In fact you might say he was just what the doctor ordered.

Later on, when I was on my own give or take a few teenagers, Stella asked me if I regretted my association with him. But I can't honestly say I regret anything.

I didn't actually go off to Paris as Dr Lewis had suggested. But I did find the courage to join the local dramatic society, a thing I'd been longing to do for ages.

They met in a little old church that had been deconsecrated, just down the road from us. I passed it every time I went into town. Norman, I think it was. Very old anyway. It made a grand little theatre. We'd been to see one or two of their productions, and damn good they were too. Almost professional.

I'd established the right to a life of my own by now. It was all of three years since I started at the art class, so that was no problem. But it was still a bit of an ordeal barging into this boisterous self-assured circle, the Dramatic Society.

They were rehearsing Chekhov, I remember, the night I first plucked up courage to turn the big iron ring in that heavy studded door to join them.

Ted was the producer. He was certainly a distinguished figure. No getting away from it. Very tall and very thin, with a mane of straight blond hair, pure Michael Heseltine. And Denis Healey eye-brows. He was sitting in the front row directing operations with his arm round a young girl whom I assumed in my innocence to be his wife, inspite of the disparity in age.

Over the phone, I'd offered to lend a hand painting scenery and so on, and I was pleased to be found a job there and then helping a couple of students from the Art School with a back-cloth for the summer garden scene. From now on the Little Theatre became the centre of my life. I was swept into a polka of dramatic events.

There were rehearsals three nights a week at first, and more often than that as the opening drew near. There were workshop nights, with long late discussions in the bar afterwards. And technical rehearsals. And frequent coffee parties in people's flats or bed-sits after the theatre lights were out.

Much to my delight I was given a small part in *The Three Sisters*. A maid. I didn't have any lines, of course. I simply had to shuffle across the stage carrying a heavy samovar that had been borrowed from an exiled Russian Countess for the production.

Oh - how I loved it! Being part of this lively colourful group. Having a part to play, a contribution to make, no matter how small.

Pete wasn't too happy that I was out every night, but once I'd got a whiff of that grease paint there was no stopping me.

The play was a tremendous success, predictably, and I shuffled on and off a treat.

There was a notice pinned in the Green Room inviting us all to the Last Night Party at the producer's house.

"How are you going to get over to Ted's tomorrow?" one of the scene shifters asked me on the Friday night.

"Well - I don't think I'll be going," I stammered diffidently. I hadn't been to a party since our college days, all but twenty years back. And I'd nothing remotely party-ish to wear.

"Rubbish!" said Stan. "Course you'll be going. Everyone goes. I'll give you a lift."

I still half hoped I might get out of it and slip quietly away after the final triumphant curtain call. But no such luck.

"I'm just nipping home to get tidied up," Stan said, collaring me by the door. "I'll give a blast on the old horn outside your place in about an hour. I know where you live. Make sure you're ready."

So that was that.

It was funny getting dolled up to go out at that time of night. Pete was in his study marking a batch of Open University papers. He merely grunted when I told him I was going to a bit of a get-together at the theatre and I didn't know how late I'd be.

Rummaging desperately through my wardrobe - well, my chest-of-drawers actually, we'd never got round to a wardrobe - I fished out an old cotton nightie checked in lovely shades of blue and green and purple. It was in a kind of Jane Austen style with a high waist, little puffed sleeves, and a deep flounce round the hem. It was the only thing I had that was in the least bit suitable. But I was still covered in those hideous boils. My arms and throat were a terrible mess. So I put a roll-necked jersey underneath the nightgown, and it didn't look too bad.

Ted lived on the outskirts of the town in a large detached house which was absolutely bursting with people by the time Stan and I arrived. A trestle table was set up in the hall for all the bottles that had been brought along, and there was help-yourself food in the kitchen.

I felt very much the new girl, and when Richard Elton began to tell me about the play he was writing for the autumn production, I settled down on the hearthrug beside him, thankful to be no longer conspicuously alone.

There was music coming from somewhere. I could hear it now and again above the chatter.

"Would you like to dance?" asked Richard, struggling to his feet in the crush.

"No. No, I'm not really a dancer. And anyway it's time I was going. My husband will be wondering where I am."

"I'll run you home if you like. I'm about ready to leave myself."

Among the mountains of things on somebody's bed I managed to find my coat. There were as many people upstairs as down, as far as I could tell. There seemed to be a lot of giggling and squealing going on behind closed doors, and a pile of bodies on the landing.

Just as well we're going, I thought to myself with a little sniff of disapproval. This definitely wasn't my scene.

"Thank you for having me, Ted."

"Hold on! You can't be leaving already? Things are just beginning to warm up. And I haven't had a dance with you yet."

"I'm a hopeless dancer," I said, all innocence. "And Richard's waiting to give me a lift."

"He'll wait. You can't go until we've had a dance. It's the producer's prerogative."

And in spite of my protests he hustled me into the darkness of the Dancing Room.

"Close the door, dammit!" yelled a voice.

And, "Christ! I'm not doing *that*, darling!" from someone else.

The room was packed. Never mind dancing, no-one could do more than sway about on the spot. Not that it seemed to matter much.

Ted manoeuvred me into a secluded spot, wedging us in behind the piano. He nibbled my ear. "Relax. Relax and enjoy it," he whispered as he plunged one hand down my demure bodice, and fumbled his way up my skirt with the other.

"Oh, for heaven's sake!" I spluttered. "What do you take me for? Get off!"

"Where's the harm, dear," he soothed, going merrily on with his explorations. "Let yourself go. This is a party."

Of course I should like to be able to relate at this point that I slapped the fellow's face, and escaped to the lighted hall. But I'm afraid I didn't.

In one way I was outraged at this casual seduction, but after all I was longing for excitement. For some colour in my life. And this could well be it. I'd waited long enough to join the Dramatic Society, and it was drama I was looking for, no use denying it. Was I now going to run away from the first bit of innocent fun (as he was busy persuading me to call it)?

Good God, I thought, as mine host nibbled his way down to my navel, is this what goes on at parties?

"Go up to the bathroom and strip off," he whispered eagerly. "Go on. I'll come and tap on the door in a couple of minutes. Go on, there's a good girl."

"Bloody hell! You're barmy!"

But he steered me masterfully to the door, and murmuring "Two minutes, now," pushed me towards the stairs.

I went up, found the bathroom, locked the door and had a wee. Glancing in the mirror as I washed my hands I suddenly saw sense. What was I thinking about? I was still plain, mousey, and covered with boils. For heaven's sake! Adultery simply wasn't my line.

Quickly before Ted arrived, I unlocked the door and ran down to look for Richard-the-playwright and my coat.

"Goodnight! Goodnight!" I called, with unfamiliar confidence. "Goodnight, Ted. It was a lovely party."

He came out onto the drive and opened the door of Richard's car for me.

"I haven't finished with you yet, my girl," he hissed in my ear. "Not by a long way."

Chapter Six

It was five years before I visited that house again, and this time it was Ted's wife I was going to see.

I knew Jeannie fairly well by now. I'd talked to her a time or two at the theatre, and he had spoken about her, of course. She had come along to a Last Night Party at our house once, after the Peter Schaeffer comedy, and she'd gone into raptures about my performance as Miss Webster.

"I saw the play in the West End, my dear, and quite honestly you were every bit as funny as Beryl Reid."

"Oh, rubbish, Jeannie! I wasn't acting at all. It was type casting. They all know what a staid old maid I am at heart." This while I was deeply embroiled with her husband, mind. I was a real cow, you can see I was.

Now suddenly we were thrown together in a little drama of our own. I met her in Sainsbury's one crowded Thursday evening. Stella had given me a lift down, so I was scuttling round trying not to hold her up.

"Why, hello dear," Ted's Jeannie called, on tip-toes to catch my attention among the fruit and vegetables. "Still active at the Little Theatre are you?"

"I never go near the place nowadays. I'm far too busy. And it's not so handy now we've moved up to the other end of town . . ."

"I didn't know you'd moved," she said pinning me in a convenient lay-by between the dairy produce and the bacon counter.

"We sold the house when our divorce went through. I live up by the Common now."

"Divorce! Goodness me, I'd no idea you were divorced. You always seemed such a happy couple. I am sorry to hear it."

"There's no need to be sorry, Jeannie. If I'd had any sense I'd have left him years ago. It's marvellous to be on my own. Alone apart from the kids, that is."

"Oh, but it's always such a shame when a family splits up, isn't it."

"I must be going," I said. Stella was already queuing at the check-out. She had picked me up straight from work, and had to get home to cook supper for her lot. "My friend is waiting for me. See you around!" And I steered my trolley back into the main stream.

The next night Jeannie phoned me.

"I wish you'd come over," she told me. "I could use a bit of advice. You know what Ted's like. Everyone knows. I've decided I'm a fool to put up with it any longer. Twenty-seven years we've been married, and for most of that time he's been mucking about with other women. Quite blatantly."

"Oh, Jeannie..." But she wouldn't let me get a word in.

"Hearing about your divorce has made me realise that I must take action. I'm sixty-three, you know. I can't go on like this."

"Of course you can't. He's an absolute wolf."

"I wondered whether you would come over. I'm sure you are the one to help me. Come and have a cup of coffee, won't you? In the morning? He's never home on Saturdays. He spends the weekend with his latest girlfriend."

"Oh, Jeannie..."

"No more now. We'll talk in the morning. I feel better already. The first step's always the most difficult."

Which is how I came to be ringing her doorbell next morning, breathless from the hill, and from the conflicting emotions the visit stirred in me.

"I want nothing further to do with you," I'd yelled at Ted that last evening. "And this time I bloody mean it."

"Don't be cruel, my dear," he'd pleaded in a very convincing imitation of a wounded lover. "I've grown used to you. I can't manage without you."

"Don't give me that crap. Any bloody body would do for you. Half the time you're not even sure *who* you're screwing."

He'd never once called me by name, not even in the heat of the action. He daren't in case he'd mixed me up with one of his other women.

"I've had enough. Last night was the bleeding end."

"I can explain, if you'll allow me to."

"Don't waste your breath, man. I wish to God this had never started."

But that wasn't strictly true. I had enjoyed most of it. The illicit meetings. The subterfuge. The secrecy. He had almost persuaded me over to his sterile philosophy, that physical pleasure is all, and emotional involvement an unfortunate by-product to be avoided at all costs, like pregnancy.

"I know I could simply go and see a lawyer," Jeannie was saying as she made the coffee. "But Ted is so clever. He won't admit a thing. I know perfectly well what he's up to, what he's always been up to, but he'll deny everything. I'm going to need evidence, aren't I?"

"But you can cite me, Jeannie. I'll gladly give you the necessary evidence."

"No, no - we can't fake it . . . "

"I don't mean fake it."

"You?" She didn't understand immediately.

"I'm sorry. I felt sure you knew."

"You!"

"Believe me, I'm sorry . . . "

"YOU!"

All of a sudden and much to our surprise we found ourselves dancing round the kitchen table, arms round one another's necks, shrieking with laughter.

"You should slap my face, by rights. Scratch my eyes out."

"But why should I do that to my chief witness," she gasped, collapsing into a chair.

"I am sorry, Jeannie," I said again. "I was certain you knew. Thought that was why you asked me round."

"Why, no. I'd no idea. I think this calls for a celebration, don't you, my dear?" And she dragged me through to the sittingroom. "Come on. We're going to treat ourselves to a bottle of his special export-only gin. He brings it back from the States. I know very well where he hides the key of the sideboard. I can't think why I haven't indulged myself before." And pouring us each another, "You don't seem the type."

The type. Any old type does for Ted. And actually he was rather keen on dowdy little wives with boring marriages. Women with pretty restricted horizons. He knew how flattered they would be, how thrilled at the prospect of a bit of an adventure. "I'm *just* his type really."

"Oh, come on - you're not like that at all."

I was then though. Down-trodden, colourless, and longing for some excitement.

He had phoned me, I remembered, the Monday after that first Last Night Party.

"Why, hello!" he began in his husky Oxford accent. "I'm sorry you rushed off like that on Saturday night. Just when things were beginning to warm up. I was wondering whether you'd like to come out for a drink tonight?"

"No. I'm sorry, Ted, but you've completely misjudged me. I'm not that sort of woman at all."

"Oh, come on! We could find a quiet country pub. All perfectly above board. I wouldn't like us to be bad friends. Please say you'll come."

"No. There's really no point."

"Look, I feel I should explain my behaviour at the party. Please do come." And sensing my indecision, "I'll pick you up by the Blue Boar at eight-fifteen."

I found I was all of a dither when I put the phone down. I must have known very well what I was letting myself in for, though I wouldn't have admitted it. Why else did I run myself a furtive bath before the children came in from school.

"I'm going down to the theatre later on," I mentioned casually to Peter. "The producer is taking everyone out for a drink. All the cast and that . . . "

"I wouldn't have thought you counted," he grunted into his casserole. "I honestly can't understand what you see in it. Out every night for weeks, for that pathetic appearance."

If he'd been more friendly then I still might not have gone.

"The kids are all watching the Norman Wisdom film. Charlie says she'll put the little ones to bed, so you won't have to worry."

"I wasn't going to worry, I can assure you. I have a great deal of school work to get through tonight. As long as I'm left in peace . . . "

You're bringing it on yourself, Pete, I thought bitterly as I scurried down the road soon after eight, cutting through the park to our rendez-vous. But I was only trying to justify things to my conscience.

Guilty as hell, but dizzy with excitement, I reached the far gate of the park which would bring me out onto the London Road opposite the Blue Boar. And here, I am pleased to record, my qualms almost got the better of me. In fact I lurked in the bushes and watched the big green Rover cruising by a time or two.

He'll have given me up by now, I told myself, coming out in the open and strolling nonchalantly towards the spot.

"Hello there!" he said in that deep cultured voice of his. "I'm sorry I'm a little late."

"Look, Ted," I said crouching down beside the passenger door, "I've only come to tell you I'm *not* coming."

Rather to my surprise, to my disappointment, he didn't argue or try to persuade me. "That's up to you," he said calmly. "Jump in and I'll run you home."

And that was that, of course!

He drove straight out of town, soothing my indignation with his soft tongue. "Surely we can pull off the road and talk for a minute. I think you owe me that. You did agree to come. I've been looking forward to it all afternoon. Have a drink with me, at least. I've brought a bottle and some glasses. Don't be unfriendly."

I guess that's one of my problems. I never want to be unfriendly. Never like to appear to distrust the other fellow. Hurt anyone's feelings. It's got me into a fair bit of trouble one way or another.

We drew into the deserted car park on Cheesefoot Head, looking out across the April countryside. He fetched glasses and gin and tonic from the boot, and we sat demurely in the front seats discussing various erudite subjects including Chekhov, marriage and loyalty, freedom of choice, virtue, and that quaint Victorian concept known as adultery.

"Where's the harm in it?" he whispered, stroking a particularly vulnerable spot on the back of my neck. "It's such a little thing when all's said and done. And who's to know, for God's sake!"

Chapter Seven

And Ted was right. Who was to know? It need have made no difference whatsoever. But somehow I couldn't keep this incredible turn of events to myself. I confided in Stella the very next day.

"But you don't even like it," she reminded me with a mixture of disbelief and envy.

"I don't like it with a husband who expects it as his damn right, no." But this was something else.

Stella knew about husbands, and their demands. She had slipped up to our house in the early hours only the week before, sickened and humiliated by Bob's demands.

"Can I doss down on your sofa?" she begged over a comforting cup of tea. "If I go back there'll be another outburst."

Like us, they had been married a good many years. Their two children were about the same age as Henry and Claire. And every night of her life, every night of their marriage, Bob had demanded his rights.

"There's no loving in it," Stella had told me time and again. "He insists he can't sleep unless he's had it. Like cleaning his teeth or having a wee. I'm not part of the experience. It leaves me feeling *dirty!*"

She had tried to talk to him. Explaining how she felt. But he didn't seem to care.

"If I don't have it I can't sleep. You know that. For Christ's sake, why else would a fellow walk up the aisle?"

They had frequent rows. The odd time she did refuse him he would sit up in bed reading till dawn, while she tossed about unable to sleep but desperate not to let him see she was still awake. Sometimes she took the eiderdown and crawled off to sleep on the sittingroom floor or crept into bed with one of the children. But there would be ructions next morning, and she wouldn't be the only one to suffer.

She had been to see the doctor about it once, saying she could not stand it, she felt like a piss-pot, a receptacle, a masturbation device.

"Count yourself lucky," he told her shortly. "Most women who come to see me are complaining that their husbands no longer want them." This was *not* my kind Dr Lewis, but a smart young man not long out of medical school. He fancied himself as a bit of a sex-therapist.

"But what if Pete finds out?" she whispered, remembering how violent her Bob had become when he discovered she had invited her driving instructor in for a cup of coffee, the week he was down in Swanage with his Fourth Year Geography group. He'd come back on the Thursday unexpectedly, having had to bring one of the kids home with a sprained ankle.

"He won't find out," I promised her. Though I had to admit I felt as if it was branded on my forehead : ADULTRESS.

It was not so easy to keep it to myself, however. I had to fight this incredible urge to publish it abroad, shout it from the rooftop. "I'm not quite such a boring little woman after all. I have a lover, would you believe! I'm actually having an affair!"

I found myself singing over the washing-up, humming contentedly as I tackled a pile of ironing, holding my shoulders back and my head high for the first time in years.

"Stand up straight!" they had shouted at me at school.

"You must hold yourself better, dear," from my disappointed mother as I slouched around the house, refusing to accept the nasty tricks that my body was playing on me. "Anyone would think you were ashamed of growing into a woman."

Now I felt very much a woman. Now my life revolved around Ted. Around Monday evenings. Between six-forty-five and seven I would hover anxiously, innocently near the phone, knowing he would call me from the station when he got off the train from Town.

"Hello," he'd whisper conspiratorially. "Are you free tonight?" Free? My week started and finished on Monday evenings. The rest was no more than a grey blur. "Eight-fifteen, then? In the usual place."

And we'd whirl off into the sweet summer countryside to find a convenient lay-by, a secluded copse, a quiet cart-track where we could pull off the road.

I always had an alibi ready. Usually to do with the theatre, though sometimes I made out I was going sketching with the art class. Pete showed no sign of suspicion. The children accepted by now that I had a life of my own.

I didn't feel I could deceive Angus, however.

Angus Armstrong was (as Prue Sarn might have said in *Precious Bane*) my very dear acquaintance. I had met him two or three years earlier. His wife had come along to the Young Wives Group, and had attached herself firmly to me. She was a sad bitter creature, was Alice Armstrong. Full of anger, hatred and self-pity.

"Nothing has gone right for me," she moaned, following me up the garden to the washing line, "not since I married that arse-hole Armstrong."

It's a mistake to show sympathy or compassion to some people. They thrive on it. Alice certainly did. She became a fixture in the house, often arriving before I'd got the children off to school. Sometimes still there when they came home at four o'clock.

"I've so much to do," she'd complain, while I loaded the washing machine and tidied the kitchen.

"I really haven't time to talk today, but . . . " she'd start off ominously, settling herself down in the window seat while I made pastry.

She was older than me. Older than Angus. They had no children, and she had no interests apart from belittling her long-suffering husband.

It was some time before we actually met the monster she described so vividly. She turned up one Sunday afternoon, I remember. I was doing the garden.

Tom came to find me. "That awful creature is here, Mum. And God Almighty - you should just see her!"

There was Alice wearing a bitter expression as usual. And what appeared to be football shorts, high-heeled sandals and a skimpy flowery bra. Nothing else.

"He's gone to cricket!" she exploded. "The selfish pig! I don't know how I'm supposed to amuse myself. He never thinks of anything but himself. I left him a note to pick me up here when the match is over. He's a right arse-hole, that Armstrong!"

It was a long afternoon.

As I weeded the rockery she gave me the full story, for the umpteenth time, of her deprived childhood in a Glasgow slum. She droned on inaudibly while I mowed the grass, saving the gory details of her father's untimely death (in his seventy-eighth year) until I was clipping the edges, crawling round behind me to be certain I should miss none of them.

When I went in to get tea for the family she sat on the high stool by the stove enlarging angrily on the latest crimes of "that arse-hole Armstrong," while Charlie made drop scones and I cut bread and butter.

The least I can do is show her a little sympathy, I thought. She seems to have had her fair share of misfortune.

And then he arrived, and we all fell in love with him. Angus Armstrong, cricketer, hockey captain, geophysicist. Liberal supporter, crazy enthusiast. Heaven knows how he had survived the years with that mean-minded self-centred Alice. But survive them he had. And gloriously.

Even Pete responded to Angus and his warmth and gaiety, and always welcomed him to the house with genuine pleasure. He was an enrichment to all our lives. Angus Armstrong.

The children found in this delightful new 'uncle' the warmth and fun and excitement that their own father was incapable of providing. He had a car, for one thing, and sometimes took us all off into the New Forest for a picnic, or down to Southampton baths for a swim on Sunday mornings. Whatever it was, if Angus was with us it would be a success.

"I'm sorry, Angus," Pete told him when he came to collect us for a trip to the beach one fine Sunday, "but I won't be able to come along today. I've all this Open University marking to finish. It must be in the post tomorrow. A pity, but there it is . . . "

"Well, at least I'm taking this noisy rabble off your hands for an hour or two. Don't work too hard, old chap."

The normal procedure was for Angus to come and collect us first, and then pick Alice up as we passed their house on the way out of town.

"She's not coming either," he announced, jumping back into the car, rather red in the face. She was in bed with a migraine or something. Hoping Angus would cancel the outing, I suspect. But he didn't. "Spread out everybody. Plenty of room for a change."

Not that much really, what with all the kids, our two dogs, and his funny little terrier bitch. But it was an estate car, and no-one was complaining. Certainly not me.

We paddled on a deserted sandy shore. Ate our picnic on a grassy headland looking across to the Isle of Wight. And played French Cricket afterwards, with the dogs as fielders.

He paid for us all to go round some beautiful gardens, rich in rhododendrons, with a yew hedge two yards thick between us and the cliff edge. There was a ping-pong table on a deserted patio, and although I expected to be shoo-ed off every minute by the irate owner, Angus gaily organised a doubles tournament, drawing other casual visitors into his magnetic field until a riotous match brought half-a-dozen teenagers out of the house to join in the fun.

We stopped at a pub on the journey home and sat out in the courtyard in the twilight with a big plate of ham sandwiches, coke for the kids and red wine for us.

"I love you, Angus Armstrong, and I shall marry you one day," announced five year old Claire, hugging him fiercely.

And, oh boy - how I longed to say the same!

Chapter Eight

I would have married him, too. Or run away with him. If he hadn't been so jolly honourable. Yes, that summer, while the madness was on me, I'd have left them all for Angus. Pete and the children. Hearth and home. Without much more than a bat of the eyelids, I'd have gone off with him. To Canada. To Timbuktu. Anywhere.

It was the year Pete got his Master's Degree, I remember. The presentation ceremony was being held at London University one evening in May. He'd hired all the regalia and Angus came up the Sunday before to take a photo of the Master of Education to send to his proud parents.

"I could meet you both for lunch on Tuesday," Angus suggested warmly. "My office isn't far from Waterloo. It would be fun."

"Well, thanks mate," said Pete in his painfully jocular way, "but Tuesday will be a normal school day for me. We'll be travelling up on the five o'clock train. That should give us plenty of time. As long as I'm robed and in my seat by seven-fifteen..."

"But surely you can take the day off. The afternoon at least." Angus was clearly astonished.

"I do have a fairly responsible job, you know. I can't just go gadding off to London in school hours."

"Oh come off it, Pete. It is rather a special occasion. Give yourself a break, man."

But it was no good. Pete was adamant. In all the years we had lived down here, only an hour from Waterloo, we'd never once been up to Town. And now when we had a wonderful excuse for a trip, he was intending to go up on the five o'clock, and come home right after the ceremony.

I didn't care a hoot for his flipping M.Ed. which might sound like sour grapes, but honestly! This would be his third degree, and I was heartily sick of Wolvesey Hall and its correspondence courses, and the long hours Pete was shut away studying. Not that I'd actually been up to one of these presentations myself. I'd always been heavily pregnant at the time. But his parents had travelled down from their midland mining village to sit beaming in wonder at their brilliant son.

"Don't let your mother struggle about with buckets of coal, Pete," I'd nagged the first few times I visited his family before we were married.

"Oh, we don't expect our Pete to do aught around the house. Our Pete's a reader, sithee."

Funny how you don't spot the warning lights. I must have been an idiot.

"But *you* could come up earlier in the day," Angus said to me, quite casually.

Halleluyah!

"How about coming up in time for lunch? I'll meet you off the train. You can amuse yourself in the afternoon, pottering around the shops or something till Pete arrives. Why not?"

And here we were, as easy as that, drifting down the Thames on a River Bus, drunk with our steak and chianti and the balmy day.

"I've taken the afternoon off," Angus told me over coffee in the enchanting bistro he had found with tables on the pavement and striped umbrellas, just like abroad. "It seemed a pity to waste such an opportunity. I thought we could go on the river."

If nothing else happens in my whole damn life, there will have been this, I thought blissfully, as we strolled along the Embankment. There will have been the river with cottonwool clouds floating in it, and the bustling crowds drawn out into the streets by the soft spring sunshine. And Angus and I alone among them.

On Waterloo Bridge, right there with the trains going by, he hugged me to him. "Hell! I'm glad Pete's so bloody conscientious!" he shouted. And hand in hand, laughing like loonies, we danced across to the Festival Hall and reality. Angus to catch his usual train home and I to wait innocently with a cup of tea in a snackbar until Pete arrived at six.

"I found I simply couldn't bear to go home though," he told me afterwards. "I saw Pete come through the barrier, and instead of catching my train I slipped back to the office and mooched about until it got to ten-thirty. I'm sorry. I just had to see you again. I couldn't bear the day, *our* day to end."

As if I was complaining!

There we were, the ceremony safely behind us, sitting glumly waiting for the train home to pull out of Waterloo. Pete was going over the high-points of his evening, with the odd deprecating sniff as he recalled some trite or ill-judged remark he had overheard, some brilliant observation of his own, while I did a video playback of my afternoon, taking some parts over and over again in delicious slow motion, when into our compartment burst, yes, Angus himself!

"Hello, hello!" he exclaimed, as if surprised to see us. "How did it go then, Pete? Great. Great." And then to me, "Sorry I had to rush away after lunch. Busy time for us at the minute. I've only just finished now. Did you have a nice afternoon? Did you get yourself to Carnaby Street?"

Poor darling Angus - he was a feeble liar. But Pete was happy to have a captive ear, and chatted animatedly all the way home, oblivious of the high voltage in the carriage.

That was the beginning of an idyllic period for me. I gladly suffered Alice Armstrong's visits, the dreary sagas of her husband's short-comings, her malice and self-pity, because as long as she and I were friends, Angus and I could keep in touch.

I'm not too proud about this part of the story. Talk about *underhand*! Not only did I tolerate her neurotic outbursts, I positively encouraged them.

"God, you've no idea what I've put up with from that arsehole Armstrong." And she'd launch into a vivid description of their intimate life. The low-down on his foibles and frailties. Which I drank in, enchanted.

It was that summer that we took a cottage in Devon for a week, sharing it with Angus and Alice. It was our first seaside holiday. Our one-and-only seaside holiday. That's one of the things that I most regret, that we didn't give the children holidays to look back on.

Once in Norfolk I had taken Tom and Charlie on the Sunday School Outing to Great Yarmouth. I left Henry, who was about a year old, with dear Mrs Rudd-Along-the-Row so that Pete could have the day to himself.

"Now you must all come," said Mrs French, the Rector's wife. "The coach leaves from the school gate at nine-fifteen. A change will do you good, dear. You've been looking a little peaky lately."

(I was pregnant again. Claire would be born at Christmas.)

I found the 7/6d fare out of the Family Allowance. The kids went free.

"We'll need some money with us, Pete. It'll be a long day."

"Don't keep on about it. I'll give you some money, of course I will."

"I thought we might treat ourselves to fish-and-chips," I suggested. "They've never had them. Not proper fish-and-chips. It would be a treat."

"Fish-and-chips! Oh, goodie-goodie! Mum's going to get us fish-and-chips at Yarmouth, Tommy."

"We were merely discussing the possibility, thank you. If you two don't go to bed soon, your mother will be going to Yarmouth on her own tomorrow."

"I had fish-and-chips once, Mum," Tom whispered when I went up to tuck them in. "When Granny and Grandpa took me to Norwich last summer."

"Well, we'll have some tomorrow sitting on the beach. Won't that be lovely. No more talking now. Get to sleep, there's good children."

We'd need sandwiches as well, of course, and apples and biscuits. I got everything ready early before taking the baby along to Mrs Rudd.

"Now don't you go a-worryin' about young Henry, Missus. Him'll be grand wi' Oi," she said, enfolding him in her ample bosom.

"Hurry up, Mum!" they were yelling. "The coach is coming."

"I've got the bag of swimming things . . . "

"And I've got the buckets and spades . . . "

They weren't very old. She was five-and-a-half. He was just seven.

"Are you going to give us some money then, Pete? We're off now. The bus is waiting."

"Yes, yes - I'll give you some money. Let's see you safely aboard first." And having handed up the bags and buckets, and swung Charlie up after them into the Sunday School coach, he scrabbled around in his pocket and with a flourish brought out - *a one pound note.*

It was a beautiful day. A beautiful drive to Yarmouth. No-one was sick and there were no quarrels.

"Can we have a go on the roundabout, Mum?"

"Please, please, can we have a go on the trampoline?"

"Oh, look - ices with flaky bars sticking out at the top!"

"Look . . . "

"Look . . . "

"Mummy . . . "

" Mummy, look . . . "

They dug in the sand and paddled and were delighted with their first sight of the sea, their introduction to shells and ships and seagulls.

"They sound like Henry when his teeth were pushing through," said Charlie, staring solemnly at a flight of gulls screaming and wheeling overhead.

"I shall be a sailor when I grow up," said her big brother. "I shall sail right round the world and home again."

It was lunchtime. The Sunday School families were leaving the beach, dribbling back into town.

"Dawny!" called Mrs Dixon. "Come along, chick. Let Mummy put your sandals on. We're going to get us fish-and-chip dinners."

"We're having fish-and-chips too, Dawny Dixon," announced Charlie, struggling into her dry knickers.

We made our way along the front, tired now and hungry. Weighed down with shells and seaweed and soggy bathing suits. The fish-and-chip cafes were crowded. We found a clean though modest establishment in a side street. The proprietor let us dump our bags round a table in the window while we tidied ourselves up in the Ladies.

"Fish and chips for three, please," I told him when we were organised.

"That will be 3/6 each, love. Will there be anything else?"

I was doing some frantic arithmetic in my head. "No, no thanks. That will be fine. Small portions for the children, if you do them, please."

It was delicious, and they ate every scrap, Charlie wiping a surreptitious finger round her plate to savour the last of the salt and vinegar. Tom had wolfed down the adult portion and sneaked a couple of chips off my plate as well.

"I'm thirsty, Mum. I'm so thirsty."

"So am I. Can we have a drink?"

"Can we have some orange, Mum?"

"Please, *please*!"

He brought the bill with their orange squash. 12/11d. Oh, my God! 12/11d.

I tipped the contents of my purse out onto my lap under cover of the table. Three half-crowns, one florin, three sixpences, a handful of copper and a threepenny bit. Twelve shillings exactly.

"Have you any money, Tommy? Charlie, have you?"

"No, I've got nuffink."

"I only had ten pence left over from my birthday money and I spent it on the switchback."

"It's all right. It doesn't matter. I just wondered how much we had between us." I rummaged in my pockets without success. "Take Charlie up to the loo, love, and see that she has a wee and washes her hands."

"I'm sorry," I choked, when the children were safely out of the way. "I'm terribly sorry . . . I shouldn't have let them have their squash. I'm afraid, I'm afraid I haven't got enough to pay the bill . . . "

A pound, I was thinking. A fucking pound. For the three of us. And their first trip to the sea.

It had gone very quiet in that crowded cafe. Apart from my sobs of shame.

"I'll wash up or something . . . "

"Don't you worry, Lady. You've all-but got it." And scooping up the handful of change he pushed a florin back across the counter to me. "Now, now - no need to take on so. It doesn't do to be penniless with bairns at the seaside."

Penniless. That's what we always seemed to be, penniless.

"And it's all your damn fault," Pete would accuse me, whenever there was a crisis. "I'd live on a pittance if it wasn't for you bloody lot."

We had a lovely afternoon. We went to the quay where the fishing boats were moored and watched all the comings and goings. The kids danced along the seawall, following the leader with their old stripy sunhats on. Swinging their arms, and singing the first two lines of some crazy song :

"Ha-ha-ha he-he-he
An elephant's nest in a rhubarb tree."

They were still singing it sleepily when we disembarked at the School House. They were itchy from the sunshine, and when they got undressed for the bath sand trickled out of their socks and knickers.

Pete had the table set for supper. The children ate Weetabix, Charlie sitting on my knee being the baby again.

"I'll have the change," he said, "before you blue it."

"Was Henry good with Mrs Rudd?" I asked, ignoring the hand he was holding out to me expectantly. "I'll pop up and look at him before I tuck the others in."

While I was upstairs I took that two-shilling piece and hid it under my hankies.

"Mummy," a drowsy voice called out later when they were all in bed, "fish-and-chips is lovely."

Chapter Nine

"Smoked salmon, or turkey?" asked Walter, ordering Danish sandwiches for us after the theatre.

"Oh, Walter - you do spoil me. What a day it's been."

"We were due for a celebration, my dear. It's sounds as though *Penguin* like your illustrations. I'll keep my fingers crossed for you. Now then, which is it to be?"

We'd been to see *Equus* at the Festival Theatre. Such a powerful play. We had put it on at the Little Theatre soon after the Ted thing started. I was involved in all their productions by then, though I still wasn't comfortable in that extrovert group.

"Yes, I'll prompt if you like. If no-one else wants the job."

But no-one ever did. It's quite a responsibility, prompting. You must keep your eyes glued to the text. Sure as fate, if your attention wanders, that's the moment someone forgets their lines. I tried *not* to prompt. I mean, I always waited as long as I dared before giving the cue. They can get very funny about prompts, especially the Stars.

"I didn't need a prompt in Act One, thank you. That was a deliberate pause."

And the very next minute I'd be in trouble for not coming to the rescue quickly enough.

"What were you doing back there, wasn't it obvious I was stuck?"

But it was all worth it, to be part of the team. To contribute in some small way to the drama, the illusion. Perched on my stool behind the right hand flap I'd wait breathless for the houselights to go down, for the curtain cue in the overture, for the magic to begin.

It was during our production of *Equus* that Ernest Jagger, Grandfather of the Dramatic Society, came into the story. He had a minor part (I can't even remember what it was now), and only appeared in the final scene. He took to sitting backstage with me. Not distracting me, mind. Just sitting beside me in a friendly sort of way, waiting for his entrance. Now and again he'd slip me a peppermint cream or some other little treat, and after the final curtain call he'd waylay me as I made my way through to the Green Room.

"Why do you always scuttle off, my dear?"

"It's so late. I must get home. I have to be up for work in the morning."

I couldn't tell him of the excruciating shyness that seemed to smother me. My sense of total inadequacy among such glittering company.

"Just wait till I change," Ernest said, "and we'll have a little drink together."

But even that was difficult. I didn't want Ted thinking I was hanging around on his account. Normally he ignored me completely at the theatre. To allay suspicion, he assured me. I was too green to see that I was scarcely a feather in his cap. In any case, the last thing he wanted was to be publicly committed to anyone. Ted liked to keep his options open.

"What will it be, then?"

"Oh, that's very kind of you, Ernest. A half of cider, please."

"I'm not buying cider for a lady. Come along, have something special."

"Well, could I have a gin and tonic, perhaps."

Ted leered at me from the other end of the bar. I was getting quite a taste for gin and tonic since he introduced me to it on the back seat of his Rover. It was suddenly friendly, leaning on the bar, being included in the banter, joining in the laughter and the gossip.

"You two were having a good time of it tonight, James. Thought we'd have the vice squad down on us."

"You said to make it realistic."

"Last orders. Last orders."

"Can I persuade you to have another one, dear."

"Oh, no. No thank you. I must be going. I really must."

"In that case I shall accompany you home, if I may. I'm on my bike tonight unfortunately, or I could have offered you a lift. Perhaps you'll let me walk along with you."

Such a gentleman Ernest was. One of the old school.

"No, no - I couldn't let you do that. But thank you for the drink."

He escorted me out nevertheless, collecting his bike from the store-room as we went past.

"Talk about devotion, folks!" I heard someone screech. "Such an ordinary little soul - how *does* she do it?"

There was no answer to that, but devoted he certainly was. Still is, come to that, now I'm on my own. Coming round to give me advice on everything from mending my bike to growing sweet-peas. I've only to mention a problem and he's over here with his toolbag. Take shelves, for instance. A dripping tap. A door that drags on the carpet. Grass clippers that have lost their bite. It isn't *Jim'll Fix It* in this house. It's dear old Ernest every time.

And *old* Ernest is right. He was in his eighties then when our paths first crossed. He's never actually told me his age, but he was in the First War. Invalided out in 1915 with a serious leg wound. He still limps.

There was the traditional Last Night Party after *Equus*. Ernest made a great fuss of me, escorting me round, not letting me out of his sight. But all the time I was waiting for a signal from Ted.

I was still thinking of us as 'lovers', Ted and I. I suppose it was because I so desperately needed some love in my life (especially now that Angus had moved back to Edinburgh to finish his life sentence with Alice up there), that I deluded myself in this way. I was seeing him most Mondays, though he wouldn't commit himself even that much.

"Next week, as usual?" I'd say without thinking as I hopped out of his car at the end of our road.

"We'll see. We'll see. I'll be in touch."

"Couldn't we see each other more often?" I asked once naively.

"We mustn't be greedy," he said. "I don't want to get bored with you."

God! What a chauvinist! But still I didn't choose to see it.

Invariably on those Monday nights we'd drive out into the countryside, draw into some secluded lay-by or copse, transfer to the back seat with the gin and tonic from the boot, and after a perfunctory chat he'd get down to business.

"You lasted as long as any of his girlfriends," Jeannie told me later. "Three years - that must be a record."

Perhaps the old fox cared for me a little, after all, I wondered. But it wasn't that. Of course it wasn't. It was his pride, his prowess, his track record, that kept us together.

I'm what you might call a slow worker, you see. Desperately slow. In his diplomatic career, Ted had swept through Latin America, India and Scandinavia as the Foreign Office directed, whipping up orgasms as he went. But with me he got nowhere, much to his chagrin. His skill and determination, his professionalism produced not a thing. Not the slightest shudder of excitement. All his handwork, all the gymnastics were wasted on me.

"I'll get there in the end," I heard him mutter once. "I've not been beaten yet."

It's not manual dexterity that counts, I thought. It's a matter of psychology.

"If you could say something friendly, Ted. That might help."

But he was incapable of such a thing. Afraid of committing himself to something rash in the heat of the moment, he worked away in silence. Total silence. Not even my name escaped his thin lips. But then, he probably couldn't remember from one night to the next who he was with.

"Darling Betty . . . er, Mary . . . er, Susan! What night of the week is it, for Christ's sake!"

Poor old Ted.

In spite of all this, he had hinted that we could sneak off after the *Equus* party and besport ourselves till dawn. So anxiously, besottedly I waited for his signal.

He was looking incredibly distinguished that night in an ice blue safari jacket that exactly echoed the colour of his eyes. His thick blond hair was fresh-washed and fluffy. His dramatic eyebrows twitched lasciviously as he danced and drank the hours away.

Eventually the party began to disintegrate, but still there was no signal from Ted.

"I really must take you home, my dear," said Ernest looking at his watch. "Come along. It's well after two. I've got the car tonight."

"Don't worry about me," I stalled, eager for him to leave. For Ted to claim me. "I'll be fine. Someone will drop me off."

"I wouldn't think of leaving you to the mercy of this wild lot," he insisted. "Everyone's leaving more or less."

As Ernest and I shuffled out, Ted was chatting animatedly to Sylvie, the sexy pianist. He didn't give me a glance. Damn him, I thought. He wouldn't find me such a co-operative little piece in future. Him and his bloody games!

"I hope I won't be breathalysed," said Ernest as we drove through the empty streets. "They can stop anyone at this time of night, without provocation."

Someone was tailing us, headlights full on.

"Thank you for a lovely evening," he said, gripping my hand passionately. "Perhaps I may be allowed a kiss."

I gave him a peck on the cheek and opened the car door. The other car had drawn up fifty yards behind us, lights still blazing.

"I'll phone you, if I may," Ernest was saying. "Perhaps we could meet for coffee one day." With this production over there would be no more cosy evenings in the theatre bar.

"Yes. Lovely. Yes." I scrambled out, gathering up my long skirt for fear of tripping. The house was dark, of course. Dark and silent. I stood at the gate waving Ernest off. And waiting. Waiting for the other car which I now recognised as the big green Rover to slide quietly alongside.

"Ah! Thought I wasn't going to make it in time. Thought that old fool was going to force himself on you first. Jump in!"

Was it a face I glimpsed at our bedroom window as we glided off into the dawn? Had Pete lain awake waiting for my return? Who cares, I thought, as we swept up the road to the open countryside. Who bloody cares?

"Why did you ignore me all night, Ted?" I asked afterwards, as we buttoned ourselves together again in a rabbity cornfield.

"I'm only trying to protect your reputation, my dear," he assured me.

And I was mollified.

Chapter Ten

I was easily mollified in those days.

"Couldn't we have an evening out, Ted?" I asked him once. "Properly out? Couldn't we go to the sea? While the heatwave lasts?"

"By the time I get back from Town it's far too late to go gallivanting off - you know it is."

"Oh, come on, you old misery." It would be heavenly to walk along by the sea in the dusk. Roamin' in the gloamin' and all that. "Do let's go."

"We'll see, we'll see," he said stroking the back of my neck impatiently.

A couple of times I did persuade him to have a quick walk through the woods before getting down to business, or to sit a few minutes beside a chalk stream and watch the trout snatching at flies, but that was only to placate me when I was threatening to back out of the relationship. Oh, yes - daft as I was, I didn't take it all lying down.

"Look here, Ted, I've had enough of your bloody games. I waited nearly half an hour last night. In the freezing fog. You could have let me know. Could have phoned me at work. You didn't have to leave me hanging around. I must be an idiot to bother with you. You're a flaming chauvinist. But *that's it* - this time I've had enough. You can find someone else for your Monday slot. Good bloody bye!" And I slammed down the phone.

Funnily enough this was the surest way to elicit a little affection from him. He couldn't bear rejection.

"Oh, look, please - please don't be like that," he begged, phoning straight back. "My sister died yesterday. My youngest sister, Marian. She had multiple sclerosis - I told you about her. She died in her sleep. Without any warning.

I had to dash over to Reading. From the office. I wasn't home till midnight. I was very fond of her. It was a terrible shock. Everything else went out of my head."

"Oh, hell! I'm sorry. Poor old thing." And we'd drift on to the next crisis.

"But it did last three years," Jeannie reminded me. "Three years was a long time for Ted."

"A very long time," said the private detective Jeannie employed to trail him. "You were in fact his mistress."

Yes, I suppose I was. Especially once we had moved our activities into the house. Then I really felt like a mistress.

"I've got a surprise for us tonight, he announced one foggy evening that first November, and he headed the car back into town, drawing up outside a terrace of Victorian cottages. Unlocking the door of Number 15 he ushered me in.

"But, whose place is it? Ted . . . ?"

"It's *my* place," he explained with glee. "It's *our* place."

Our place. Oh what comforting words! All the slights and indignities of the past months evaporated there and then. This was our place. Just for us, for Ted and me.

He showed me round. There were two flats. The upstairs one a love nest for our secret pleasures, the groundfloor flat to be rented out.

"I'll advertise for tenants," he said, "but don't worry, I shall choose very carefully. There'll be no chance of our being denounced."

It was all freshly decorated, with luxurious bathrooms and kitchens. The top flat was bright and cheerful, mainly orange.

"I've been working at it for weeks. I wanted to surprise you."

He did that all right. I sank onto the large bouncy bed and pulled him down beside me. "Oh, Ted, you're the limit! I guess this makes me into your mistress. A scarlet woman!" And we rolled about laughing.

Maybe I'm a fool to believe it, but as far as I know no other woman ever came to Number Fifteen, not during my 'term of office.' He'd bought it through a London solicitor, incognito. No one else knew about it. Jeannie didn't, that's for sure.

"We used to meet in the Albemarle Street flat," I told her later when everything was coming out in the open. I had been promoted by then. Mondays and Fridays were my nights. Twice a week! I was Royal Favourite for a time."

Jeannie couldn't believe it. She was wild at him.

"But it must have been my money he bought the place with. The money my poor father left me. Ted said he'd invest it for me. Invest it!"

We were sitting on the wall outside Number Fifteen, that Saturday morning after my divorce. After I'd told her about me and Ted.

"He had several different lots of tenants in the bottom flat. None of them stayed very long. The place got pretty smelly. One couple had dozens of cats that were never let out as far as we could tell."

"But what's it like in his flat?" Jeannie persisted. "I wish I could get in and see for myself."

"It was nice at the start. All so clean. Freshly painted. Everything orange and white. But it soon got scruffy. He didn't bother to look after it. Piles of litter in the kitchen. Bottles. Papers. Mostly bottles. Yes, it was squalid, really squalid the last time I saw it."

I remembered it vividly.

There was an Olde Time Music Hall on at the Little Theatre. I wasn't in it myself, but Ted was doing a comic song and a melodramatic monologue. What with rehearsals and various problems at my end we had not visited our love nest for a week or two.

"I can escape after the first scene," he told me, phoning from work. "Wait for me by the bridge and I'll run you up to Albemarle Street as soon as I come off stage. I'll have to be back in time for my spot in the second half. You can be keeping the bed warm for us."

It was bitterly cold. I felt conspicuous hanging around at that time of night.

"Sorry," he said, when he eventually rolled up. "Got waylaid in the bar. Didn't want to arouse suspicion."

As usual, we parked the car round the corner from Number Fifteen and while he approached it from one direction I walked round the block and approached it from the other.

"God! It's arctic up here!" And he put the electric fire on. At one time he had brought logs and we'd sat snugly together on the hearthrug with our gin and tonics. But not now. Now it was the electric fire, the electric blanket, and straight down to business.

"Bloody hell! My monologue!" He scrambled back into his clothes and fled. "Don't go away. I'll only be an hour or so."

I could have done with a cup of coffee, but there would be nothing in the flat except gin and tonic and beer, I knew that. I switched on the second bar of the fire and snuggled down under the grubby orange blankets.

Hang about. Don't go away. Be sure to wait. That was the pattern of my life with Ted. Waiting for phone calls. Lurking in the shadows waiting for a lift. Waiting for him to remember my birthday. To whisper sweet nothings. To use my name. Always waiting . . .

What a fool I'd been. A right bloody fool.

There'd been the time I found myself in London and very unwisely phoned him at the Ministry.

"It's me, Ted." Naively.

"Ah - hello." Guardedly.

"I'm up here for the day. Had to see Aunt Edith safely onto her train to Edinburgh. I just wondered . . ."

"What a pity I didn't know sooner," coldly. "I'm completely tied up unfortunately. All day."

" . . . a quick lunch together?" Idiotically.

"I've arranged to have lunch with a colleague. It would have been nice, but not today. Goodbye, now."

I somehow never got to understand the rules. Ted's rules.

One evening I persuaded him to drive over to visit Kate, my youngest sister, who was living 18 miles away, over towards Petersfield, at the time. Her husband was working out in Saudi Arabia. They lived in a smartly modernised cottage in the grounds of a Victorian mansion. Eventually the house would be converted into sixteen luxury flats, but for the present it was a derelict shell, awaiting planning permission or something. Apart from Alasdair who was only a couple of months old and their two large Alsatians, Kate was entirely alone on the estate.

I had confided in her too about Ted.

"Why don't you ask him to bring you over one evening. It would be good to have company. I'll make you a meal."

"Yes," he said when I suggested it. "Yes, if I get the earlier train for once, perhaps we could drive over. I like Kate. She's always looked to me as if she'd be game for a bit of the other."

You got used to remarks like that. Ted was a born hunter, and it was no use pretending otherwise.

It was a strange evening. He was at his most dashing. For Kate's benefit, of course. He followed her through to the kitchen at every opportunity, and when he was in the loo she signalled to me that he'd been making a pass at her. He made a note of her phone number while she was changing the baby, and behaved in a most derisory manner to me.

"Awfully attractive girl, Katie. No-one would guess you were sisters."

I gave Kate a quick hug as we left. "I'll ring you tomorrow," I told her, regretting having inflicted him on her.

Ted gave her a hug too, fondling her quite blatantly.

"Get off," she told him, furious. "*She's* supposed to be your little friend, remember. Keep your mucky hands to yourself, will you." Rex and Queenie snarled and bared their teeth.

On the way home he was taken ill. Every mile or so he had to stop the car and vomit in the hedge. It was dangerous on that busy road, dangerous and disgusting. I didn't feel in the least bit sorry for him. I just hoped to God we'd get home in one piece.

And then, in the last lay-by before town, having spewed up yet again, he pulled me roughly onto his lap and took his reward, his 'taxi fare' you might call it. Like that. Smelling of vomit. Clammy and weak from his attack. Like that.

"Kate excited me," he explained, surprised I should resist him. "Come on - I need it."

He's an animal, a pig, I thought now, lying waiting for him to come back from the Old Time Music Hall and take his pleasure of me again.

There had been good times, though. At the beginning mainly. We did actually get to the seaside during that heatwave. We had a swim and fish and chips and happened on a Barn Dance at the back of a pub we called at on our journey home.

"Oh, Ted - let's have a dance, shall we?"

I'd only just discovered dancing. Disco-ing I suppose you'd call it. I was hopeless at any other sort. Ballroom and all that stuff they used to try to teach us at school. Great gawky girls clutching one another grimly in the gym, while Miss Pickwick called out : "*One* two three, *one* two three, *left* two three, keep the rhythm now, girls." I was stiff with anxiety then, and all feet.

But *this* is something else! It's mad at my age, I know. But, oh boy! Do I love it!

There's always dancing at these weekend courses I go on. 'Saturday Night : Social and Dancing' it says on the programme. The first time or two I sat meekly on the fringe of things longing for someone to ask me to dance never did. So few men. So many ravishing girls. Who's going to bother with a funny old bat like me!

After a bit I worked out that only about a third of the women were dancing. The rest of us were forced to sit there smiling fixedly like something out of Jane Austen, for Christ's sake! Trying to disguise our feelings of rejection, our feet tapping irrepressibly to that insistent music.

Bugger this, I thought. And I got up and started dancing on my own. Took some courage, I can tell you, but I didn't care. I simply had to dance. As I spun round, weaving between the polite couples, I swept up one or two of my fellow wallflowers.

"Come on. Come and dance."

Before long there wasn't a soul sitting out. Every damned artist on our *Landscapes in Winter* course was dancing. And I'll tell you something else. The men were none too pleased. We had deprived them of their traditional right, to confer on a chosen few the privilege of sharing in the dance.

To hell with that! This is the Dance of Life. Like it says in the song :

Dance, dance, wherever you may be,
For I am the Lord of the Dance, said he . . .

Nothing to do with flirting or wooing. Nothing to do with finding a fleeting bed-fellow. This is the rhythm of life, and we've been left out long enough. We're joining in, in force. Wild and abandoned, for the sheer joy of it. And willy-bloody-nilly!

"Why not?" said Ted, on that summer night by the sea. "Why not!" And we whirled madly into the fray.

"I didn't know you were a dancer," he whispered into my hair as we drew into a convenient lay-by for our *nightcap*. And for once, I felt it was me he was making love to, crouching so uncomfortably on the back seat. I almost caught him breathing my name.

I guess he's no worse than the rest of them, I comforted myself, jumping out of bed with a shiver now in the Love Nest, and helping myself to a good stiff gin and tonic. They're all led by the genitals.

In the church tower at the corner the clock struck the hour. I looked at my watch. Midnight! The show would have been over hours ago. He must be chatting up some promising little creature in the Theatre Bar. There was a troop of gorgeous can-can dancers in the programme. That would be it.

I remembered the time we were both in the pantomime, Ted and I. He was interested in one of the chorus girls then. I was the back-end of the flipping horse! He was mauling her blatantly in the Green Room, abandoning his usual discretion. He saw me eyeing him and set to with greater enthusiasm than before.

Now this girl's husband always collected her after the show so there would be no opportunity for Ted to get her on her own. Frustrated, he sought me out.

"Can I give you a lift home?" he asked sweetly.

"No thanks. I've got a lift. Phil goes right past my place."

"Oh, come on now - there's no need to be put out, just because I was having a drink with young Carol. Possessiveness is such an ugly emotion."

I can scarcely bear to record what happened next. It fills me with shame to this day. Shame and disgust. But I've started so I'll finish. Yes, I let him drive me home. I shouldn't have allowed it, but I did. He stopped by the park gates.

"I don't like to see you upset, my dear. Let's have a little walk and talk it over."

This was so uncharacteristic, I should have been on my guard. But I preferred to think he was truly contrite.

At one end of the park there are steep steps among the trees. He guided me over to them and steered me up one step above him.

"Stay there!" he commanded, his voice think with lust. "No, don't struggle!" And he took me like that, like a dog, from behind. Exactly like a dog. Treating me to the passion young Carol had aroused in him. Yuk!

My God. What a fool I am, I thought now, draining my glass and coming to a decision at last.

I got up. Got dressed. Crept down through the groundfloor hall and out into the bitter January night. I'd have to walk home, but that didn't matter. It wasn't much more than a mile and the street lights were still on.

A young man passed me, racing happily home from his girlfriend's on his bike. It was Thomas. My son Thomas. He wouldn't recognise me, not in the dark, and me with the hood of my dufflecoat pulled up over my head. Surely he wouldn't recognise his mother, skulking around at dead of night like a street walker, like a slut.

Christ, I thought. What have I come to? I must get away somewhere. Get away and sort myself out.

Chapter Eleven

I did manage to get away on my own a time or two in the last couple of years before our divorce. The family was shrinking rapidly, and with it, my responsibilities. Thomas was away at University, and Charlotte had gone to Australia.

My cousin Robert and his wife Liz had stayed with us for three months while they tried to decide whether or not to buy a village shop and settle in Dorset. They had both emigrated to Australia in their teens, Robert going out at nineteen as a freshly qualified chef. Liz sailing on the Canberra with her parents when she was thirteen. They seemed doomed to wander back and forth for ever, like restless spirits denied eternal peace. While they were out there they were desperately homesick for England but when they returned on one of their regular attempts to repatriate themselves they were invariably disillusioned with things here : the economic situation, the strength of the trade unions, the growing number of immigrants (yes, even in Dorset), and were soon booking their flights back to New South Wales.

"But you're immigrants yourselves," Tom told them heatedly in his Left Wing period.

"We'd be delighted to have Charlotte out here for a spell," Liz wrote soon after they had opened their Service Station and Restaurant on the Pacific Highway north of Sydney. "She'd be a great help to us . . . "

"Looking after that flaming kid of theirs," Henry grunted into his cornflakes.

"Mark's OK, Henry. He can't help his parents."

" . . . and it would be a tremendous opportunity for her."

"As long as you don't go and settle out there, Charlie. It's the other side of the flaming earth."

"Henry! Don't keep using that flaming word. And get a move on, you'll miss your bus. What do you think, Pete?"

"Hm," he said grudgingly. "Decent of them to offer to pay your fare, Charlotte. They must be doing well."

"I don't know that we should let you go, love. What if things don't work out. They're a funny pair. It's so far away."

They had just about driven me round the bend, Robert and Liz, while they were with us. Scattering their belongings throughout the house in spite of having Charlie's lovely big groundfloor room to spread themselves in. Criticising the way I ran things. Always rowing over two year old Mark.

"Robert! What are you doing up there?" Liz would yell. "Don't excite that child. Get him bathed quietly. I've got one of my heads coming on."

I suffered more with migraine during those three months than ever before or since, but that's by the way.

"It's only for six months, Mum," Charlie said. "I am seventeen."

We saw her off one golden September evening. Kate came to hold the fort till we got back.

"We don't need a baby-sitter, Mum. Goodness, we can manage. We're not kids, you know."

"It's all arranged. She's bringing Alasdair over after lunch. They'll just stay till we get back from Heathrow."

This was soon after Pete had been persuaded to learn to drive. He'd bought a car from friends, a huge hungry thing that was constantly breaking down.

"We were better off without it," he complained, stamping in yet again to phone Harold for instructions. "It's nothing more than a liability."

But at least we could drive Charlie up to Heathrow.

"This time tomorrow you'll be somewhere over the Pacific," said Kate as we labelled the suitcases.

"Don't forget, Robert said you could phone as soon as you get there, lovey. We won't go to bed until you've rung tomorrow night."

"Oh, Gawd! Remember how they used to row?"

"But only with each other. They're very good hearted, both of them."

"Six months is a hell of a time . . . "

"It's nothing. It'll flash by."

"At least you'll miss the winter. It's the best time of the year to be going."

"I like the winter, actually. I like it."

"Come on, let's put the kettle on. We've time for a cup of tea before we set out, and Dad'll want one when he gets in from school."

"You'll be sure to write, won't you, Mum," she said, coming through to help me in the kitchen. "And tell me everything that's happening. Everything. OK?"

"Hey, come on! Cheer up! It's going to be one hell of an adventure. I wish I was going with you."

"So do I, Mum. So do I."

"Carry the tray through for me. There's some of Clair's special flapjack in the tin. I think I'll put my lovely record on to cheer us all up."

Una Paloma blanca, it began. *I'm just a bird in the sky.* And we were off, jigging madly round to the irresistible tune.

Alasdair was a great dancer, balancing uncertainly on his fat little legs, swaying seductively from side to side as he waved his hands above his head, mesmerised by the music.

Una paloma blanca, over the mountains I fly . . .

"A very suitable send-off," Kate pointed out, bellowing above the band. "Whoops!" as Alasdair plonked down in a heap. "He could probably walk if he'd only risk it."

No-one can take my freedom away. Dah, dah, dah, dah, daaaaah.

That's the bit I like, I thought, starting it off again. *No-one can take my freedom away.*

"Great!" We flopped around exhausted.

"I kept thinking about that," Charlie wrote in her first airmail home. "Halfway round the world it was singing in my head. Kate was right. It was a good send-off. *My white dove.* I like that. *I fly off to the sun.* That was me all right. It's really boiling here, I can tell you. My skin's gone all funny. My lips and fingers are covered in gungy sores. Liz says it's Solar Eczema probably. I hope it won't get any worse. If it's this bad in the spring, what's it going to be like in the summer?"

I missed Charlie badly.

Tom had set off for Exeter and the rather dreary digs he'd found, sharing a room in a council house on the outskirts of town with a fellow student.

"She's got crinoline ladies everywhere," he told me, phoning for extra socks and jerseys. "It's pretty excruciating. And she's so bloody fussy. We have to book a bath. And pay for it. Twenty-five pence. And she puts secret marks on the coffee jar in case we're sneaking a cup while she's out." Pip-pip-pip. "I've no more money. Don't forget the woollies, Mum. See you soon. Bye."

"Crumbs! I wouldn't fancy sharing, specially with a flaming stranger."

"Henry!"

"I'll make jolly sure I get a place in a hostel when I go to college."

"Go on, who says you're going to get through your O Levels, eh? Never mind anything else," said Claire, a very raw First Former at King Alfred's Comprehensive.

They were both bigger than me already, the little ones, and quite able to look after themselves for a few days.

"There's a painting course at Earnley, Pete. Sussex Landscapes." Eddie had been talking about it at the class. "At the beginning of November."

"Hm," he said, shuffling through his marking.

"I thought I might go. I've never been away on my own."

"And what about us?" he said, looking up in astonishment.

"I'll leave you plenty of stuff ready in the fridge. Things that are easy to heat up. It's only for two nights. You won't even miss me."

"Well, as long as I'm not expected to cough up, you go. Why not? Yes, you go and enjoy yourself."

So off I went, simple as that. I was working full time by then so the money wasn't a problem. And what a weekend it was, my first taste of un-married life in twenty years. With a room to myself. Time to think. Space in which to stretch and breathe and grow.

"Coming for a walk?" they asked when the bar closed on the Friday night. "It's only ten minutes down the lane to the sea."

And, "Who's for coffee?" when we got back wild and exhilarated by our freedom. "We can help ourselves, you know."

It was like being back at college, but wiser with it. Sitting round the log fire in the Common Room discussing Art and Life and Personal Relationships, Sex and Literature till the kitchen staff came through with an urn of early morning tea.

"How long have you been painting, kid?" Ben, the tutor, asked me at the end of the afternoon session. "I think you've got something. Good feeling for atmosphere. Make sure you stick at it. You could just go places."

He's only trying to encourage me, I told myself soberly, though I had to admit I was quite as good as anyone else on the course. It did me good that. Gave me a bit of confidence.

"Hey, that's great, Mum. Flaming great!"

They had survived at home without me.

"Mm! The perspective is good," Pete allowed, casting a perfunctory eye over my Winter Landscape. "Yes, not bad for a beginner. I can scarcely draw a straight line."

With Charlie out in Australia, I had commandeered her bedroom as my studio.

"Just while you're away," I wrote to her. "I hope you don't mind. The light's good, and it's nice looking out onto the garden. I won't interfere with your things."

It was blissful having a corner to myself. A room of my own. Old Virginia Woolf knew what she was talking about there, even if she did go off her rocker in the end. Once you've got a bit of space, space and quiet and solitude, that's when a woman can begin to live, begin to blossom. We all need space, don't we? Men and women. Pity it's such a rare ingredient in marriage. There might be more chance of surviving together if we could each establish our right to a little personal space.

Now I'd taken the room over, very often I'd sleep down there in Charlie's bed, especially if I had been working late, struggling to get the mistiness right, the early-morning-ness that is my particular strength, I've discovered. New every morning and all that.

"I seem to be leading a celibate life these days," Pete complained, poking his head round the door to tell me he was off to bed.

"I'd only disturb you when I came up." I didn't care. I was giddy with creativity.

Having launched myself into the world of residential courses for adults there was no holding me. Lincolnshire Landscapes at Horncastle, I went to next. Wessex Watercolour Weekend. Abstracts in Oils at Oxford.

I like abstracts, though I don't often have time to do one these days. I enjoy painting them. You discover things in an abstract, your own abstract. Things you didn't realise you wanted to say.

"Here we see an artist's struggle to express her individuality vividly yet subtly conveyed," they were to write in the Sunday Colour Supplements later, after my first

London Show. "Here we see the dilemma of a woman torn between family responsibility and her own latent talent."

But I wasn't torn any longer. I was mending fast.

"Una paloma blanca," I sang as I mixed the viridian with a touch of cobalt for my summer dawn.

"Una paloma blanca
I'm just a bird in the sky,
over the mountains I fly
No-one can take my freedom away."
No-one can take my new-found freedom away.

Chapter Twelve

It wasn't only painting courses I went on. There were Self-Discovery ones, Spontaneous-Interaction ones, New-Age Share-ins, and God knows what else.

Pete had found himself a Special Friend by this time, and I couldn't blame him in the least. He knew about Ted, after all, and one or two other little adventures besides.

"Oh, no," he groaned, when he discovered what went on backstage at the Little Theatre. "I just can't believe you'd behave like that. After all these years together. I thought we were happy enough. Where's it all gone wrong?" He was sitting at the kitchen table, weeping like a child. I did feel bad then. I really did.

"Come on, love. Cheer up. You'll get used to it."

"Used to it! You are my wife, for Christ's sake! Whatever has happened to us?"

He wiped his tears on his sleeve like a lost five year old, and I passed him a box of Kleenex.

"Oh - sorry!" Claire popped her head round the door. She must have been sent to see whether the storm was abating. "We're going to take the dogs up the hill. Came for the leads. Sorry."

"He's *crying*!" I heard her whisper to the others. They trooped off silently. Even the dogs had picked up the atmosphere and were curbing their natural exuberance at the prospect of a walk.

"Oh, kid," he sobbed. "I'm sorry. I really am sorry. I'd no idea that you were unhappy. I've done my best, you know. We can only do our best."

And it was true. According to his light, Pete had done his best. It was simply that we had such very different expectations.

All human suffering stems from our attachments, said the Lord Buddha. Expectations, attachments - I guess he was right.

"It's probably something to do with our backgrounds, Pete." That had definitely been part of the trouble.

My mother had tried to tell me the first time I took him home.

We met at college up in Leeds. We were both training to be teachers. In those days the students at Teacher Training College fell into two distinct categories. All the women seemed to come from comfortable middle-class families like my own. Teaching was a nice respectable career for your average Grammar School product.

"She's bound to marry," they would decide for their daughters. "She can always pick teaching up again later, once her own children are at school."

The men students, on the other hand, were from northern working-class communities. Almost without exception. Teaching was a step up the ladder for these bright young men from the coalfields, the steel towns, the heavy industry of Middlesbrough and Sheffield. The simplest route into the comparative affluence of the professional world.

"Ooh! Your Jimmy's doing well then, Annie. Going to be a teacher, i'nt he?"

Pete's Dad was a Nottinghamshire miner. His Grandfather had spent sixty years underground too. Not hewing coal, but as a colliery blacksmith, shoeing the pit ponies, repairing machinery, maintaining equipment in the mine.

"But our lad's not goin' down t'pit," he'd tell you with pride. "He's reet sharp is our young Pete. Him's a-gooin' to college, sirrah!"

"He's probably the brightest man in his year," I'd told my parents. "I'm sure you'll like him."

I wasn't at all sure, but it's best to look on the bright side. So far, I'd only seen Pete in the college environment where we were free to establish our own criteria. It was a different matter having him in the bosom of my family over Easter.

"Well?" I asked anxiously afterwards.

"We did try to tell you, dear," my mother says now. "But it wasn't easy."

As a mother of teenagers, I understand what she means. Trying to point things out to love sick offspring is not easy.

"Oh, you're just being snobby about him, Mum. About his accent and everything."

"But he's not our sort of boy, darling." Poor old Daddy! There were to be six other stormy stretches for him to navigate before all of us were settled, but mine was the first.

"Well, I'm not your sort of *girl*, then!" And I'd slammed out of the sittingroom to sob myself to sleep.

"I'll change, kid," he promised now, sipping the good strong tea I'd made to comfort us. "I'll have driving lessons for a start. Yes, and I'll talk to Harold about that old car of his. It would be something to learn in. And we'll have a holiday this summer, all of us. We'll start all over again." Awkwardly, shyly my husband put his arms around me and wept into my hair.

He did try, it's true. He really made an effort to put things right.

"What's happened to Pete?" people asked in astonishment. "Whatever's come over him?"

It could well be that, emotionally handicapped as he was by his mother's bitterness, his father's dumb misery, poor old Pete was coming to life at last. In his fortieth year, the pain of my betrayal had jolted him awake.

"I think that was the first genuine emotion he'd ever felt," I was to say later. His tears were certainly genuine. And so was his anguish. But nevertheless, though I record it with shame, I couldn't give up Ted and all that I still chose to think he symbolised : freedom, self-determination, excitement, *life*!

"You can divorce me if you like," I told him. "You have ample grounds, that's for sure."

"But I don't want a divorce. What would I do without you? You may find it hard to believe, but I love you. In spite of everything, I love you." He got up and tipped a scuttleful of coke into the stove. "Where would you go, for Christ's sake? That sod's married, isn't he? Not much hope of running to him."

So in our wisdom we decided to stay together, keep the family together, let things ride.

"And if you find yourself a girlfriend, that'll be fine by me, Pete. We can both be discreet about it. In France everyone has an extra-marital relationship." (One of Ted's persuasive lines, this, but not necessarily true.) "It's the normal thing."

Pete took his new role very seriously. He lost a lot of weight and became quite youthful and handsome again. He took me out sometimes. To dances and theatres. He went off to things on his own - to socials, clubs. discos - at which (I suspected) he was miserably out of place, a middle-aged academic posing as one of your Bright Young Things. It was pathetic to see the effort he put into dressing up for a night on the town. And his dejection afterwards.

"I had a lot of fun tonight," he'd tell me brightly, peeling off his tight jeans, the psychedelic cravat he'd selected so carefully for this particular occasion.

He learnt to drive. He learnt to play the guitar. He abandoned his eternal studying and joined the Squash Club with Steve Hughes.

"You were right," he said a few months after the crisis, "I'm having a whale of a time, in spite of Ted. I might even give the bloody chap a medal."

So we jogged along happily enough, each with our private friends and affairs. It looked as if we might survive after all.

The Encounter Group was advertised in the local paper. *Explore your inner self*, the notice said. *Release your unrecognised potential. Experience a deeper more meaningful awareness. Live*!

"Yes, still a few places," they told me when I phoned. "We'll be glad to have you with us. Twenty pounds for the full weekend. We start at seven."

Perhaps you went to one of these Encounter Groups. They were all the rage just then. This one was weird, I can tell you. It was being held in a ramshackle farmhouse a couple of miles from town. Pete kindly dropped me there on the way to his Folk Evening.

About fifteen people were sitting on the floor round a cheerful log fire. Clive, a young man who claimed to be a psychologist was in charge.

"There isn't enough physical contact these days," he trilled. "We're all becoming physically inhibited. We're a generation of untouchables."

He got us playing various simple games aimed at releasing us from our terrible crippling hang-ups.

"Now then, I want you to choose a partner, sit opposite him on the floor, and look into his eyes. *Really* look at him. Now - doesn't that feel better?"

Slowly we progressed from looking to touching. Fingers first, shyly. Then hands. Hugging, embracing, kissing. It was quite something. Then came the bosom-baring session.

"I want you all to share your problems. Offer them to the group. Don't let shame or embarrassment hold you back. Let's share a great big beautiful psychological *crap*. Let's evacuate the waste products from our minds."

They picked on Cynthia to start the ball rolling. A nervous, dumpy, dingy little woman, Cynthia was suffering from a difficult marriage and a serious heart condition.

"My life's so restricted," she offered, horrified at having to take the floor. "I can't get a job. My health is too poor. Apart from my little car, I'm pretty well confined to the house. We scarcely speak any more, me and Bill. I sometimes wonder what the point of it all is."

Clive was radiant at having discovered such a splendid case so soon. He swelled with professional assurance.

"Ah! The *point*. That's what we're after this weekend. The point of it all. To find your particular answer, Sylvia..."

"Er, *Cynthia*, actually..."

"The point we're looking for in your case, Cynthia, lies somewhere in your past. How long have you been ill?"

"All my life practically. Since I was in my teens. I had the rheumatic fever when I was twelve. Never been much good since."

"*Clive*. 'Since I was twelve, *Clive*.' We must overcome our social inhibitions as well as our physical ones, Cynthia. Christian names from now on. And that means *use* them, please. All use them now. Yes, now! That's it. Come along. Don't be shy."

We sat there like dummies, paralysed with embarrassment.

"Each one of you turn to your neighbour and tell him your name. Your nickname if you like. Right. After me, round the group, one-by-one - yes. The people on both sides of you. 'Hello Phil. Hello Mary.' You see, it's not difficult. Off we go then..."

Eventually we drifted back to Cynthia and her confessed problem.

"Now Cynthia, I want you to look back into your childhood. Way back before you were ill. Tell me, Cynthia," all in a most condescending tone, "what were you good at then? What did you most enjoy?"

"Oh, er - I hardly like to say, er, Clive. It sounds so silly."

"Come along now, Cynthia. We're all being very-very honest this evening. That's why we are here together. Remember?"

"Well, then, when I was little I loved standing on my head. Doing cartwheels, handstands. I don't suppose I was that good, but I loved it. Gymnastics and all that stuff. I really loved it."

This was a jewel for our bright young analyst.

"Right then. What we're going to do is help you to do a handstand now. That's it - *now*! Come along. I need some help. You give me a hand. And you. And you."

With a team of eager helpers Clive proceeded to force poor bewildered Cynthia to stand on her head. "Together we will help you to re-discover your purpose in life, Sylvia."

"You'll kill me," she tried to tell him, struggling to get her feet back on the ground. "Put me down! Please put me down!"

"I'm not even allowed to lie flat in bed," she told me afterwards. In addition to the heart problem and rheumatoid arthritis, her innards were all adrift. poor soul. "I have to sleep bolt upright with six pillows behind me."

Suddenly I came to my senses. "Put her down!" I ordered with incredible command. "You'll have her death on your hands. Put her down at once or I shall call the police." I had crawled across and grabbed the phone that was on the window ledge. "Psychologist, my foot! You're irresponsible. You're a bloody menace."

They dropped Cynthia flat on her face with her problems and turned on me.

"You are obviously a woman with enormous personality deficiencies," Clive told me sourly. "Sit here," and he pushed me roughly down onto this cushion in the centre of the circle, "and one-by-one we will vocalise our reactions to your inadequacies."

"But . . ."

"No, *you* are not allowed to speak."

This was clearly not going to be my weekend. And somehow, I wasn't holding out much hope of enlightenment.

Chapter Thirteen

"I can see you were slowly emerging from your shell," said Walter, pouring us some more wine.

"Well, believe it or not, in a funny way my sordid affair with Ted was a help. Gave me a bit of self-confidence. I've got to give him that."

I was staying the night with Walter. He had taken me to a concert - Mozart, Elgar, Schubert - and then on to a little French restaurant that served excellent onion soup and *crepes florentines*.

"Raspberries would be nice to finish with, wouldn't they. Raspberries and cream, please. And liqueurs with our coffee, I think. Tia Maria, lass? Cointreau? Tia Maria."

"Walter, you're so good to me." I reached across the red and white checked tablecloth and squeezed his hand.

"Rubbish, my dear! I'm a thoroughly selfish creature, I can assure you. I'm only good to people who amuse me. People I enjoy. Now, what were we talking about . . . ?"

Having a job made a difference, of course. Having some money in my pocket.

"If you're seriously thinking of divorcing him," my father said the time I rushed over to Bristol to pour it all out to them, "then the important thing is to get yourself organised financially. Find a job. That's the first step."

"Oh, Gawd! No way could I face a class of kids. I was never much good in the classroom, but *now* I'd be a disaster."

"Plenty of other things you could do," my mother chipped in. "No reason to be snooty about office work. I worked in an office myself for a while during the war. Something to do with the evacuees, keeping a record of where everyone was billeted, the children who'd been sent out of the city. It was interesting. I quite enjoyed it."

Which is how I came to be in the Manpower Employment Agency the morning Mr Grimshaw rang them for help..

"I've got myself a job," I told them at tea time. "Only temporary. With a central heating firm. Up on Jewry Street. I'm to start tomorrow."

"Hm," Pete grunted into his baked potato. "I can't see what use you'll be to them, but it'll make a nice change having someone to share the financial burdens with me at last."

"But it means you'll all have to share the domestic burdens with *me*. This great place won't run itself."

And they did. On Saturday mornings everyone rallied round, and between us we got things ship-shape.

"You're a good organiser," said Mr Grimshaw after the first couple of weeks. "The filing system has never been in such good order. I'm very pleased with you. I'd like to offer you a permanent job here, if you're happy with *us*."

I'd very quickly learnt that all those intimidating items on the Agency questionnaire did indeed require little more than the ability to sort things into alphabetical order. That plus a tidy mind and a modicum of maths. Child's play compared with coping with the multifarious demands of family life. With running a shabby five bedroomed Victorian semi. On a shoestring. With the kids and the dogs and Henry's white mice and Claire's rabbits. Not to mention the difficult husband.

"But it means we'd expect you to do the same hours as everyone else," added Mr Fletcher, the Senior Partner. "Eight-thirty till five. That shouldn't be too much for you, should it? You've had time to adjust to a working routine."

"Oh, yes. Thank you for offering me the post. I do appreciate it. And I understand about the hours. I'll manage. I'll manage somehow."

But *how*, I was thinking. *How*? It was already a struggle to survive *part*-time. To keep us all afloat. Even with them all doing their bit on a Saturday.

"Change your sheets this morning, all of you. Strip the beds for me."

"I've made mine already. And I'm meeting Maria at eleven. Sorry, but I haven't time this week."

"Tom had an excuse last Saturday as well, Mum. His sheets stink . . ."

"Yeh, his room stinks, Ma. I'm nearly flaming gassed next door."

"Oh, shut up, Henry. You make me sick. And anyway, it's not my job, changing sheets. That's the mother's job. Do it yourself. I'm going out."

"Hey! Don't you talk to Mum like that. You think you're so big, don't you. You can help the same as the rest of us."

"Oh, piss off! Creep!"

It isn't easy being a working mother. It's no better than a treadmill. In fact it's worse. It's like being on one of those exercise machines that they were demonstrating on *Blue Peter* not so long ago. A treadmill that gets faster and steeper as you run.

It's not that I'm madly houseproud or anything, but like a lot of other people, I function best in an orderly environment. In spite of their help, Saturday seemed to get eaten up by washing, shopping, cooking, ironing - and Sunday was often worse.

"Who's taking the dogs for a walk, then?"

"Oh, no peace for the flaming wicked!"

"And don't forget the grass needs cutting, will you Tom."

"All right. All right. Just don't nag me, Mum."

"Here, Charlie - help me hang these sheets out, will you?"

"But you know what Miss Harris said . . ."

"I can't help it. Sunday or not. There's a good wind this morning. They'll soon dry. Can you move your stuff off the table, Claire. I'll make some scones while the oven's on for dinner."

And after tea :

"Knickers! I'm sick of this rubbish. Can't get it into my bloody head. I'm not bloody doing it. Knickers!"

"Come on, Tommy. It's not that bad. If Italian toddlers managed to pick it up . . . "

"Oh yes, very funny!"

"Come through to the kitchen and I'll test you while I do the ironing."

"Mum - I forgot to put my football gear out for the wash. I'm in the team tomorrow. Sir said we had to look bloody smart or else . . . "

"*Bloody* smart! Mr Evans? He never did, Mum."

"I've got to have them for tomorrow. I've got to have them *clean*."

"O.K. Bring them down. Put them in a bucket and wash the worst of the mud out of them yourself. Show him, Charlie. Then they can bung in the machine tonight with the jeans. I'll dry them on the radiator for you and iron them first thing."

"Corr - you little stinker! When were they last washed, eh?"

"Bloody hell! His shorts are going mouldy, Mum!"

"Ha ha! His shorts are going mouldy!"

"Claire, it's time you were running your bath. Perhaps Charlie will wash your hair this once. I'm trying to hear Tom's Latin."

"I can't have a bath yet. I've got to see the end of the Vet programme. And I can do my own hair, *thanks*. I don't want anyone in the bathroom with me. I'm not a baby. I'm entitled to a bit of privacy, same as the rest of you."

"She hasn't cleaned her shoes yet, Mum. Come on, you'll only be late in the morning if they're not done tonight."

"Do mine while you're at it, Sis. The Doc Martens. They're on the back porch."

"Do your own. I'm not your servant."

"Hey, Mum - you know about photosynthesis, don't you? Miss Brewer wants our essays in tomorrow. Jill phoned to remind me. Well, no - actually she was hoping to pick my brains on the subject. That's the price of brilliance for you."

"If you're so brilliant, how come you need Mum to help?"

"Oh, shut your mouth! She's helping *you*, isn't she?"

"Oh, can you believe it! Claire's gone and put all the shoe-cleaning stuff away, hasn't she. We've all got ours to clean too, idiot!"

"Come on, come on! Aren't we all going to watch the vets together. The Sabbath was made for mothers, you know, as well as the rest of you. Where are those football things, Henry?"

"Could I suggest you all get on quietly, please." Pete had come through from the sittingroom. "Surely a man is entitled to a little peace and quiet in his own home. Just now and again. I'm trying to read *The Observer*."

"Don't worry too much about getting in on time," Mr Grimshaw said kindly when the high-powered Mr Fletcher had swept off to a business lunch. "Quite frankly very little work gets done before nine-thirty. I know that once you are here you're jolly well working. I don't know how you cope with all your brood."

That nearly finished me. Don't ask me why. His compassion or something. It often happens like that, doesn't it. You struggle along, keeping the lid on tight, and then one word of sympathy and it all comes pouring out. The pent up pain, the injustice, the disappointment. And the exhaustion. It only takes the silliest thing to trigger it off.

" . . . I don't know how you cope."

"Thanks," I spluttered, putting an arm momentarily round his benevolent shoulders, "but I'll manage the hours full time. It will be OK." And incoherent with grief I rushed out.

"What's got into her, Marge?" I heard Linda, Mr Fletcher's glamorous secretary, exclaim as I fled.

Where can you go for a good cry, then? The children would be in from school by now, so there wouldn't be much privacy at home. I put my sun-glasses on and dodged through the Close, intending to take the quiet route home and walk along the river bank until I had composed myself. But then, on impulse, I slipped into the West Door of the Cathedral, weaving in and out of the gawping tourists until I found a dim and deserted chapel.

This Chapel is reserved for Private Prayer, it said on the wrought-iron grille. *Please respect the silence.*

It was a grand place for a weep and I tried to do it quietly.

"Where have you been, Mum?" they chorused when I got home.

"We've had tea."

"Eggs and things."

"And the last of the gingerbread."

"Dad's gone to a meeting."

"You missed the last episode of *Tom Sawyer*."

"Granny phoned."

"Are you O.K., Mum?" Charlie asked, realising I'd been crying.

"I'm fine. Just came over a bit depressed, but I'm all right now. I'll make a pot of tea and some toast."

I must have been more than two hours in the Cathedral bawling my bloody eyes out. A casual observer might well have thought I'd suffered some devastating loss. Child, parent, husband. Luckily nobody enquired.

"I've no idea what I'm weeping for," I might have answered. "Unless it's my lost identity. What might have been."

Chapter Fourteen

"I can understand your tears," said Walter," squeezing *my* hand now. "I've felt like that myself a time or two, but it's harder for a man to cry."

We were the last customers. The good *patron* was looking restless.

"I'm sorry - I've talked too much."

"Our bill, please, Monsieur." And I watched him count out more fivers than the bank allowed me to feed the three of us for a week.

"Just a moment, please," the cashier would say when I scuttled in on a Wednesday for my allotment, calling for a junior to take my miserable cheque backstage to be vetted by Mr Dymond, the Assistant Manager.

"You can't go on like this any longer," he'd told me firmly, calling me into his office on one of these Wednesdays. "I'm sorry, but things are getting out of hand. I'm clamping down now before they get any worse. If you've any sense you'll thank me for putting the brakes on before things get totally out of control."

"I always knew you were an idiot with money," Pete would have said, had he known.

Only because I'd never had any, never handled any. Apart from the good old Family Allowance, that is.

"I think this money should go into the common fund," he had announced when Charlotte arrived and with her the Family Allowance Book. The first child didn't count in those days, though God knows we could have done with a little help.

We were living in Matlock then, in our first home. An attic flat in what had originally been an elegant Edwardian house high above the town which we rented for £8 a month, exactly a quarter of the salary Pete earned teaching at the local Primary School.

I didn't have a clue about babies or housekeeping or anything much. It's a wonder any of us survived those early years. We were mostly cold and shabby and penniless. And often hungry. Boiled eggs were our staple diet, and even those were sometimes bought on credit from the corner shop.

"Er... I've only actually got sixpence till tomorrow but do you think I could have four eggs and a small loaf, please? I'll settle up when I get my housekeeping."

"For Christ's sake!" Pete bellowed at me once when I'd asked for an extra shilling for rubber pants for Thomas who was still in nappies when his sister was born. "You can surely manage on what I give you!"

He wrote to Evelyn Home, I remember, in a fit of righteous indignation, and waited smugly for her reply.

"My dear Man, it is impossible for anyone to feed a family of four on £3 a week. Try doing the shopping yourself."

That shook him. From then on I was allowed to keep the Family Allowance. It was only eight shillings, mind, but it made a considerable difference. I could sometimes save a bob or two towards Christmas and birthdays out of it. I blued it occasionally on some wild extravagance. Currant buns, a couple of bananas, a colouring book for Tommy. Two weeks allowance went on a plate rack once.

"A plate rack!" he said, incredulous. "What do we need with a plate rack? We can't afford these luxuries. My mother never had one."

I didn't think it was an extravagance, that yellow plastic plate rack, but then it was me that was doing the washing up. Soon, with six to cater for, it was a downright necessity. I'm still using it today.

By the time Henry and Claire arrived I was drawing an allowance of £1.8.0d a week. Eight shillings for Charlotte. Ten shillings each for the little ones.

We had moved to Norfolk by then, to the School House at Eccleston. A hundred years old and more. Two up, two down and an *elsan* across the play ground.

"There's a slight problem with the house," Pete admitted, coming back radiant from his interview. "It's a bit primitive, but they've agreed to install electricity before we move in. And to build a bathroom off the kitchen."

"No electricity! No loo! How does the present Head cope?"

"Hang on - there is a cold tap in the kitchen, and one of those old fashioned coppers for heating water. You know, you light a fire under it . . . "

"Oh, that's nice. That's a comfort, that is. Sounds like something out of the Dark Ages to me, never mind promotion!"

"Don't worry. I'm sure they'll get it all organised before we move in. The place will be empty for a whole term. They gave their word."

They were the School Governors, of course. In this case that meant two doddery old parsons and the Lady of the Manor (really feudal it is, Norfolk). When we arrived, the week after Christmas in the winter of Sixty-Two, nothing had been done.

"But you said they promised. You should have been pestering them about it all these months. I knew we were idiots to trust them. How can we live in such a hovel?"

"They'll do it now we're in. They'll bloody well have to. Meanwhile, we can manage."

Anything rather than make a fuss, that was Pete. He was so overwhelmed by his appointment - a headmaster at 29 - that nothing bothered him.

That was a bleak winter, and no mistake. The winds howled across the sugar beet fields, piling the snow in dramatic drifts round the back door. The playground turned into an ice rink across which we had to venture several times a day to reach the line of privies by the fence.

"I want a pooh! Mum, I want a pooh!" Tommy was dancing about the kitchen holding his tummy, screwing up his face in misery.

"Quick then. Coats on both of you. Come on. And your wellies. Fetch the gloves, Charlie. Hurry now. Here, push your foot in, Tom. Push. Wrap this round your head, love. Right."

And like a small band of Siberian nomads we battled our way across the netball pitch, Tom five, Charlie four, and me ungainly with Henry who would be born in the spring.

"Quick now, Tommy. Let me help you with your trousies, love." But it was too late, and he just stood there howling, his smelly tartan trews round his ankles.

"I couldn't help it, Mummy. It was such a long way."

"It doesn't matter. We should have put you on the potty. I didn't realise you were so desperate."

"I hate this old place. When are we going home, Mummy? When are we going back home?"

"But it was OK in the end, wasn't it," Pete reminded me. "You loved the School House once they'd modernised it for us. Once we'd got a bathroom."

Yes, it was true. I did love it in the end. Though that might have had something to do with Dr Olaf, I guess. A bath certainly made a big difference.

"I've never known anyone have so many baths," people say to me sometimes. "Morning and evening as often as not. It's not natural."

I've been addicted to baths ever since my year in Switzerland. As an Au Pair, way back when I was seventeen.

"You English are so dirty," said Mme Hamburger with venom. (She never forgave me for winning the War.) "Baths weaken you. Baths are not necessary. Especially not for servants."

And having supervised me while I cleaned her beautiful turquoise bathroom complete with shower cabinet, bidet, basin, loo and large marble bathtub, she firmly locked the door on it again. Such a clean country, Switzerland. So bloody hygienic.

"Students can bath vonce a fortnight," explained my eighty year old employer who ran a *Pension* for students. "But *you*, you may take a bath only vonce in six weeks. Don't vorry. I vill be keeping a record. You are understanding, huh?"

It was the height of summer when I started working for her.

"Tonight you may 'ave zee bath," Madame eventually announced towards the end of August. "Come. Ve vill find you some clean bed linen, yes."

Oh, yes - clean sheets as well. How lovely.

Together we went through every sheet in the huge *armoire* on the landing, unfolding each one.

"Ach! Here is something," she said, discovering a sheet that had an enormous tear in it. "And another," putting aside a particularly threadbare specimen with a nice big hole in the middle. "You will not go to your class this afternoon, *ma chere*. (I was supposed to be taking a French Language course at the University, though it wasn't often convenient for Madam to allow me to attend.) "Today you will mend your sheets."

"But Madame . . . " I'd always been a fool with a needle.

"And I will inspect them, yes, before you put them on your bed. *Comprenez?*"

I soon came to dread bath nights in Lausanne. Madame would stand outside the bathroom door, enraged that I dared lock it on her.

"Don't you lie there like a lady, my girl," she'd yell at me. "Servants are not to use bathsalts. You have been long enough. You hear me, Miss? Quite long enough. Come out now at vonce. Come out, I say. Why are you not yet out of ze water. How dare you defy me! I vill give you such a slapping if I find you have used the talcum powder."

Bath nights with Mme Hamburger were not a lot of fun.

At least now in the School House, once the Church authorities had got round to installing it, we had a bathroom. We had a loo, and hot water, and a bath.

The washing was done in the bath. I'd leave it to soak over night, and pummel away at it in the morning, my knees braced against the side of the tub, wringing it out by hand. My hands were always red and chapped, but I had incredibly firm tummy muscles.

John Bloom had just started advertising his Electromatic twin tubs. You probably remember. He was the Freddy Laker, the Richard Branson of the washing machine. I think he went bankrupt in the end, which isn't terribly surprising. With each washing machine he was giving away another expensive gadget.

Buy a twin-tub and we give you a vacuum cleaner FREE.

Ludicrous offers like that. Still, he did me a good turn, along with ten million other penniless mums.

"Look at this," I said waving the newspaper under Pete's nose. "Only forty pounds, and six months to pay it off."

"I will not get mixed up with hire purchase, so please don't keep on about it."

"But the Family Allowance would cover it. Look, it tells you here. One-pound-eight a week."

"No. I'm sorry, but I will not allow anything into this house on credit. And I'm certainly not prepared to cough up that sort of sum for such an extravagance. My mother never had a washing machine."

"But my entire life is spent leaning over that bloody bath. A washing machine would be an absolute God-send."

"And if you had one, however would you fill your time?"

Secretly I filled in the slip in the paper, and when the sales man called I handed over the week's housekeeping, £8 by this time, in full. We lived on tick that week, and I swore to Pete that I'd managed to save the deposit from the Family Allowance.

"Sorry," I lied to Mr Jolly, when he called at the garden gate with his mobile grocery store on Thursday. "I had a hefty milk bill this week. Can I leave it till your next visit?"

"Sorry," to the butcher's boy, when he brought the mince on Friday. "My husband hasn't been able to get to the bank this week. Tell Mr Hodgson I'll settle up next time he calls."

It took several weeks to get straight with all those patient tradesmen, and that was only for the deposit. But it was worth it. I'd got my beautiful liberating twin-tub.

We needed it too. The kids were constantly going down with tummy bugs. There always seemed to be piles of vomitty bedding to put through Mr Bloom's programme for heavily soiled whites.

"I'll have the water supply analysed," said Dr Olaf, coming to check up on the row of dehydrated children on the sofa. "A pity you haven't got a fridge, you know, gal. The larder's the sunniest place in this old house."

"Mummy! Glugh!"

"Here! Good girl. All in the bucket."

"And all these damn flies from the pig farm don't help. Boil all water for the moment, and give them each a spoonful of this stuff three times a day. I'll look in again tomorrow. And don't go worrying. We'll have them back on their little legs in no time."

"The doctor suggested a fridge might be a good idea, Pete."

"He didn't suggest where the money would come from, I suppose. He's no business going round putting ideas in all your silly heads, you women. Washing machine, telly, fridge. I'd have you remember that I'm only a struggling headmaster."

I wrote to my parents.

"I could buy a fridge from the Electricity Board for £27. I wondered whether you'd lend me the money. I could send you the Family Allowance Book, right. And if you keep it for fifteen weeks there will be enough accumulated to pay you back. If I keep it here, I'll never manage to save it for you."

£27 arrived by return. They had a fair idea how things were between us. Pete accepted the story that they had had a win on 'Ernie' and were sharing their good fortune with us.

For years the Family Allowance was my only source of income. All our household goods came out of it. Bedding, towels, saucepans, china, garden tools, clothes for the children. Most of it from my friend Maggie's mail order catalogue, paid for in weekly instalments.

Shortly before our divorce Pete became really tight-fisted. I was a nervous wreck by then. And unemployed.

"No!" he barked, when I suggested that I should have housekeeping money the way I used to before I started earning a little of my own. "I never could trust you with money. If I gave it to you, you'd only spend it. I earn it and I shall decide what it goes on."

For the best part of a year I handled no money at all apart from the Child Benefit (as they now called it) of £1.50 a week. Tom and Charlie no longer qualified, which made Henry the First Child, and I drew the allowance for Claire.

That small sum was my life-line. With it I was able to pay for my art class, for paint and paper, birthday presents for the children, and the occasional trip home to visit my anxious parents.

"I think our financial difficulties were the main cause of the breakdown of our marriage," Pete suggested sadly when he saw I was serious about going ahead with the divorce. "You're congenitally extravagant, that's your trouble."

Chapter Fifteen

"No, you really can't go on like this," Mr Dymond repeated firmly. "I'm afraid you're going to have to look for a job."

Oh, Gawd! Not the old nine-to-five routine again. Anything but that.

We'd been divorced three years by now. Our rambling Edwardian semi had been sold for a good price. Pete had gone back north to a plum headship in County Durham.

"I never really felt at home down here," he said. "It's probably all for the best."

I had moved to a gem of a terraced cottage on the other side of town with Claire and Henry.

"It's not fair!" they had complained loudly. "Why do we have to move?"

"Yes, why can't we stay put. Dad can go up there and leave us here together."

"We can't afford it here. Not on our own. We'll find something cosy. you'll both have a say in it. It'll be great, just the three of us."

Claire and I walked over that Saturday morning to look at Railway Terrace. From the advert in the paper it sounded nice.

Beautifully modernised Victorian terrace, 3 beds, gas c.h. walled garden, immaculate order.

Oh no, I thought, as we leant over the low wall looking down on the row of mean little cottages. Their roofs were at street level. Steep steps led down to the front doors. Oh no - surely we're not reduced to *this*!

"Well, come on, Mum. Now we're here we might as well have a look."

And of course we both fell in love with it at once.

"I'm glad we moved here," Henry was to say later, coming back from his first term at college. "We were lucky to find it, weren't we?"

Now I have to admit that for all his faults Pete was generous when it came to this.

"Never mind about fifty-fifty," he said when we settled for Number 31 Railway Terrace. "The important thing is for us to provide a decent home for the kids. We'll pay on the nail for your house and I'll take what's left. I'm not particularly fussy, and prices are a lot lower in the north."

He was generous over the share-out of our goods and chattels too.

"You take whatever you want. I'll pick over what's left. We've got to ensure that the children don't suffer. That's the main thing."

He was generous too in the settlement he made on us. But in spite of that, I obviously had to find a job to augment the allowance he sent us each month. It would scarcely be fair to expect him to subsidise my early retirement.

Now Mr Grimshaw's training came in very useful. I worked in a lawyer's office to start with. And then in the barracks, in the regimental museum. This was followed by a spell in the City Museum as secretary to the Curator. Over the years I tried part-time, full-time and temporary jobs. But it wasn't easy, dovetailing it all - the job, the kids, the house and garden. The strain was enormous. I was invariably exhausted and often despairing.

"You've got to make more time for your painting," said Eddie, holding out one of my landscapes, squinting at it ferociously. "I've told you before. With a bit of serious application you could make it. No, I'm not kidding. You could definitely make it."

I didn't go to his classes any more, but we kept in touch. Once or twice I'd stood in for him, taking over for an evening. To my surprise, I enjoyed teaching art, I discovered. I enjoyed teaching adults.

"Oh, Eddie, it's hopeless. By the time I get in from work I'm a wreck. I very often flop off to bed right after supper. It's only at the weekends I can salvage a little time, a little energy. And not always then."

"Well, you're a fool frittering your life away like this. I've said it before and I mean it. You've got something important locked up in you. You shouldn't waste it. If you really wanted to paint you'd find a way."

He's right, I thought. There must be a way to keep us all afloat without mortgaging my soul to a nine-to-five job.

An advertisement caught my eye on the back page of The Guardian. 'Easy loans to home owners. No security. No credentials.'

I wrote off immediately.

"Could you lend me £1,000. Just £1,000. To enable me to give up my job for six months and concentrate on painting?"

But in spite of all their promises, there was nothing forthcoming for an unsupported woman in her forties with dependent children, home-owner or not.

"Unfortunately we do not have funds available for projects of this kind . . . "

It was only a thousand I was after. A measly thousand. And they claimed to have vaste fortunes at their disposal.

I put in for a Bursary that the School of Art were offering to a working artist. Artist in Residence. £7,500 and a one man exhibition at the end of the year. Seven-and-a-half thousand! More than came my way in two years normally. Two years freedom. Freedom to paint. And at the end of that time . . . who knows? I might have got myself established. I might never have to do any more dreary secretarial work for anyone. Ever.

Eddie gave me a glowing testimonial. By the time the winner was announced (another of your bright young moderns) I had deluded myself into planning my imminent freedom in loving detail.

The disappointment was shattering, but somehow I struggled on.

I tried a local money lender next, advertising in our weekly paper. 'Immediate loans offered. No security required.'

"Look," I told him uncertainly over the phone, thinking how horrified my parents would be. "I need a thousand pounds. I need it desperately. I want a chance to establish myself as an artist. I'm going to make it, you know. They tell me I'm good." I very much wished I believed it.

I could hear him grunting sceptically at the other end of the line.

"I own the house. How about helping me, eh?"

"Keep away from me, my dear," he told me bluntly. "I'll ruin you, won't I? That's my living, ruining folks. Ask your own bank. They're the people to help you."

"Thank you. It was good of you to be honest with me."

"You're not joking, love - could cost me my job, easy as wink."

I rang Lloyds Bank where my credit-worthiness was threadbare, to say the least, expecting to be laughed off the line. But no, they might agree to a loan. I was to go and see the Manager taking a portfolio of my work, Eddie's recommendation, receipts for the odd few paintings I had sold.

It took them three days to decide. Yes, they would take a risk. They would give me a chance. I wasn't going to have to spend the rest of my life doing a God-awful job, waiting until I retired to do the thing I was beginning to believe (with Eddie, bless him) that I was born to do. Lloyds Bank was prepared to sponsor me for an unspecified time. They would allow me up to £2,000 credit.

"We'll allow you to go overdrawn each month to the equivalent of your present salary. Eventually you can repay the loan as if it were a mortgage, but we'll discuss that later on. When we see how you make out."

"Oh, how splendid!" I wanted to kiss him. "I can't believe it. I won't disappoint you. You'll see. One day in some book on *Art in the Twentieth Century*, Lloyds Bank may get the credit for giving me a chance. Thankyou!" And I did kiss him.

That was in September. At the beginning of October I gave up my job at the Museum and prepared to spend the rest of my waking hours at my easel. That's what I intended. But I'd get the house in order first, I decided, so that I could devote myself to my painting with a clear conscience. Clean the cooker. Defrost the freezer. Wash the curtains. Better get the garden straight too. And then at last I would settle down with my brush and palette.

Tomorrow, that is. I surely deserved one day's grace. But *tomorrow* was already November the first.

Another problem cropped up. Exhaustion. At first I thought it was a hangover from all the frenzied preparations of the past few weeks. I felt utterly limp and lifeless. I would wake exhausted. Crawl round doing the basic chores. Stagger reluctantly to my bedroom (that doubled as studio) and sit there stupefied and lethargic for hours on end with not a dab of yellow ochre to show for myself. A trip to Sainsbury's would flatten me for the rest of the day.

I was a failure and a wreck. And here we were creeping into December, for God's sake!

"Try ginseng," Stella suggested.

"You shouldn't be drinking so much coffee," Jo advised. "One cup destroys a whole day's supply of vitamin E, you know."

Slowly, miraculously, I began to gather strength. On reflection, I think it was the accumulated weariness of twenty- five years of motherhood catching up on me. A back-log of the strain of non-stop responsibility for others. The relentless pressure to keep the washing under control and provide three meals a day for six of us. Day in, day out. Remorselessly. For a quarter of a century. Somehow, now free of pressure at last, free to sag, it had overwhelmed me, that accumulation of stress.

"I've worked out a realistic routine," I told Eddie happily. "I generally manage to settle down to work at my easel as soon as the kids go off to school. I leave housework and shopping till late afternoon when they're coming home again. Most days I get five clear hours. Sometimes more. That's about as much as I can cope with at present."

"I was beginning to think you'd never get yourself organised. Can I pop round in the morning and take a look at your work? OK?"

If it had only been Eddie, fair enough, but my precious work schedule was constantly being interrupted.

"Hi, there! Just thought I'd see how you were settling in to your new routine."

"Hello, love! Popped round to check you really are working. Felt sure there'd be a pot of coffee on the stove, what!"

"Maggie told me I *must* come and see your latest landscape. A chimney-scape she says it is. A knock-out."

Oh, please but *please* leave me alone, all of you. How am I ever going to get any serious work done.

"Don't worry," said Brenda, settling down on my bed with her knitting. "You carry on with that while we chat. I don't want to hinder progress."

Help! Help! We're well into the New Year already. There's so little time left.

"Hello, Mum! I'm coming up to talk to you. Want a cup of tea? Guess what Danny told me in Chemistry. He said..."

"Hey, Ma - come and watch this programme. Come on. It's *brill*. Whales. They talk, you know. Sing. Come on. Leave that till tomorrow."

I'm not an early bird by nature, but I began to realise this was my only hope. It wasn't easy but I was determined. Gradually, painfully, I made myself get up and get on earlier. Earlier and earlier.

"Oh, do put the telly off, you two. Do go to your beds. You're not really watching. You're just too lazy to switch it off. For God's sake get to bed."

Seven-thirty. Seven. Seven-fifteen. Six-thirty. Six o'clock. Five-thirty. That's more like it. I was actually doing a couple of hours before anyone else woke up. A quick shower to get the blood circulating. A cup of tea. And straight down to work.

It wasn't light so early. Not in February. But there were still plenty of things I could be working at. Sizing card and canvas. Sketching out the next picture. Framing finished ones. And then as soon as day broke I got down to it, painting, painting, painting. Forgetting about meals and housework and shopping. Totally absorbed and exhilarated. I was a serious painter at last.

"What shall I put on my UCA form?" asked Henry. "My university application, where it says occupation of parents?"

"They mean your father," I told him. "Put Headmaster."

"No, they mean the parent I live with."

"Well put *artist* then, silly. It's obvious, isn't it." Dear Claire!

Artist, I thought. That's me, an artist. Imagine!

But hold on, not in the eyes of the world, and unfortunately not in the eyes of the Bank Manager.

"We've given you six months," explained Mr Dymond, "but I'm sorry to say that we really can't give you any longer. You'll have to find a job, I'm afraid. And you'll have to find it quickly. Unfortunately there's now the overdraft to be re-paid. With interest. It looks as if you'd better find yourself a full-time post in order to cope with all your commitments."

Oh, Gawd! So *near*. So bloody fucking near! Shit!

"Use your wits," said Jo, my friend the writer. (You may have heard of her. She's quite well known. *She's* made it all right. Josephine Drinkwater, that's her.) "A job doesn't have to mean an office job. Nine-to-five slavery. What else can you do?"

"Not much. Housework. Gardening." Lowly work and poorly paid.

I'd worked as a gardener for six months shortly before our divorce. Jobbing gardener. Cycling round between employers. That was in the very black period when Pete would give me no money. Absolutely none. All through that last long hot summer I went out gardening and odd-jobbing, answering adverts in the paper, post cards in the window of the newsagent.

"Hello. Yes, about the gardening . . . "

"Er - we weren't expecting a woman to apply."

"I can give you references. I've several long-standing clients. They all seem perfectly satisfied with me." So humiliating, selling yourself like that. Grovelling. For a few hours back-breaking toil a week.

"I've made you a coffee, dear. I suggest you drink it out here on the back step."

"Thanks."

"Don't I know you? Isn't your husband head of Westwood Primary . . . ?"

"Where did you say you lived? Those houses have pretty large gardens, don't they? I'm surprised you haven't enough to do at home."

I somehow bluffed my way through.

Dear old Ernest Jagger could be relied upon to give me a testimonial. I'd started my gardening career with him.

"Oh, Ernest!" I'd told him the summer Claire and her cousin Jane were supposed to be going to stay in Jersey with Tony and Kate, who had gone back to live there by then. "I'm in a right fix."

My brother had sent me a cheque to pay for his daughter's ticket and left me to book the girls' flight. I put David's cheque in my empty bank account, meaning to use it for the air tickets. But somehow the money had got used up. It was the only money I had access to.

"You see, Ernest, I've spent my brother's money," I wept. "I haven't booked the children's tickets. And now I have to raise the fare for the two of them, Jane and Claire. Out of thin air."

I broke into great hicuppy sobs of shame and worry.

"Pete won't help. I daren't even mention it to him." He'd said from the start it was a ridiculously extravagant idea. "Nobody gives *me* a holiday in Jersey," he'd said.

"Now cheer up, my dear. I know what we can do. I'll give you . . ."

"No, no! Don't *give me* anything. I'm not asking for charity. I had to tell someone, that's all."

"It's not charity I'm offering. Now listen. As you know, Felicity is getting married at the end of July. We're hoping to have the reception in the garden. We're hiring a marquee and everything. What I'd like to suggest, my dear, is that I pay for the girls' tickets to Jersey. Right? And you pay me back by doing some gardening for us. We'll say £2 an hour, shall we?" (This was a very generous rate.) "And between us we'll get the garden into super shape before the Great Day."

"Oh, Ernest . . ."

"Perhaps you could come for three hours twice a week? It won't take long to pay me back."

"Bless you! What a friend you are."

"There, that's better. There's always a solution. Just a case of using the old grey matter. Now then, how much do you need for those tickets?"

"Gardening!" said Jo, horrified. "Don't be such an idiot! Where's your bloody self-confidence, woman?"

I dearly wished I knew.

"I'm only trying to be realistic, Jo. What *can* I offer, for Christ's sake?"

"Well, teaching, for one thing."

"*Teaching*!"

"Evening classes, you moron! You said yourself you enjoy teaching adults. Standing in for Eddie. You were all bubbly about it. Ring up the F.E. Centre. Go on. Do it now."

"I'm going to see if we can survive on the money Pete sends us," I told Mr Dymond. "There's a chance I'll be taking a couple of evening classes next term, and I've offered to give demonstrations to the W.I. Oils, watercolours. To get them going. Women's Institutes, The Townswomen's Guild, Young Wives groups. That sort of thing. I've sent round a letter and already had a couple of phone calls."

"It's going to be pretty tight, my dear. Are you sure you're doing the right thing? Poverty isn't much fun."

"Look. Work out how much we're allowed each week. For food, milk, papers. Once all the bills are taken care of, and the overdraft repayments. How much have we got left?"

"Fourteen-pounds-fifty a week. And absolutely nothing more. I'm taking your cheque card away so that you're not tempted to spend anything else. You can come in once a week for your money. And that's it. Good luck with your painting."

"It's not as bad as it sounds, actually," I told Stella, as we finished off the last of the sherry. "There won't be money for this sort of thing, but it should be enough to feed us. Just. If we're careful."

"Too bad you didn't make it with your painting. Bob always said it was crazy. Giving up the museum job."

"Didn't make it! What artist ever made her name in six measly months, for crying out loud! The freedom the bank gave me, that simply helped me sort myself out. In my head. I'm going to make it, don't you worry. This is only the start. You can tell your Bob. I'm going to be an artist. I promise you that."

Chapter Sixteen

By mid April I had established a pattern which I still follow today.

Here is an artist who captures in oils the iridescent quality of dawn, they were to write later in the reviews of my first One Woman Exhibition. *With a few confident strokes of her brush she distils the mystery from the morning, the spirituality from the sunrise.*

They love my misty dawns, the serious critics and the media people.

When weather conditions were right I'd be up with the sun if not earlier. With a sketch block, chalks, charcoal, my camera and a flask of tea, I'd pedal off on Claire's bike before the world was stirring. Out into the countryside in search of material.

Her paintings nearly always focus on a stream, a footpath, or a freshly ploughed furrow. Something that draws the eye tantalisingly away into the distance, eventually disappearing into those incredibly swirling mists for which she is becoming renowned.

(This from the Polish gentleman I referred to earlier. He was from *The Observer*. As you can see, he was really bowled over by my work.)

"I've never known anyone get so much out of a clump of cow-parsley," said Eric Upton at The Old Granary Gallery, taking his first batch of canvases from me. "These are going to sell. No doubt about it."

And sure enough, they did. But not yet awhile.

"I regret to advise you," said the letter from the bank, "that we have been obliged to return your cheque for £47.34 in favour of British Telecom as your account is already overdrawn by £8.07."

"Please let it go through," I begged. "There should be a cheque from one of my galleries in the next day or two. They've sold three pictures. They rang me last night. I'd be lost without the phone. And I'd never raise the money to get us re-connected."

"I knew you wouldn't be able to survive on the allowance from your husband," said Mr Dymond. "It was calculated to boost the salary you were presumed to be able to earn in a full-time job. It's not even index-linked, is it? Why not admit defeat and find yourself a secretarial post? And carry on with your painting at weekends."

"No!" said Jo. "Don't give up, not now you are beginning to sell. It's only a matter of time. All you need is one lucky break. It was the same with my writing. You struggle along getting nothing but rejections. Then all of a sudden your luck changes. Meanwhile, you've got to have faith in yourself. Faith in what you're doing . . . "

"I'm not good enough, Jo. I'm never going to make it."

"Rubbish! You can't give up now. Bugger the bank. Apply for Supplementary Benefits or something. But keep at it, for God's sake. I'll pay your bloody phone bill. As a gesture of faith. No, no - you can pay me back when Eric Upton coughs up. You're nearly there, I can feel it in my bones."

I'd a great respect for the feelings in Jo's bones. More than once she'd put me on the right track.

"I've put your name forward to speak at our Artists and Writers Seminar next month. There's going to be a discussion on sponsorship for the arts. Thought you could make a useful contribution. Tell us about the struggles you've had to keep body and soul together while you got established. Mother, Artist and Breadwinner. Something like that."

"But I've never given a talk, Jo!"

"No *buts*. Come down and stay the weekend. It might give you another string to your bow, lecturing. You'll be good. I can feel it in my bones."

"And she was right," said Walter later on. "It must be quite a lucrative side-line for you. Lecturing. One or two bookings a month. That's good. Good experience. And a help financially."

"Hey, what are you doing tomorrow?" Jo asked, ringing late one evening.

"Nothing special."

"Right. I'm bringing a friend of mine over to see you then. A writer. I'll take you both out to lunch. We'll get to your place about eleven. I feel it could be important for you two to meet."

I'd met Jo through *Link*. You've probably seen it advertised.

LINK a lively widespread group of unattached people. To make new friends and enrich your social life, give us a ring!

"Hello," I said nervously, phoning the London number. "I was wondering how much you charge . . . ?"

"Thirty-five pounds initially. That's for the first six months, dear."

"Thirty-five pounds! Oh, glory! I couldn't possibly raise that much. Sorry to waste your time . . . "

This was in the days when I was still apologising for having my foot run over by a supermarket trolley. "Ooh! I'm so sorry! No, no - my fault. I shouldn't have been in your way." And I'd limp across to the checkout.

"No, hang on," said the Link man. "How much *could* you afford?" They were clearly struggling to establish *them*selves.

"Well, certainly not more than a fiver."

"Five pounds it is then. How long have you been on your own?"

"Not long. About six months. Our divorce went through in January."

"Fine. Fine. I'll put all the bumph in the post for you. I'm sure you are going to discover a whole new world with

Link. Oh, did you give me your age group? Merely for our files, of course."

"How could we have got involved in it?" said Jo afterwards. "Neither of us was exactly friendless."

"We weren't even *man*-less, were we? You had your David, and I was drifting between Stuart and Mike."

"It must have been that feeling of panic. The feeling that no-one is ever going to love you again. Everyone seems to go through that phase . . . "

"Even when they are glad to be divorced."

"But even so, *Link*!"

The first batch of information arrived next morning, before they'd received my income-related subscription.

'Link is young at heart,' I was told. 'Live life to the full with Link. Give yourself a fresh start. Link up with like-minded unattached people.'

There was a list of forthcoming events in our area.

'Bottle Party at Brian's. Always a popular venue. Phone for an invite.' (An invite!)

'Games Night at Linda's!!!'

'Sheiks and Slave Girls Party. Bring a pitcher of wine.'

'Teddy Bears Picnic at Evelyn's. Admission : a bottle and a teddy.'

The choice was infinite. Bierkeller nights, discos, moonlit rambles. 'Chinese Nosh - welly good,' at Ian's. 'A Vicars and Tarts Party' at Paul's. Christ! What excruciating jollity!

"Don't be so bloody supercilious," Stuart was to say later, when I was poking fun at Link at one of his rather dreary supper parties. I was being abominable, of course, but I'd drunk a lot of red wine, and the talk had become pompous and intellectual. "It's easier to mingle in a silly abandoned atmosphere. That doesn't mean they are any sillier than you or me."

"But honestly! All those *slim, youthful, fun-loving, witty* and *exciting* characters! How come they were reduced to advertising for friends, eh?"

To put lonely singles in touch with one another, to create *meaningful links*, lists of subscribers were sent out, with their short pithy curriculae vitae.

"Celia - a cuddly 10 stone . . . my friends tell me I'm attractive and look young for my years."

"Patricia - Hi! I'm slim, 5'2", hazel eyes, red hair . . . I like walking, animals, travel, theatre. And I'm longing to hear from you."

"Paul - I'm 34, 5'8" . . . a bit of a character . . . non-smoker, birth sign Cancer . . . why not give me a ring?"

"Ann - hoping to make a fresh start . . . all my friends seem to be happily married . . .feel myself out on a limb . . . hoping to find a new circle of friends."

Ann was right. It is hell at first, trying to make sense of the ravelled threads, the frayed ends, and knit them back into a coherent pattern. A different pattern from the married one, but a pattern nevertheless.

'Roll up! Roll up!' ran the entry for our town. 'Inaugural Party Friday 10th. Come and help us get off to a swinging start.'

This gruesome jocularity was one of the special things about Link.

"Do you remember it?" said Jo, with horror. "All those women with freshly tinted hair . . . "

" . . . all talking so brightly, with such animation."

"And weighing up the male talent on the sly."

"Oh my Gawd! The male talent!"

It had been terribly sad really. Sixty odd women, dressed to kill. And a dozen anxious little men. Every one busily explaining away their own loneliness to anyone who would stop talking and listen.

"I've plenty of friends, of course, but somehow they all seem to come in pairs."

"That's right. And married women are none too keen to invite single girlfriends along to dinner parties."

" . . . a threat to their marriages."

"Foot loose and all that."

"On the warpath..."

"It's different for men, mind. A single fellow is always welcome."

"Not always," said the battered looking man sitting on the rug beside us. "If you're still single at thirty-five then you're out on a limb. Everyone else neatly paired off. Must be a queer or..."

"Sure. He's right. Take me for instance." This was Peter. Six-foot-two. Swarthy. With a tendency to speak with his eyes shut, as if overcome by his own audacity. "I've been abroad a lot. Out in the Oil States and that. You don't meet girls out there. Apart from other chaps' wives."

"My problem's my mother, poor old love." So many problems. So much flaming loneliness. "I've always lived with her. I'm all she's got, see. I'd like a girlfriend, but she'd have to get on with Mother."

There certainly was a need for *Link* and the like. An enormous need,

I went on a country walk with them one Sunday, and on a theatre trip to Salisbury. But it wasn't my scene. And it wasn't Jo's either.

"But at least *we* met," she says now. "And it was me that introduced you to Jim."

I liked Jo straight away. I liked her patched jeans and her wild grey curls. I liked her self-confidence, and the positive way she coped with life.

"Look," she explained hurriedly, when the big bearded writer disappeared into the *Gents*. "I want you to read Jim's manuscript. He's brought it with him. I think you two might be good for one another."

"Oh, come on, Jo! I'm not looking for romance, thankyou. Not even with a hunky specimen like him. I'm past all that. It's too damn painful."

"Not that way, stupid. Professionally."

And as usual she was right.

Chapter Seventeen

"Yes, Jo was right," yelled Jim, fifteen months later, whirling me round with delight. "She was bloody well right that time."

Jim had arrived hot foot from the New Forest, waving the letter from *Penguin* and yodelling down my garden steps.

"We did it, girl! We did it! Whoopee! We're in business!"

I'd had a letter too, of course.

We are delighted to be able to tell you ... accepting the children's book 'Flora's Holiday' ... written by James F Stansbridge and illustrated by yourself ... and our cheque is enclosed for £300 advance payment on royalties.'

Three hundred pounds! Wow!

"Coffee, Jim?" I wriggled out of his arms to put the kettle on.

"Coffee! Never mind bloody coffee! Come on to bed, love. This calls for a celebration."

"No, Jim. That's all over. Sorry, but I'm a one-man woman now. You know I am."

"Ah, well. No harm in hoping. Though I can't think what you see in that young whipper-snapper of yours. Pain in the arse, in my opinion. But never mind. I'll have to settle for coffee then."

Funny how I'd fallen for James F Stansbridge, in spite of all my good intentions.

"It's not funny at all," said Jo. "He's just your type, now isn't he. Bearded. Hunky. Crazy. Intelligent. Fun. You were bound to fall for him."

"But I'd meant it to be a strictly professional relationship. I truly did. I thought I was past all that romantic nonsense."

"Once you're past it, you might as well be dead," says my old friend David Davidson. And at ninety-one he should know. Not sex necessarily, but loving. That's what counts, that's what makes the world go round. The magic of love.

David was laid up all last winter. Some trouble with his chest.

"Do pop round," said his wife, Lucia, when I bumped into her in Marks & Spencers. "He's feeling very sorry for himself. He'd be so pleased to see you."

"Hello, David, love. How are you? I've brought you a few daffodils to cheer you up."

He lay there looking old and frail and frightened.

"Oh, how sweet of you to come. How good to see you, my dear."

"I'd no idea you'd been so poorly. Why didn't you phone me?"

"I didn't want to bother you, Know how busy you are."

"I'll make us all a cup of tea," said Lucia, bustling down to the kitchen.

"Hm!" he sighed, grasping my hand hungrily. "Kiss me. Please kiss me, darling. Quick, kiss me before she comes up with the tea."

I gave him a friendly peck and tried to change the subject.

"It's so hot in here, so terribly hot," he said, flinging back the bedclothes to reveal his trim naked body. In full.

"David!" I threw the duvet over him again. "Cover yourself up, man. Lucia's coming . . . "

"Here we are, then," she said, bringing in the tea tray. "I'll leave you two to chat if you don't mind. I'm doing some baking."

His hands shook as he drank his tea. He leered at me.

"I never wear pyjamas," he explained. "I like to be ready for action."

"Look, love - we've been over all this before. I thought we'd sorted it out. Friendship, that's what we've got. And that's how it's staying. No, you listen to me. You've got

Lucia, right? You don't need me. And anyway you're old enough to be my grandfather. Easily."

Now he was whimpering into his tea.

"I'm sorry. Forgive me, dear girl. I don't know what came over me. It's lying here all day, wondering when I'll be up and about again. *If* I'll ever be up and about again. That's what gets you down. Don't be cross. I couldn't bear it. Please forget it. Please say you forgive me."

I remembered then what he'd told me years back, when I was still married.

"I think about you every night. When Lucia's, er, working me off . . . "

"Working you off! Bloody hell, I don't want to know about your bloomin' sex life, thank you."

He told me, nevertheless.

"She just hasn't fancied me, not since the twins were born, has she."

"But they're grown men, David. They're middle-aged. Grandfathers both of them."

"They're in their fifties, yes."

"Well, I guess that's normal. Sex and marriage just don't seem compatible. Or only very rarely."

"She's a good wife to me, mind - Lucia. She's looked after my comfort. You know, that way. There's never been a night, not a single night when she hasn't, you know, made sure I was, well, *comfortable* before she goes to sleep. On one condition, mind . . . "

"Go on - tell me."

"I have to shave it. Every day. Same as my chin. She couldn't stand it otherwise. She couldn't handle it hairy."

Poor old David. No wonder he needed someone to fantasise about.

Jim's story was a fantasy. A beautiful rollicking fairy tale. Full of archetypal characters. Dressed up in modern clothes.

It's a fairy story for discerning adults, wrote The Guardian reviewer. *And the illustrations are a delight.*

That was me. His illustrator. That's what Jo had been wanting me to do.

"But I've never done illustrations," I protested. "I wouldn't know how to begin."

"Then bloody well find out. Eddie will know. He'll be able to help. Or he'll know someone who can."

And he did.

"My friend Bill's an illustrator. He's quite successful. I'll invite him over to meet you."

"The main thing is that you really feel for the story," Bill explained. "Unless you're in tune with the writer it's hopeless, a total waste of time."

"Damn good job we turned out to be so beautifully, erotically, totally in harmony then," said Jim, stroking the seat of my jeans wistfully. "I still say we should have had a celebration. Just a quick one, for old time's sake. To hell with your young Romeo."

Jim was married. Happily married. He lived down near Lymington. Running a small-holding and writing children's books in his spare time.

"You smell of goat," I told him the first time, surprised. Sniffing his big hairy torso.

"Oh, Christ!" said Jo. "I can't trust you with anyone. This was supposed to be a professional relationship. Remember."

"It just sort of happened, Jo. Where's the harm, as long as she doesn't find out." I was beginning to sound like Ted.

"But Eva's my friend. I feel responsible. It was me that bloody introduced you two. Don't go breaking everything up for them, will you. I'd never forgive you."

But that was the last thing I wanted to do. It was fun. It was exciting. It was what Erica Jong was calling 'the zipless fuck,' a filthy expression for a beautiful spontaneous affair, with no preconceptions or attachments. No fears for the future. No guilt. Heaven!

"It's so easy with you," he declared, nuzzling down beside me. "Kind of . . . kind of un-pre-meditated. No wonder I'm into prize-winning fiction at the moment."

All through that summer it went on, his married-ness adding a little spice. I don't think Eva ever found out. I'd have heard about it from Jo if she had. She was perfectly friendly at the publication party. I really liked her.

"She did look gorgeous, Jim. She's a beauty, your Eva."

"She always looks good in those Indian dresses. Soft and voluminous. They suit her, in spite of her size."

"She's like a Botticelli Madonna - stunning."

"Yes, I'm lucky," said Jim. "Two lovely women in my life."

I'd slept with a good few men by then, before and after our divorce. But Jim was the first one who seemed to love me. It was an idyllic period. He couldn't get over to see me very often, though there were always the illustrations for an excuse.

"I don't want to over do it, love. Don't want Eva to get suspicious."

We went to the seaside once and swam naked in the starlight. The beach was deserted by that time, the day trippers streaming back to town and everyone else enjoying their hotel dinners.

We had a day in London. The day we delivered *Flora* to his agent. A meal in the Chinese quarter. Jim kept rummaging in the industrial rubbish skips along the back streets.

"Hey - look at this!" he'd shout, unearthing some ludicrous prize from the debris. "A brand new piece of rope. Just what I was needing for *The Mary Ann*."

He wasn't hard up, my Jim, even before the book. But he couldn't bear waste. Once he turned up looking frightfully smart.

"Wow! Going to a wedding?"

"I found the shirt . . . "

"*Found* it?"

"In a polythene bag on Waterloo Station. Seventeen good shirts. And all my size, would you believe! What do you think, eh? Pretty damn classy, what!" He swaggered about, delighted with himself.

"And the suit? Don't tell me you found that too. On the tip? It fits like it was made for you."

"It was. It was. I sold my grand-dad's watch and chain. I told you. So I thought I'd treat myself to a really posh suit. Moss Bros, no less. Hand stitched. Look at the label."

"You're impossible, Jim!" A Moss Bros suit and a shirt from a rubbish bin.

It was always a hoot with Jim. He was like an overgrown kid. Full of madness. Racing round in search of adventure. Making love in haystacks, in his tiny boat, on the kitchen table, in the bath. It was a wild and wonderful affair while it lasted.

"Don't worry, darling," he said cheerfully, the night he turned up unexpectedly, to find my sister Peggy here with her two girls. "The children are old enough to be left alone for an hour or so, aren't they? After supper I'll take you and Peggy out for a drink. I'd like that."

"Oh, Jim, it's such a shame. You've never escaped for the night before."

"There'll be other times," he said confidently. "We've a life-time before us, love. And there's no reason why this shouldn't last for ever, me and my two darlings. Is there?"

Chapter Eighteen

"While it lasted!" said Walter in amazement. "I thought you were still in the thick of it."

"No - no," I told him awkwardly. "There's been the most incredible development in my life recently. I couldn't mention it in my letter. I didn't want to shock you."

"Have I ever been shocked, my girl?" He was driving us home this July evening after a good day's painting in the Sussex Downlands. "Now, have I?"

And he never had. Not even when I'd confided in him the humiliating story of my infatuation for the distinguished Edward Hill, and that was pretty gruesome, I can tell you.

Every year since the divorce, no matter how hard up we were, I somehow contrived to put aside the fees for the Artists' Summer School at Wentworth Hall. I wouldn't have missed it for anything. It was fantastic.

"You may not get a place," Eddie warned me, encouraging me to apply. "There's fierce competition to get in."

But I was lucky first time. I got a place that year, and I've managed to get one every year since. This will be my sixth Summer School. I led a discussion group one year. And next year with all the hoo-ha about Jim's book, *our* book, I've been invited to lecture.

"But what's so special about Wentworth Hall?" Jim asked once. "Personally I can think of nothing worse than being cooped up for an entire week with a gaggle of artists. Or *writers*, in my case. Creative people are usually such frightful egotists. They've got to be, I guess, to get anywhere. But three-hundred-plus under one roof for a whole week. Bloody hell!"

Henry and Claire were too young to cope on their own the first year I went.

"We'll be OK," they said, clearly imagining a week of bliss. Fish and chips every night, unsupervised parties, long lazy lie-ins. "We'll be fine."

"Oh, no," I said. "Next year perhaps. But this time Dad'll have to come down and hold the fort. It's months since he saw either of you."

"You've left us before, Ma . . . "

"A whole week is different."

"We wouldn't get up to anything."

"If I know your father, the minute school breaks up he'll be down here anyway. He usually is."

Incredibly enough, every school holiday since he moved up north Pete came rolling 'home'. Just like that.

"Hello! Is Mum there? Ah, just ringing to confirm that we break up on Wednesday this time so I'm planning to come down to you on Thursday. I must fit in a visit to my mother sometime and I'll need a couple of days in school before we start back next term. I'll have about ten days with you. All right?"

"All right!" I groaned to Stella. "It's not all right at all. Why does he think I went to all that trouble divorcing him, for Christ's sake!"

"Well, tell him, then," she said. "Tell him you're busy."

"Well, tell him, then," said Jo. "Tell him your boyfriend's moved in with you. Tell him he's no longer in the picture."

But somehow I couldn't tell him. For the first couple of years, the minute the schools broke up, Pete arrived on the doorstep. It was excruciating. For me, anyway. The kids seemed to cope more happily.

"Ah - here we are again, folks! Your old Dad turning up like the bad penny."

"Hello, Dad."

"Hello, Daddy."

Poor man. He'd stand there making bright brittle conversation. To cover his pain, I guess. His pain at *not* being met at the station, at *not* being welcomed like the Prodigal Father with hugs and kisses and squeals of delight.

"Supper's just about ready, Pete. Dump your bags and have a wash while I'm dishing out."

"You should have gone to meet him, Mum," they accused me guiltily before he emerged from the bathroom. "Someone should have been there to meet him."

"You could have gone, Henry. Either one of you could have gone. He is your father."

"I had my Chemistry to finish . . . "

"And I've only this minute got in from netball practice."

These visits of Pete's were a strain on all of us. Claire withdrew in an embarrassed silence. Henry was ultra polite and subdued.

"Well, how's school going, Dad? Settling into your new house, are you? Do you get to any football matches these days?"

Long ago, when we were still one big happy family, Henry had been football crazy. For three or four seasons. Between the fishing phase and his first girl friend. He and Tom would go off to the Dell every possible Saturday afternoon. One year they managed to save up for tickets for Wembley.

Saturday night was sacrosanct then. A bag of chips, a bottle of coke, and *Match of the Day* on the telly.

"Blimey, what a row!" Charlie had said, the first Saturday after she got home from Australia. "What's going on in there?"

"It's only Henry watching his football," Claire explained. "You've heard nothing yet."

"Do you remember, Henry?" they tease him now. "You'd sit there in your pyjamas with your arsenal scarf on . . . "

"And the woolly hat I'd knitted you . . . "

"Cheering and shouting . . . "

"And whirling that bloody rattle above your head when they got a goal."

"You were a real fanatic."

It was *then* Pete should have been sharing his ten year old son's interest. *Then*. Angus would come up and watch with Henry occasionally. He wasn't allowed to watch at home.

"Liverpool!" we'd hear them yelling.

"Up the Saints!"

Sharing the chips and the excitement.

"No, I haven't been to a match since I moved up there," Pete replied stiffly. "Seen quite a bit on the box though. Notts Forest seem to be doing pretty well at the moment. Did you see them last week?"

"No, no I didn't actually. I must have been out."

The myth that Henry was still interested in football was quietly kept alive to give them, Henry and his father, something to talk about.

Once I'd tried to get through to Pete, tried to make him see that there might be more to the father's role than simply winning the bread. It was triggered off by an incident on Claire's sixth birthday.

Angus looked in on his way home from the train, bringing the Birthday Girl a knobbly parcel from Hamley's, the famous London toy shop.

"Here's for my little princess!" he said sweeping her up for a piggy-back.

"Ooh! How lovely. Look, Mummy - how pretty! Ooh Angus!"

He'd brought her a necklace of bright glass daisies. A tiny tin in the shape of a thatched cottage. A Dutch doll small enough to fit in a pocket. And two rainbow hair-slides.

"Oh, Angus . . . " I said, interpreting it in part as a token of his feelings for *me*. "You are a dear. You are generous." It must have taken his entire lunch hour, crossing town to find these treasures for Claire.

Pete came down from his study to see what all the excitement was about.

"Look. Look what Angus brought me, Daddy. *Look*!"

"Ah! Bet you thought your old Dad had forgotten your birthday, eh?"

There was an awkward silence. He was never one for making a song and dance about things. Not birthdays, anniversaries, Christmas . . . they'd never bothered where he came from.

"Well, you could be wrong there, Claire. Your old Dad might just have got a surprise hidden away upstairs. I suggest you go and take a look in the bottom drawer of my desk."

We all went. Tom and Charlie, Henry and Claire, Angus and me and the two dogs, Bruno and Cilla, barking their heads off with excitement. All of us rushing upstairs one behind the other to look for the birthday surprise.

But there wasn't one. There was nothing in the desk drawer. Nothing but the jumble of used envelopes he was saving for a rainy day.

"How could you have played such a mean trick on the poor kid?" I asked him later, when Claire's tears had dried, and the hubbub had died down at last, and everyone was in bed. "That was really nasty of you, really unkind."

"It was only a joke," he said. "Can't anyone in this house take a joke?"

"Well, I think it was rotten of you. Cruel."

"I suppose I was jealous of Angus. All the fuss everyone was making of him."

"But he's such fun. They all love him,"

"What about me, then? I'm the one who pays the bloody bills. The one that keeps us all going. I reckon I deserve a lot more love than I seem to get. From them. From you, come to think of it."

"Nobody *deserves* love, Pete. No-one's *entitled* to it. You've got to love *them* before they can love *you*."

He must have taken it to heart because after this he made a big effort for a while, contributing in his own special way to the tea table chatter.

"Oh, Jeeze! You should have heard Old Jonesy carrying on in Assembly today," Henry might say, swigging back another mug of milk.

"Ah! Jonesy, eh. Did he mention your Old Dad, I wonder? Did he refer to the Westwood contingency, and the educational benefits they had received from Yours Truly?"

"Marmite, please. Claire! Marmite!"

"And what did you do at school today, Charlotte? Did you miss your Daddy?" He was determined to share in the banter.

It was pathetic. The kids were dumb with embarrassment. Utterly bewildered, they tried to ignore his facetious jokes.

"I can't wash up tonight, Mum. It's Bruno's training night. I'll have to start my homework straight away, or I won't be ready by eight."

"So, as I predicted, our young dog handler is finding it difficult to cope. I hope it doesn't mean that the flea-bitten creature will miss tonight's class. He's impossible to live with as he is. I gave you three months, I seem to remember. I'm keeping a strict record, son."

Son! Forgetting the bonhomie, he was suddenly switching to his *Pater Familias* part. But unfortunately his offspring had fled.

"I did try," he was to weep later. "You don't know how desperately I tried."

"But that was the problem - they knew you were having to try, Pete. Fake friendliness is no good. They knew you weren't really interested in them."

"You're not being very friendly, Mum," they scolded me now. "Poor old Dad. He comes all this way to visit us, and then you pretty well ignore him."

"Yes, she's right. You keep going off to read or paint or something, and leave us to entertain him. It's obvious he's not welcome."

"You're being horrid to him, poor Dad."

"Look, I'm doing my best to be civilised. It's not exactly easy for me either, you know."

Most fellows would have the wit to keep away, I thought. Most divorced fellows. Having gone through all the agony of divorcing someone you hardly expect him to turn up all the time. Turn up *and crawl into bed with you*, for Christ's sake.

"Honestly!" My mother was disgusted. "I can't understand you. If he's got to come and stay, why can't he sleep on the sofa."

Poor old Mother. She was still struggling to come to terms with pre-marital sex, and here we had the post-marital variety to contend with.

"He seems to assume he's entitled to share my bed. Our old bed," I explained rather feebly to Charlie, married herself by this time, and home from Doncaster for a few days on her own. "Stuffs his pyjamas under the pillow as if nothing had changed. We lie there like effigies on a medieval tomb." Terrified of inadvertently touching one another and disturbing a gaggle of domestic ghosts.

"He can't accept that the divorce is for real, Ma. He's telling everyone it's some kind of feminist game you're playing."

"Ah - the divorce," he was saying with a sour little smile. "That's just her latest fad. It suits her image. The new independent female and all that. It doesn't mean anything. I go down there every holiday. Friendly as can be."

"It's no good," I told him after a string of sleepless nights. "I can't share a bed any longer. Sorry. No ill will, but I'm going to sleep on the sofa."

"I get the feeling you don't love me any more," he said over his cornflakes. "I can't understand what I've done to deserve it." And he dashed through to the bathroom and closed the door with painful care.

"But it's obvious, Pete," I said later on, as we walked Cilla across the Common. "If I still loved you I wouldn't have divorced you. I wouldn't have gone off with Ted. You're an idiot. I tolerate your visits for the sake of the kids. But quite frankly, why can't you arrange something for the three of you? Adventures together. Find a cottage on the coast. Hire a barge. Take them to France. Anything. Give them some exciting times to look back on. Quality time with Daddy. Holidays you have taken the trouble to organise for them."

But he never did.

Chapter Nineteen

"And Edward Hill?" asked the young man driving me to the New Age party. "You haven't told me about him."

"No, Rupert, I haven't. And I don't think I could." Not you, with your principles, your intensity and integrity. Not you, lovey.

Edward Hill was gorgeous. Tall, distinguished, with a mane of curly grey hair and a beard to match. The first year he came to Summer School was the year Lyn and I decided we'd had enough of segregation.

As always at these things, there were three times as many women artists as men. This gave the minority a kind of mystical superiority. As always. A man was usually to be found at the centre of an admiring little circle of women who laughed too loudly at his jokes, vying with one another to be the most outspoken, outrageous, perceptive or bewitching.

"Don't they make you sick," said Lyn, a miniaturist of considerable talent. I'd chummed up with her at my very first Wentworth week. "Why do women have to demean themselves in this stupid way? Look at them, playing all the old sexist games. Though they enjoy it, the men aren't to blame. It's the flaming women."

"A pity really," I said. "There are some lovely fellows here this year. And quite a lot of talent."

"Oh, don't you start . . . "

"No! *Creative* talent. I wish it was easier to mingle without all this seduction rubbish."

"Right! We'll initiate the non-sexual con-spiracy."

"Conspiracy? Sounds rather unsavoury."

"Not that kind of conspiracy, stupid. A harmonious concurrence, Happy role-free mingling. Get it?"

It wasn't easy, not with all those sexual charades going on around us, but we persevered.

"We'll try to speak with every man here - OK. Sit by a different one when ever we can," Lyn decided. "At meals. In lectures. On the terrace."

"It won't do much for our reputations. As independent feminists."

"We won't be fluttering our bloody eye-lashes, *darling*. Simpering, tossing back our hair provocatively. We'll be treating them as fellow artists. Equal. Equally interesting. Got it?"

So that's what we did. Between us we managed to sit by, talk to, mingle with, about ninety of the hundred-odd males at the Summer School. We learnt a lot. We learnt that most of them enjoy the androcentric role their womenfolk give them. That they are flattered, naturally enough, by our primitive mating games. That they suffer as much from feelings of inadequacy, rejection, shyness as the rest of us.

We also learnt a great deal about the Public School system. Life in Her Majesty's Forces, the Oedipus thing, adolescent homosexuality as opposed to the real thing, marital disappointments of the masculine variety, bread-winner frustration and stress. This last was especially common among would-be artists struggling to work out a compromise between their talents and their responsibilities, much like the harassed housewife but less vocal. And, to our astonishment, from one of the Conference Stewards, a well-established portrait painter, we learnt about the quarter century he had spent in Dartmoor.

"Well, that was an interesting week," I said to Lyn as we packed our bags and canvases into the boot of her mini. "Let's have a Con-spiracy every year."

"Jolly exhausting, mind. I've felt duty-bound to cover the whole field. Know what I mean? No time to slope off for a snooze or anything."

I hadn't taken it *that* seriously. I'd swum two or three times a day in the (mostly freezing) open air pool. I'd indulged in my usual free-style dancing each night. And I hate to admit it, I'd found time to fall under the spell of Edward Hill.

"I haven't seen you here before. Is it your first Wentworth week?"

It was. He had only recently begun to paint but had already sold a few of his wildlife pictures. Birds were his thing (Ha!). He somehow captured their movement with a very original treatment of the wings.

"It's a bit reminiscent of high-speed photography. Like they use in natural history films. To analyse the mechanics of flight. You know, in slow motion," I said, trying to describe the magic of Edward's technique to Walter afterwards.

Marvellous paintings. He has made quite a name for himself already which is not in the least surprising.

"Remember his owl, captured as it pounced on its prey?" said Lyn recently.

"And that kingfisher hovering over a trout stream."

During that week of Con-spiracy, Edward and I talked several times. At that stage he was incredibly shy and self-denigrating.

"Oh, no - I really don't know any other artists. I'm very much a beginner."

Brazenedly, when I got home I sent him the details of the winter weekend I was helping to organise over at Donnington. For landscape and wildlife painters.

"Why not come?" I wrote on the back of the application form. "You'd love it, I'm sure. We're always short of fellas, and anyway I'd like to get to know you better."

"Oh, come on!" said Lyn. "Don't start playing those gruesome sexist games. I thought we were above all that, you and me."

Edward didn't come to Donnington. But he wrote once or twice between then and the next Wentworth week.

"I thought I wasn't going to get a place. They said I was on the reserve list. Thank goodness someone dropped out." Lyn was in America. It was probably her place he got. "I'm so looking forward to seeing you again."

And there he was hanging around in the foyer when I arrived, apparently waiting for me. I mean, for *me*! This gorgeous hulk - imagine!

"I've thought about you such a lot," he whispered, sitting on my bed. Stroking that particularly vulnerable spot on the back of my neck.

I felt terribly shy with him. Indeed I found myself avoiding him the first couple of days. Scuttling out of the side door of the Conference Hall to make certain our paths didn't cross in the stampede for the bar.

"I'm feeling rather sore about you," he said, coming over to sit beside me at the lecture on Acrylics. "I was hoping something might blossom between us this year."

"I feel so shy," I whispered, going red and silly as if to demonstrate what shyness does to you. "I've never had a . . . a *special friend* at Summer School." I didn't know how to handle it.

"We'd better have a chat about it," he said, giving my hand a quick squeeze. "You know my room number. Slip up and see me tonight. I've got a bottle of Bordeaux under my bed."

I didn't take in much that the *Winsor & Newton* representative was trying to tell us about the brilliant colour range in this new medium.

Slip up and see me. Bottle under the bed. Better talk about it. Oh, heavens - how the speaker droned on. And all those damn fool questions afterwards. For God's sake, get on with it, man.

"See you later, then," he said as we trooped out to the coffee trolleys on the moonlit terrace.

I didn't bother with coffee, but scurried away to make preparations. A long hot soak before the rush on bathrooms began. A few minutes meditation to calm my split nerves.

I can't just creep up to the men's floor, I thought. Not in cold blood.

But of course I did. Once the house had settled down a bit. Once the late night coffee party on the central staircase had moved into somebody's bedroom.

And I needn't have worried. Anyone who was abroad at that time of night was most probably up to something equally illicit. No-one was going to stop and ask questions.

"You came!" he said, gathering me to him with delight. "I'd nearly given up hope."

We squeezed into the two-foot-six bed and sipped wine from his tooth mug.

"I've thought about you so often since last year . . . been working tremendously hard . . . stuff hanging in several galleries now . . . sold quite a few . . ."

He re-filled the tumbler. "Well, what are we waiting for, then?"

He searched me out at breakfast. "Did you sleep well?" he asked innocently over the porridge. I didn't see him in the first lecture and slipped away for a sleep myself instead of choosing a discussion group after the coffee break. Of course, it's the Excursion Afternoon, I thought. The place will be deserted.

Before people came back to tidy up for lunch, I sneaked up to the top floor again, and left a note stuck to his mirror.

We don't have to go on the Dove Dale walk! Could we think of some better way of spending the afternoon?

What an idiotic thing to do. I never remember the bloody rules. Nice girls never take the initiative.

"I'd already put my name down for a trip to Chatsworth," he said, leaning over from the next table at lunch. "A pity, but . . ."

"Pass the water, please."

I suppose he assumed I would be going on the healthy walk. I always had done before. Dove Dale, Monsal Dale, Ashford-in-the-Water where I taught twelve mixed infants for one term when we were first married, giving up thankfully at Christmas with Thomas well on the way. Wherever they chose for the Healthy Walk it was familiar territory to me. Peopled with ghosts from our years in Matlock. Eyam, the plague village. Monyash. Lathkill Dale.

The walk was popular. The coach always full.

"Can I sit beside you? No-one's seat is it?"

"No. Come and sit here with me, Edna."

"I didn't have the chance to finish telling you about poor Nan's death, did I? Well... and afterwards... and of course I said... but Keith reckoned... womb trouble... that trouble myself... I know how she must have suffered..."

Oh, leave me alone. Please, please shut up. Let me face up to my past. Let me remember awhile.

This time I decided not to go with the coach party to Dove Holes and the Blue John mines at Castleton. I would stay behind and have a swim. Wash my hair. Possibly do a sketch from the far side of the tennis courts of the distant Derbyshire hills. It was wild and unkempt over there, well off the beat of the motor mower.

I didn't do much. Just lay in the long grass, dozing and dreaming the afternoon away. I'd better not tell Lyn about Edward. Not after last year's great con-spiracy. I was letting the feminist side down good and proper.

"Ah!" he'd breathed in his cramped little bed, hot and sticky with desire. "You're just a wild and beautiful animal. Generous. Spontaneous. And madly exciting. Aaaah!"

I could hear him saying it now. Clear as clear.

"... generous, spontaneous, madly exciting..."

With a nasty jolt I realised he *was* saying it now. Here and now! The very same patter. The very same Aaaah! Right there on the other side of the hedge.

I lay perfectly still, drowning in the heavy grasses. The poppies and groundsel. The thistles and cow parsley. The shame and humiliation of it.

"He was so beautiful," I was to tell Walter later. How could he have been so fickle!

"When you get to know them, beautiful people are often disappointing. Everything comes too easily to them. It's better to be plain and honest in the end."

Yes, that's worth remembering, I thought, sneaking a joyful glance at the slender fellow at the wheel beside me now. I must not let myself be dazzled in that way again.

Chapter Twenty

I can't quite remember how I came to be mixed up with the New Age lot. Unless it had to do with my extra-terrestrial experience.

"Oh, come on, lass!" said Walter. "You don't honestly expect me to swallow *that*!"

But it's true. I promise you. I had an encounter with a UFO. And a very close encounter it was too.

"We often notice that a sighting brings about a deep and meaningful change in the lives of the people involved," said our eminent UFO-ologist, signalling to me to switch the lights off ready for him to show his slides.

I had been coerced into launching a local branch of the Wessex Investigators, an organisation run by a young man in Exeter for the study of such things as Ley Lines, Re-incarnation, Holistic Health, Psycho-expansion, the Turin Shroud. Not *new age* so much as ancient, primeval, eternal.

"Do you think it effected *your* life in any way?" asked Dr Henkel, as he tucked into my excellent bean pot after the lecture.

"No, I can't think that it made any difference," I said putting the kettle on for camomile tea.

But afterwards, I wondered. I wondered a great deal.

It was the year before our divorce. I was curled up in bed with a book.

"Oh, yes, madam," drawled the policeman when I phoned to report what I had seen. "Science Fiction, was it?"

"It was not," I told him fiercely. "I never read Science Fiction. It was a pretty weighty tome on Vernacular Architecture, if you must know."

That flattened him. He'd no idea what Vernacular Architecture is. That much was obvious. Well, not that many people care about old domestic buildings, farm buildings. Cottages, barns, pigsties, granaries. Especially granaries.

I'd just discovered granaries. Granaries on staddle stones. You know? Those mushroom shaped stones that you're more likely to see gracing someone's pretentious driveway these days than supporting the traditional grain store. I've found loads of them round here, since I became addicted. I've painted several of them. Commissioned by the owner in two or three cases. They're so simple, granaries. So darned functional. I like that.

Anyway, that's what I was reading when it appeared to me. I say *to me* because no-one else seems to have noticed it, though heaven knows it was large enough. And conspicuous enough too.

There I was sitting up in bed with my hot drink . . .

"Could it have been the hot drink, I wonder, madam?" suggested our clay-footed police sergeant.

"Hot milk and honey, same as always."

"Right, I've got that. Please go on, then."

"It sounds pretty far fetched, I grant you, but . . . "

"Yes?"

"Well, the first thing I noticed was this bright pink light. Kind of flashing across my book."

I had looked up to see what could possibly be producing a light of such intensity, and there was this huge, well, saucer-shape. A UFO hovering outside the window. Right outside the bedroom window.

"Describe it to me, please," said the sergeant sceptically.

"All I can tell you is that it was huge, pink . . . "

"Pink?"

"Pink and spherical, well a *flattened* sphere, actually." What was the word for it? "Elliptical. Your typical flying saucer. It was pulsating strongly . . . "

"Pulsating?"

"Yes. As the pulse died away you could see . . . "

"Who could?"

"Oh - *I* could. Between flashes of light I could see the outline of the, er, space craft quite clearly. Then when the pulse came again all you, er, I could see was this almost blinding pinkness."

On reflection, it must have been an incredibly bright light. I mean, it takes a lot, for a light to show up in a lighted room. When the source of the new light is outside. Outside in the darkness. Think about it. Whatever this pink light was, it was mighty powerful.

Afraid I was dreaming, I got out of bed and keeping my eye firmly on the space ship (or whatever you like to call it) I yelled for the children to come and take a look. By the time they arrived, grumbling at being woken up and grumbling even more at having missed it, my extra terrestrial visitor had gone. Not in the proverbial flash. Not at all. It had simply floated calmly, rather majestically out of sight.

Unfortunately this was one of the nights Pete was over at Avril's. Typical. The one time I could have done with someone in bed with me to corroborate my story, and he's off with his girl friend.

"It's gone round the side of the house and up over the hill," I told the sergeant. "If you send someone up onto the roof of the Station it's probably still visible."

"I've got a right one here," I could hear him muttering to a colleague. "Says there's a blooming space ship up over St Swithun's Hill."

"Never mind the funny stuff," I yelled into the mouthpiece. "Send someone to have a look."

But it was too late, of course. Whatever it was that had hovered outside my window that February night had vanished.

Was it a friendly Space Man, perhaps, writing an anthropology thesis? A team of Time Travellers suddenly nostalgic for their homes and families?

I phoned the police again next morning to make certain the sighting had been entered in the Log Book. It had. And they'd contacted the Army to check whether there had been any night manoeuvres (firing of flares, for instance) that could account for what I had seen. But there hadn't been a thing.

I wrote to the Daily Mirror which I discovered was running a series on UFOs at the time, and was told our house lay on what was known as 'The Solent Loop', a regular flight path for UFOs.

Apart from that, I kept quiet. For fear of ridicule. The knowing wink. The supercilious smirk. But now among my New Age friends unidentifiable flying objects were utterly respectable. (Mine had been respectable all along, mind. You can tell, can't you!)

"And did it effect your life?" asked my young friend Rupert, helping with the washing-up after Dr Henkel and everyone else had left. "Luscious bean pot!"

"In fact it might have done. It was soon after that that I started agitating for the divorce which was to change everything. And it was round then that I became seriously interested in the supernatural. All our New Age stuff. There could be a connection."

"That was lucky, then."

"Lucky?"

"Lucky for me. Otherwise I might never have met you."

"Idiot! Come on, let's make some real coffee for a change, and take it out into the garden, shall we."

"I wasn't joking," he said solemnly as we sat under the white lilac drinking in the sweet scents of the summer twilight. "You're the dearest friend I've ever had."

"I know what you're after, young man. Another mug of coffee and a piece of that chocolate marzipan. You and your wiles!" And I gave him a motherly hug.

Funny old life, I thought, going in to re-fill the coffee mugs. This really is the most astonishing thing that ever came my way. UFOs included. And at my age, for Heaven's sake!

Chapter Twenty-One

Having so little myself, I've always been a sucker for beauty. At school I'd had *pashes* on first the Head Girl and then the gym mistress.

"Mum! Head *Girl*! Gymn *Mistress*! Females?"

"Yuck! And you say I'm perverted!"

But it was the accepted thing in those days, the pre-promiscuous forties. Prefects and teachers were the objects of our silent worship, our adolescent adoration. There was no harm in it. It was simply the fashion. It's all a question of fashion. Look at your ancient Greeks.

And they were all beautiful, all my, um . . . my Special Friends. Each in his own sweet way. Doctor Olaf, Angus, Ted, Jim.

"Jim's scrumptious! Remember he took us out for a drink once, Peggy?"

"Oh, him! He was the spitting image of Doctor Zhivago, wasn't he."

"Right down to his wandering eye."

We were letting our hair down together, Peggy and I. Poor Peg. Her marriage was in rags as mine had been.

"Can I come over with the girls for a couple of nights?" she'd begged, phoning from work. "We'll bring sleeping bags. Won't be any trouble."

"Great."

The kids were all settling down for a serious night's telly.

"Come on, Peg - let's barricade ourselves into my room. Bring the rest of the wine."

"Be good, all of you," she yelled over the *Dallas* theme tune. "No arguing!"

"Shh!" they said impatiently. "Don't keep interrupting."

And to one another :

"Ooh, I like this next bit."

"JR comes in in a minute..."

"... and gets really nasty."

"They've seen it already," she explained wearily, flopping down on my bed with her mug of Beaujolais. "That's all they ever do these days, escape to their playroom and watch the portable."

"I shouldn't worry. It's only a phase. Probably their way of blotting out what's going on. Between you and Douglas."

"I can't think straight any more. Not with him around. I know I'm going to have to do something about it, but I can't seem to muster the energy. Do you know what I mean?"

I did indeed. I hadn't forgotten the steady loss of initiative. The weathering away of protest.

"What I'm terrified of is drifting along like this until it somehow all becomes acceptable. Normal. Inevitable."

We had an orgy of honesty that night, my sister and I. When the first bottle was empty she staggered down to the off-licence to fetch another.

"Coke for the kids," she said, dumping it all on the kitchen table. "Mars Bars all round. Crisps. And whisky for us."

She wasn't short of money, anyway. That wasn't Peg's problem. In a way it was the opposite.

"He was never easy," she told me now, pouring us both generous measures of Scotch. "But since he came into all that money..." She waved her arms dramatically above her head.

"Steady on! No point wasting it."

"He does nothing. Absolutely nothing but sit in that smelly old chair..."

"Not the one his mother left him?"

"That's the one. It's threadbare and filthy, but he refuses to have it recovered or anything. He sits there all day. Reading."

"Well, he always was a bit of an intellectual, Douglas."

"Intellectual! It's porn. Real hard porn. That's partly why the girls are confined to the old playroom. Don't want them getting their hands on Daddy's *homework*."

Douglas was an academic. A classicist. Almost as intellectual as Peggy herself.

"Oh, come on! I don't believe it. He may be a sod, but *pornography*! Douglas! For heaven's sake!"

But it was true, apparently. Now there was no need for him to work, his baser nature seemed to have surfaced.

"When he found out how much his father had left him, he expected me to give up my job too." She swilled back the dregs of her whisky. "I drew the line at that. Or we'd both be suffering from Rigor Mortis by now. Forty-five last birthday and dead. *Dead*!" She began to weep quietly into my pillow.

"Hey, cheer up! I'll make us some coffee."

"They've all fallen asleep round the box," I told her, bringing our coffee through. "I've left it on or they'd wake up immediately."

"It isn't only that," she snuffled, dragging herself back from an intoxicated dream. "It's - you know - *the other*. The bed bit."

It always comes down to that in the end, doesn't it. Once you've lost respect for him you can't go through with it. Not unless you're prepared to pretend.

"Pretend?" My young friend Janet had been genuinely astounded. "Who's going to pretend over a thing like that? Either you're enjoying it, or you're not. No room for pretence."

Her generation had not been indoctrinated as ours had.

I couldn't explain it to her. It sounded so feeble. *It's a wife's duty to appear to enjoy it. It means so much to a man. It's little enough to ask, when all's said and done.* That's the sort of stuff we were brought up on. *His* marital rights. *His* pleasure. They should be a good woman's chief concern.

"It's an insult to a fellow, pretending. Faking orgasms and stuff like that. And it's downright disgusting."

Janet too was part of the New Age Scene. Bursting with idealism and curiosity. About Zen Buddhism, Ley Lines, Spiritual Healing, Atlantis, and the dawning of the Age of Aquarius. I admired her, and all the rest of them, for their dedication to the quest. The quest for enlightenment.

"I'm surprised at you," said Peg, while we were still lucid. "I didn't know you were into that sort of thing."

"I'm fascinated by it. The supernatural and all that. Always have been. Certainly since I saw my jolly old UFO."

"Be serious!"

"Suit yourself. I honestly *think* I saw it."

"Good God! Give us the rest of that wine!"

"I believe you, Swami," Rupert had said sitting with me under the lilac tree. "There are sure to be some hoaxers in the field, but that doesn't invalidate all the evidence. Not all sightings can be dismissed out of hand. In my opinion UFOs merit some serious investigation."

"That's how you met this young man of yours, isn't it?"

I was surprised that Peggy was still with me, sprawled on her tummy on my bed.

"Yes, he was one of the group. I've known him for some time."

"Funny how pointless it all seems now," he said to me recently. "We were swept away, all of us, weren't we? Walking the Ley Lines, Mystical Dancing under the full moon - it was all so fearfully significant. Remember?"

It was friendly too, and fun. The Happenings. The Share-Ins. The Meditations.

"Are you free Saturday evening? We're organising a Dream Analysis Seminar. Yes, out at the farm. And there'll be dancing after supper. On the meadow if it's fine. Can you bring a contribution to the feast? Lovely. Good. Go in peace."

Such loving, gentle, positive souls. Always looking for the best in one another. Generous. Charitable. Enthusiastic. Innocent. I thoroughly enjoyed *my* New Age.

"Until Dylan came along," Rupert reminded me dryly. "For all his madness, he made us question what we were up to, didn't he?"

"My God! Dylan! Remember the Love-Ins?"

Dylan was a young man with a mission. A New Age Prophet. A dedicated Light Worker. He brought the Sacred Dance with him from South Africa, and planned to organise a stupendous Happening around the shore of Lake Geneva.

"There will be twenty-thousand dancers circumscribing the lake, hand in hand. It will be the biggest demonstration of International Harmony the world has ever seen."

I could well imagine it. Like us, they would sway and bend, moving with a slow dignity to the haunting Greek Folk Music of the dance.

"Like a girdle of reeds at the water's edge," said Dylan, enraptured by his vision.

"I wonder if he ever made it in Switzerland? We'd have heard about it, wouldn't we?"

"I doubt whether *you* would, Swami," said Rupert. "Not after your outburst."

I'd fallen out of favour with Dylan and his followers. Irrevocably.

"It's the Saggitarian in you," he had conceded, forgiving me. "Your forthrightness. You still have a long way to travel on the path to enlightenment, Sister. But never fear, we are holding you in the light."

Yes, I thought. And my path will be a different one from yours, Brother Dylan. That much I have discovered.

Chapter Twenty-Two

As I've told you, Rupert was one of the New Age group. He's a dentist, of all things, of tremendous zeal and integrity. He's tall and lean, with a fierce intelligence behind the gentle vulnerable face of a child. And when I first knew him he was thirty-two.

"They were a lovely bunch," I told Peg. "Even if some of their games were hard to swallow."

Meditation was fine, but meditating on specially selected hill tops in the hope of conjuring up the angels, well, that was something else.

Positive thought forms were fine too, though committing myself to *beaming light* for half an hour a day onto the troubled world in the belief that our efforts might possibly tip the scales in favour of love, joy and peace was not really my thing.

"But it works," they insisted. "It worked on Iona last Summer, didn't it, when Sir George asked us all to visualise a fine sunny afternoon..."

"For our pilgrimage around the island..."

"And lo-and-behold it worked!"

"Even though it hadn't stopped pouring all week."

"And rain was forecast again."

"So you see..."

"Yes, but..."

We were sitting cross-legged in a circle on Old Winchester Hill. It was polling day in a north London by-election, and a testing time for the newly formed SDP/Liberal Alliance.

"We'll give ourselves an extra ten minutes today," said Letitia, the most experienced Light Worker among us. "We must concentrate on beaming in on the constituency and shedding light on the *Don't Knows*."

"But you can't seriously expect our efforts to influence the result, Lettuce!"

"The power of thought is infinite, my dear girl. With faith, anything can be achieved. Uri Geller's just doing party tricks. The air is full of unseen influences. Radio waves. Television signals. Brain waves are no more difficult to believe in."

"But, come on! Who's to say the Liberals are the Children of God? It seems arrogant to me, presuming to engineer things. Whether it works or not. I'm sorry, but Liberal as I am, I'm going to sit this one out."

I had never really been a committed Light Worker. I'd always had my doubts, they knew that, and lovingly made allowance for my shortcomings. Previously, I'd been content to sit in their Circle of Enlightenment, drinking in the Spring sunshine, the pattern of ploughing in the valley below us, the woolly clouds drifting above. They could worship in their way. I would in mine.

A car load of us zoomed up to Oxford one Sunday for a seminar on *The Search for the Meaning of Life*, no less. I listened respectfully to the learned and enlightened speakers who had all travelled along vastly different paths in their quest for the grail, the Holy Grail. All day they agonised above our heads (certainly above mine), about chakra points, the esoteric versus the exoteric, selfless awareness, mystical reality, the Kabala, wholism and holism, till I was dizzy.

Does it have to be so difficult, I thought, picturing a bluebell wood I'd walked through with Walter a few days earlier. Surely the answer's all around us, under our bloody noses. As simple as the Green Cross Code. Stop, look and listen! Nothing could be simpler.

"Watch it!" said Rupert, who had dropped in for a cup of tea with the post mortem next day. "Now who's being arrogant?"

I should have remembered that at Dylan's WESAK Festival. I should have kept my big mouth shut.

In his generous way, at his first visitation, Rupert had put Dylan up. "Though I must admit I hadn't expected him to stay the entire winter."

"He's a shameless sponger," said Letitia indignantly.

"I quite enjoy his company," said Rupert. "He's a bit mad, but harmless."

"Lettuce is right," said Polly, who strongly disapproved of the colourful prophet. "He'll disrupt our nice little circle if we're not watchful." (*Watchful* was part of our New Age jargon.) "He's a negative influence."

"But the dancing's rather jolly . . . "

"Jolly! It's positively *pagan*!"

"He's a dangerously deluded fellow, if you ask me."

But which one of us isn't, I thought cynically. In one way or another.

"I pick up some nasty vibes from young Dylan, I know that."

"We mustn't succumb to his charm . . . "

Dylan was causing a good deal of anxiety among the Bretheren.

"He's coming back after Easter," Rupert told me. "That's when I'll be out in Thailand. I've offered him the house while I'm away. Better than leaving it empty."

Which is how the WESAK Festival came to be celebrated in Puddle Down Cottage that year. There were about a dozen of us there. The floor was spread with mats and cushions and the scene nicely set for Dylan's particular brand of waffle.

In the north-east corner (carefully checked with a compass) an altar had been set up, a shrine with candles and a jug of daisies, some mystical postcards, and pieces of driftwood and rock. The centre-piece was a goldfish bowl of holy (Vichy!) water in which two chunks of crystal had been immersed to produce good magic. On the wall was a highly significant diagram with a lot of esoteric/exoteric/cryptic symbolism including the telling slogan,

TAURUS :
LET THE EYE SEE AND THE LIGHT POUR IN.

We took it in turns to read aloud from Dylan's book on the WESAK business, which I'd never heard of. About this secret valley in Tibet where every Taurus New Moon millions of souls gather (some living, some dreaming, some dead) to witness the descent of the Buddha from the heavens. As he floats down from the clouds in his traditional lotus posture, Jesus and two other guys are there to receive him. Then the assembled multitudes join in drinking the holy water from the spring, and tremendous fun is had by all. That's what it said in the book, anyway.

Now Dylan took us on a guided tour of the Astral Realms, the chakra points of Mother Earth, and his own radiant soul. Suzie read out a special invocation in very slow and meaningful tones, which the believers among us echoed sonorously, phrase by phrase. We all *ommed* a great deal.

(Note for the un-initiated : OMMING is a matter of taking a deep breath and humming steadily on one note through closed lips to produce a prolonged vibrating MMMMMMMMMMMMMMMMMM. Omming is most effective when undertaken in unison.)

Janet intoned the Great Invocation in a funereal voice, which again we were invited to echo phrase by mystical phrase. This was followed by your actual meditation, during which a Brother whom I thought of as the Bearded Pixie fidgeted and snorted incessantly as did his excruciating but unbearded wife. This behaviour was of course perfectly acceptable from such Very Enlightened Beings.

Now purified by Dylan's magic and the lumps of Blue John and Selenite, the holy water was ladled into plastic mugs and distributed among the faithful.

I had sat quietly through all this. Not omming. Not echoing. But nevertheless appreciating the intensity of feeling, the circle of eager faces in the candlelight. Not to mention Dylan's dramatic powers, the simple charm of the ritual and the friendly if slightly infatuated atmosphere.

Over the herbal tea and digestive biscuits, Dylan outlined his plans for bringing enlightenment to our little old town. Through Sacred Dance, Healing Circles, Meditation, and the omnipotent *Om*. He was quite carried away by his own zeal, and the others sat dewy-eyed at his feet.

Earlier, when the omming started in earnest, I had almost got myself out of it. It was just a matter of muttering something about needing the loo, and escaping quietly into the night. But the chance slipped by.

"Omming," we were being told, "is the only hope for the future. Properly studied and practiced regularly, omming will change the world, bringing about social and spiritual revolution. Ushering in the Age of Aquarius."

Suddenly I'd had enough. "What a load of humbug!" I shouted. "I never heard such waffle. Come on, Dylan - who the hell are you kidding!"

That did it. They were all so mad at me, for attacking their pet guru.

"You are too insensitive to understand."

"I never trusted you . . . "

"You brought bad vibes with you . . . "

"Right from the start I knew you were trouble."

"Look what you've done, you've destroyed the beautiful harmony that darling Dylan has worked so hard to create for us."

"You're a destroyer . . . "

"Yes, yes," I said. "Yes, you're right." Which only added fuel to the fire, and in the uproar I escaped thankfully into the two-o'clock streets upon which the Taurus New Moon winked innocently down.

"What with Dylan's circus, Lettuce and her magic triangles, manifesting Buddhas and God knows what else, I'm leaving the New Age stage, whatever it was, to the truly enlightened," I explained to Rupert, home at last, more beautiful than ever with his Thai tan.

"You've got to be exaggerating."

"Believe me, I'm only telling you half of it. I'm happy to settle for the good old material world. A Schubert Quartet. And a chocolate marzipan bar to share with a friend. That'll do me fine."

"Dylan certainly left his mark on the cottage. There are cryptic diagrams everywhere and messages of great spiritual significance (I assume). I'll have to have the place fumigated. Spiritually, of course!"

"Not much hope of getting rid of it that easily! Dylan's antics will have been absorbed into the woodwork."

"Oh, surely not!"

"Jess was telling me . . . "

Jessica is a friend from my museum days. She was studying for her Museums Diploma. Medieval floor tiles were her speciality. There were crates of them in the basement store at work, salvaged from the ruins of a Norman Abbey.

"I sneaked a few home," she told me. "I shouldn't have done, mind. Against all the rules. But I was writing this paper for my Diploma and I was late with it. As usual."

"Yes?"

"Well, just at that time I kept hearing all this singing. In the night. It woke me three or four nights on the trot. Plainsong. You know, chanting. Like they sing the psalms in Church."

Jess lives round near the College. She thought it was the boys processing round the streets, singing. That it was some ancient ceremony that they observed every spring. One night when the singing woke her she actually went out onto the street to yell at them for disturbing honest citizens at such an ungodly hour. But there was no-one there.

"The singing came in waves," she told me. "Rising and falling. Sometimes fading away completely, and then starting up again a couple of minutes later." Jess took off her shoes and curled up on the sofa. "Well, I finished my essay, right. And smuggled the tiles back into the museum. Back into the store."

"Right."

"And at coffee break Dave and Teddy were talking about this programme they'd heard on the radio, right, the night before. Honest, I nearly passed out."

"What? Why?"

"These blokes had invented this machine, right, that could pick up the location of pottery under the ground. Like a metal detector. A *pottery* detector, right. They'd been swinging it round in the cellar of some old house in York - I think it was York . . ."

"Get on with it!"

"But instead of the high pitched whistle they were expecting . . ."

"That would tell them there were archaeological remains under the floor."

"Right."

"Well?"

"It gave out *voices*. Human voices! Voices coming out of the brickwork, for Christ's sake. Voices speaking some gobbledegook that on analysis turned out to be Anglo-Saxon."

"Wow!"

"The theory was that the voices had been absorbed into the fabric of the building . . ."

"The walls and beams and . . ."

"And the brick floor. And somehow their machine had picked it up, tuned into it, and played it back. After all those centuries."

"So we reckoned the same thing must have been happening with her floor tiles," I told Rupert. "We reckoned

Jess must have released something in them. By studying them so intensely. Handling them, drawing them, thinking about them for her essay. By loving them, if you like, she'd switched them on and released the plain song chanting that was somehow stored within them."

"It doesn't surprise me in the least. I'm certain that everything that happens is somehow recorded in the environment. Most things aren't cut too deep. Just a superficial impression is left . . ."

"An echo . . ."

"But more dramatic events . . ."

"Murders and all that."

"Yes, crimes. Tragedies. Accidents. Those would leave such a sharp, such a deep impression that it would last for years."

"For ever."

"Like a video recording of the event, yes. And that's your . . ."

"That's your haunting. Your ghosts. A tape, if you like. A video recording of the dastardly deed or whatever."

"And in this case, Jess would hear the chanting in waves, as she put it, because the particular tile she had *switched on* . . ."

"Activated."

"Yes. That particular tile would have *heard*, would have picked up the chanting in waves. Loudly as the monks walked over it. Softer and softer as the procession moved on down the aisle. Wow!"

"Well, dear old Dylan has made a pretty deep and permanent impression on Puddle Down Cottage, by the sound of it. You've got him with you for ever. Into eternity."

"Oh, no!"

"Never mind Dylan. How about a plain and simple earthy and unenlightened cuddle, young man. You've been away a terrible long time."

Chapter Twenty-Three

"Funny old life!" I said to Walter. "Who'd have thought that a young chap like that, so bright, so beautiful, would come along and take a fancy to an old frump like me!" I could scarcely believe it.

"Am I going to be allowed to meet this, er . . . "

"Rupert. Well, it's Thomas, actually. But I call him Rupert."

To call him Thomas was just too painful . . .

My Thomas, Tommy my first born, had stormed off at the time of our divorce.

"That's it!" he'd shrieked at me as he moved out to some grotty digs on the other side of town. "Bloody fine mother you've been!"

"Tom's an idiot," Charlie said. "Don't worry, Mum. He'll come round. He'll be back. Give him a chance to cool down. It's only his pride . . . "

"It's his damn Maria," said Henry. "Stirring it as usual. What on earth did he ever see in her?"

"Well he's stuck with her now," said Claire, grimacing. "Come on - I'm going to make a pot of tea."

We'd just had a mysterious phone call. A girl using a carefully disguised voice . . .

"It's obvious who it was," said Henry.

. . . a girl ringing from a phone box. She'd asked for me.

"Your Thomas, he was married this morning," she informed me bluntly. You'll never see him again. And you'll never see your grandchildren, if I can help it." And she hung up.

"It isn't only that we weren't invited," Claire pointed out in her sensible way as she poured the tea. "They wanted to make damn certain we *knew* we weren't invited."

"Yes, that's the bitchy bit," said Charlie, who was home from Doncaster for a few days.

"Not that I'd have gone, mind," Henry assured me loyally. "Not unless you were invited along too, Ma."

And there was little fear of that.

It was four years since I had last seen my eldest son. Soon after he finished at University, it was. A wicked summer it had been for all of us with the divorce brewing and the family in disarray. The house was up for sale and so far we hadn't found anywhere I could move to with Henry and Claire. Tom came home with a respectable Second, but without a job, and apparently without any serious intention of looking for one.

"I'll just hang around till something turns up," he explained airily when I tried to discuss his plans with him. "I can do with a rest."

He did get temporary work on a farm, it's true. And then took himself off to Europe on a Student Runabout Ticket with Maria.

"I suppose you don't feel like coughing up a hundred quid or so towards the trip?" he asked a few days before they left. "We're going to have a problem surviving the month . . ."

"A hundred pounds, Tom! You must be joking. I haven't got a bloody bean." Pete was insisting on doing the shopping himself at this time. As he earned it, he'd damn well decide what it was to be spent on. Apart from the few quid I was earning as a jobbing gardener, the only money I ever handled was the Family Allowance. "And I've never seen a hundred pounds in my life."

British Rail got in touch the week after they'd left. Tom's cheque had bounced and the pair of them would be arrested at their next stop if funds were not immediately found to meet the deficit. Maria's father saved the day, and I read the riot act when the travellers eventually returned.

"Bloody irresponsible, you are!" I bellowed. "They were threatening to arrest you both. You knew there wasn't enough in your account to pay for the tickets. I can't believe that you'd be so stupid."

"Well, you should have helped us out. You knew we were tight. A month is a long time."

"Damn right it is. Which of us ever had a month's holiday, I should like to know."

That was the beginning of the end, really. Tom didn't see why he should demean himself getting a job unless it was tailor-made for him.

"I'm not having you loafing around indefinitely. If you're moving over to Railway Terrace with us you'll jolly well have to pay your whack."

"None of my friends have got jobs. Their parents aren't bullying them. I need a rest. Nobody seems to appreciate that I've been studying non-stop since I was a kid. Since I got the bloody eleven-plus."

"I'm sorry, love. We've done our best for you. Seen you through college. Now it's up to you. I won't be in a position to subsidise anyone. It's going to be a job surviving, if you must know."

"You chose to divorce him. Don't start complaining."

It was a terrible summer. Pete was still in the house, but cycling over most nights to see his latest girlfriend, Avril, though God knows what use he was to her after his fifteen mile ride, and coming home with the morning papers.

"Hello, love," he'd say sheepishly. "Cup of tea?"

"Did you have fun, then?"

We never rowed. That was part of the trouble, I guess.

"At least you'll have that fine great son to back you up," people said to me, but by the time the divorce went through Tom had left.

"Don't worry, Mum. He'll be back," Charlie had said. Give him a chance to cool down and he'll be back."

But she was wrong. I've never seen him since. Apart from once. It was Christmas Eve. A year after he'd left. I ran into him in Marks & Spencers.

"Why, Tom..." I said, hardly recognising the handsome young accountant at the foot of the escalator, so smart and trim.

"Er - ah - " he stammered, looking round desperately for a cue from Maria. "Uh, hello, Mum."

She was beside him instantly, homing in from the sock counter to extricate him from my clutches. "Come on, Tom. We mustn't keep Daddy waiting." And she steered him firmly through the Christmas crush, her mop of flaming curls bobbing indignantly towards the exit.

Perhaps that's where I went wrong, I thought sadly now on his wedding day. Perhaps he needed someone like Maria to steer him devotedly through the rapids. It was difficult with the four of them, and their father not much cop. I did my best.

"Don't let it bug you, Mum," said Henry cheerfully. "You've got us. You can't win 'em all."

Thomas only had eighteen months to himself before the next one came along. There was never a time that he can remember when he was the apple of anyone's eye. I suppose that's hard, though plenty of us survive it.

"Charlie never ever had you to herself, Ma," said Claire.

"And I didn't either, come to that," said Henry.

"That probably accounts for some of your personality weaknesses, eh." The girls fell about laughing.

"At least Claire'll be OK," Charlie comforted me. "Now *she*'s got you all to herself." Henry was at University by this time.

"The first baby's always difficult," said Claire with all the wisdom of her first week's Sociology at the Sixth Form College. "There's going to be trouble in China in a few years. No-one's allowed to have more than one child. They are going to be a nation of only children. Can you imagine - forty million spoilt brats. It's true. We did it on Wednesday."

"Oh, shut up, Sis. We didn't ask for a flaming lecture. I thought you said there were some chocolate biscuits, Mum? Come on, then." And there was a stampede to the kitchen.

Yes the first baby is difficult, I thought. We should be wearing *L Plates*, by rights. It's a wonder any of them survive. First-borns.

"My mother says poor Tom had a deprived childhood," Maria told me once with that incredible red-headed cheek of hers. "But I intend to make up for what he's missed."

What confidence! What righteous indignation. And from a fifteen year old at that!

He was seventeen, three years older than her, when they first met. He'd never had a girlfriend before.

"And she made sure he never had another," Claire reminded us.

We were glad he was getting a bit more fun out of life in the Lower Sixth after those grinding Grammar School years.

"Oh, Tommy - it's nearly half-past ten. You should be in bed, love."

"I'm still on my bloody Latin. The Algebra took me hours tonight."

It wasn't only the slog either. There was the discrimination to cope with. They'd all had a rough ride through Primary School with their father the Headmaster.

"I should have insisted on sending them to another school," I told Walter once. "But it was a job standing up to Pete."

"There isn't a better primary in the town," he would declare. "You seem to forget that Westwood has the best qualified Head in the county. No question of sending my own kids anywhere else."

Tom suffered more than the rest of them. He was a studious little chap, and always an enthusiast. For trains, and big ships, and Arsenal football team. And eventually for Maria.

He would save his pocket money for a trip to Southampton where he'd mooch round the docks studying the liners. Sometimes treating himself to a trip on the harbour launch that took him right alongside the proud vessels. Setting out at dawn to see the QE2 off on her maiden voyage.

Oh, Tommy . . .

I remember, years before, in our Matlock days, trailing down to the station every afternoon (just about), with the pair of them, Tom and Charlie strapped side-by-side in the heavy old twin push-chair. To watch the trains passing through on their way from Derby to the north.

But he doesn't. He only remember the bad times, it seems.

There was that awful day, the last day of the Christmas term, when I was late back from the shops and they were all locked out in the cold.

"What made you lock the door, Mum?" they ask now. The door was never locked.

Tom had been working on a Very Special Surprise for Mummy. When I arrived home at last, breathless and contrite and laden with shopping the others were sitting happily in Mrs Cross-next-door's, recounting hair-raising adventures for her over orange squash and Jaffa Cakes. Tom was crouching in misery on the back porch, his delicate table decoration (a snow scene made from a fir cone lovingly sprayed with sparkly frost) lay trampled at his feet.

"Where were you, Mum? Why were you late? Why ever were you late?"

He was the first Eleven-Plus success at Westwood for a generation (it was a very poor catchment area). The local lads made Tom suffer for it.

"They'd lie in wait for me," he told me later, when he was able to mention it calmly. "Jeer at me. 'Who's a little creep, then?' 'And is his daddy the headmaster, eh?' "

And I didn't help much, I'm afraid.

"Why can't you manage to walk home without dropping something in the river?" If it wasn't his cap it was his chemistry book, his gymn shoes, his PE kit. "We can't keep replacing it all. Money doesn't grow on trees."

Money. Money. Always the same old problem. That was why he suffered those short trousers, for God's sake.

"Bloody hell, Mum! how could you have been so simple? I was the only one in the school in short trousers. The only one. What a fool I felt. It was agony."

"But why didn't you say something? Why didn't you tell us, love. *Then*. At the time. We didn't know. You were the first eleven year old we'd had, don't forget."

"I didn't know myself, did I? Not till I bloomin' got there. And then it was too late. You were always so hard up. How could I ask for *another* pair of trousers. Good job I grew out of the bloody things pretty quick. The first term was grim, I can tell you. What with that and my old mates from Westwood lying in wait for me every night, taunting me, throwing my stuff in the river whenever they could."

Oh, Tom - who'd be a mother!

It was about this time that we got Bruno, our beautiful Alsatian puppy. My sister Kate brought him over from Jersey, the last of Queenie's litter, and gave him to Tom for his twelfth birthday.

"I'm not sharing my house with bloody animals," Pete shouted. "I've enough on my plate as it is without a damn great dog to feed."

"But I'll be responsible for him, Dad. I really will. I'll take him to training classes. You won't know he's around."

There were endless rows about poor Bruno.

"Thomas!" his father would bellow. "Do I have to pick my way through piles of dog shit in my own front hall?"

"He's only a baby," Charlie would declare indignantly. "Even you were probably a baby once." She stood up to her father.

Now on top of all the other aggro in his life, my pale intense son was carrying responsibility for this boisterous addition to the family. For his training and grooming, for exercising and disciplining him. And if he failed - God help Bruno.

Once when Tom was home from University we had a party.

"A *party*?" Pete had not been enthusiastic. "What the hell do we want a party for?"

It was coming up to my birthday. My *fortieth* birthday. As I'd never had a party in my whole damn life, not a grown-up party anyway, I decided I'd jolly well have one now. I was getting a lot bolder.

All the theatre crowd came. I baked seventy-five potatoes, and there were none left over.

"There you are," I told Pete next day, "it didn't cost much. Everyone brought a bottle. In fact," (taking a quick inventory of what was left on the sideboard) "I think we've probably done rather well out of it."

"Ah - shlovely!" said Pete, reeling playfully round the kitchen. "Tonight - hick! - we can have another party!"

Pete was a great one for playing drunk, even after half-a-pint in a pub. It may have helped him disguise his social inadequacies. Anyway, at the party he'd had no need to pretend. He ladled out the punch till he became maudlin and pathetic.

"Meet my eldest son," he confided to anyone who cared to listen. "My mediocre son, right. Thinks, thinks he's actually, actually going somewhere in life. Poor misguided fellow. No bleeding chance. Ha! Got his A's. Thomas. Sure, he's got his A's. But university, that's something else . . ."

"Shove over, man!" No-one was listening. They pushed past him, climbed over him, as he sat there burbling on the stairs. "Where's the dancing then?"

"It was in my bedroom," Claire remembered now. "That's the night we learned the facts of life, isn't it, Henry?"

"Yeh, yeh! We were hiding on the top bunk. Bloody hell . . ."

"You shouldn't have been there, either of you, young and innocent as you were."

"It was my bedroom."

"I'm leaving, Mum," Tom had wept, coming to find me in the kitchen. "Have you heard what Dad's saying?"

"He's drunk, lovey. He's not in his right mind."

"That's when people say what they really think, when they're drunk. I always knew he hadn't much faith in me, but now . . . I can't stay here any longer. I can't live with him after this. I'm off."

"Tom, no! Take no notice. You know how he is about qualifications. He can't bear to admit you'll be as well-qualified as he is. One day soon."

But when the time came, we weren't even informed that he'd got through his finals, let alone invited to the degree ceremony.

Oh dear - no wonder the poor kid pushed off, vowing that he'd never cross the threshold again. His anger aimed at me in the end.

"Bloody fine mother you've been!"

True. Too true. I remembered his first few days, when he wouldn't feed but screamed with hunger and frustration. How I was alone with him all day in our bleak bare flat. The mid-wife would make me a cup of tea before she left and a hot-water bottle, calling round morning and afternoon, knowing there was no-one else who would come.

"But surely you'd got some friends up there, Mum? Even if you were miles from your family."

We'd only been there a few months. With both of us teaching out of town there somehow hadn't been time to get to know anyone. A neighbour was kind, Pat in the next flat. But I was very lonely.

Lonely, incompetent, with scarcely enough to feed let alone clothe us all. Living on boiled eggs and Nescafe.

Exhausted. Always limp with exhaustion. And even more so with the next baby on the way . . .

"See, you were a right menace from the start, Charlie!"

"Shut up, you! How about making us some fresh coffee? Put that incredible talent of yours to some good use."

"For a change!"

. . . flopping asleep in the afternoon once young Tommy was tucked up in his cot, to struggle guiltily back to life as daylight failed, the fire nearly out and Pete due home from school for his tea.

"Crumbs, Ma! Sounds like a barrel of fun, motherhood!"

"Remind me not to go in for it myself, OK!"

Once, I remember, Tommy had filled his nappy as I slept, and wiped it up with the end of the curtain that hung beside his cot. While I slept.

"Yah! I always said he was a pig."

I thought it showed great resourcefulness, myself. He was only about a year old.

Once we nearly lost him, when waking from my pregnant under-nourished sleep, I discovered him with the remains of a bottle of aspirin.

"Ooh, those lovely orange-y baby aspirins. I remember them."

"Did he have to be pumped out and all that, like we saw on telly?"

How near we had come to losing our first born, to never knowing the storms ahead.

"But look, Tom - I can't afford anything bigger. Railway Terrace will be fine. You're welcome to come there with us, but you'll have to share a room with Henry. I'm sorry, but it's the best I can do. In any case, you'll be off as soon as you find a job, won't you. It would only be temporary."

"I'm not waiting till then, thank you. I'm off *now*! And with any luck our paths will never cross again, *Mother dear*!"

Chapter Twenty-Four

"It's pretty painful, isn't it?" I said to Walter. "Perhaps he'll swallow his pride and come to my funeral."

"It is a matter of pride," he agreed sadly. "Burying hatchets is never easy."

Walter had three children, two sons and a daughter. At nineteen the girl had run off and married a Canadian, a musician. A would-be pop star and composer.

"Not that he ever composed a solitary thing that I heard of. He'd strum about on a guitar, the same as most of his generation. Even twenty-odd years back when we knew him, he was full of aggression for a world that refused to recognise his talent. It was obviously going to be a disaster."

"And . . . ?"

"And it has been. She does keep in touch with one of her brothers. A letter a year perhaps. He went to see her once. They're living in a tumble down cottage in Yorkshire. On Social Security and the odd bit she can earn. Working on the land. Currant picking, potato lifting, anything really."

"Oh, Walter . . ."

"Last I heard she had a vegetable stall on the market."

We were sitting on one of the stone benches in the porch of a tiny Norman Church deep in the Sussex downs. I put out my hand, stained with oil paint and blackberry juice, and held tight on to his.

"There are five children. Five. And I've never set eyes on any of them."

He lifted my hand and holding it up counted them off on my fingers.

"Emma, Hudson, Paddington, Tollie and Karn."

"Paddington!"

"Not after the bear. After the station."

"She never forgave us for lumbering her with *Victoria*. 'It's not after the Queen,' she'd tell people. 'They called me after the station.' "

The laughter eased the pain.

"I could do with a drink," said Walter, as we collected up our gear and left the churchyard and its legitimate occupants in peace in the sunshine. "How about sampling what the Saracen's Head has to offer? It begins to feel like lunchtime."

"Now, tell me about this young friend of yours," he said, as we tucked into our steak and kidney, served from a two-gallon pie-dish on the bar. Home-made to the last delicious spoonful of gravy.

"It's a kind of a secret," I told him bashfully. "No-one's supposed to know."

"Why ever not? He surely can't be ashamed of you?"

"It's not that exactly. It's the age thing. I could be his mother. I really could. There's seventeen years between us. People don't approve of that sort of relationship, do they?"

"Hm!" Walter sipped his cyder thoughtfully. "From what you've said, I'm surprised it bothers him. Tell me about him."

As I've said, Rupert was one of our New Age group. Though I hadn't particularly noticed him. until he accosted me in the street one day.

"Hi! I was just on my way to visit you. I've a message for you from Adam."

"Oh - that's lucky then. Saved yourself the walk." I'd no idea who he was.

"Adam says if you want a lift to Springhead with us on Sunday there'll be room in the car. It's the lecture on Atlantis, remember. Sounds interesting."

"How did you know me?"

"I was at the meeting the other night, wasn't I. When you told us about your epilepsy."

It's a wonder I hadn't noticed him. So lean and dark, so intense. So darned beautiful. We'd had a Faith Healer from Cornwall to tell us about his work.

"Has anyone here received healing of this kind?" he'd asked us before beginning his talk.

Two or three hands went up shyly.

"I was losing my sight a few years back. They told me there was nothing more they could do. A friend knew of a spiritual healer in London. She took me along and . . . well, he cured me. I don't even wear reading glasses now."

"My mother's cancer appears to have been cured by prayer. The doctors had only given her six months to live. Her X-rays are perfectly clear now. The hospital say it's pretty well miraculous. But then again, she has been to see Dr Forbes in Bristol and still follows his diet."

"I had epilepsy as a child," I volunteered. "They tell me I was cured by the laying-on-of-hands, but I can't remember anything about it."

That was a funny thing. I couldn't remember anything about *anything* before I was healed. It took me a long time to realise it.

"You remember," my mother would say (as mothers do), "the summer Great Aunt Ann came over from San Francisco and took us all across to Barry Island on a day trip - remember?"

" . . . the time Daddy dislocated his kneee?"

" . . . the sand pit parties?" When all the kids in the street would come and help transfer the mountain of sand that we'd had delivered from the pavement where the builders had dumped it through to the sand pit in the back garden. "You must remember. Sand and sandwich parties, we used to call them."

"Remember the orchard in Lustleigh," my big brother David would say. "Remember how we'd damn the stream? And swing on the gate telling the passers-by that our cruel parents beat us? Surely you remember. You were a big girl. You were three at least. Maybe four. You must remember."

But I didn't. It was as if my life only started when the epilepsy left me. I was a twelve year old infant. A child masquerading as a grown-up. Perhaps that's why I made so many mistakes, I thought later.

"How peculiar," Rupert said, when I told them about it the next Sunday, on the way back from Springhead and the Atlantis lecture. "I can remember right back to the beginning. I can clearly remember lying in my pram and screaming with fury at being stuck out in the garden on my own. Missing everything that was going on in the house."

"Oh, *honestly*!" Rosemary was driving the rickety old Volkswagon. She was very much the traditionalist, the rationalist. Quite happy for Adam to dabble in dowsing, biorhythms, yoga, ley line tracking, and a little harmless ESP. But that didn't mean that she was going to swallow a whole load of esoteric waffle herself. "I'll come along for the drive," she'd say, glad of an excuse to escape from her demanding household for a few hours : goats, geese, lame ducks, off-spring. "No sense having an Au Pair if I can't leave her in charge now and again."

"It's true, Rosie - I can remember right back to the cradle. Honest."

"Plenty of people remember back to the womb . . . "

"It's a well-researched phenomenon, Rosie . . . "

"And if we're to believe what we were told this afternoon," Adam reminded us, "under hypnosis, most of us could recall a life in Atlantis."

"Huh!" Rosemary put her foot down hard, but kept her thoughts to herself.

"It is true, I promise you," Rupert was to tell me later. "I just happen to have this incredibly good memory."

But not always strictly accurate, young man.

"I've never initiated a sexual relationship," he assured me once. "There've been a fair number of women in my life, and invariably they have made the overtures. Not that I haven't been a willing participant, mind."

Which just shows how poor my own memory is.

"Such an incredible fellow has come into my life," I wrote to Dr Olaf in Norfolk.

After the Atlantis outing, he and Suzy his girlfriend used to come round a lot. We'd often sit talking half the night. About philosophy, religion, sex, life. She'd been causing him quite a lot of aggro with her fierce possessiveness and he wasn't terribly sorry when she went off with someone else. Rupert still came round on his own. And we'd get through gallons of coffee as we set the world to rights. Dissecting the strengths and weaknesses of every religion devised by man to solve the mysteries of life and death.

One night during the big freeze-up he was still here talking very late. At half-past one I started to push him off home, but he begged me to let him stay. Said he couldn't face driving home to his cold empty house. Empty now that Suzy had abandoned him.

"There's a sleeping bag in the airing cupboard," I said. "You can snuggle down on the sofa."

But that wasn't what he had in mind at all.

Heavens! I really couldn't believe it. So young and lean and tender! What had I done to deserve him?

"Oh, lordy!" I said next day, when he phoned me from the surgery. So loving. So passionate. "I shouldn't have allowed that to happen, my dear. At my age, I should have known better."

"Why? What difference does age make, my love. You're free. I'm free. What's the problem?"

There were my kids for a start. Claire accepted the situation, though grudgingly.

"I really shouldn't have to be worrying about my mother's morals," she told me, taking a break from her Geography revision. "Not on top of everything else. I've enough aggro with my flippin' A Levels!"

It was a different matter with Henry. He was at university by this time so it wasn't until the Easter holidays that he and Rupert crossed swords.

"Why's that fellow hanging around, Mum?" he muttered aggressively as he waited for the kettle. "It's bleeding midnight. Shoo him off, can't you."

"We put up with your friends till all hours. Be fair."

Claire must have put him in the picture then, because after a brief consultation with her he made his disapproval loud and clear, crashing around the kitchen, playing his loudest angriest rock music, calling out lewd comments to his sister for my benefit.

"I'd better go," said Rupert. "I get the feeling I'm not too welcome."

"I'll talk some sense into him. It'll be all right."

But of course it wasn't. It was never quite the same again.

"Look, Mum!" Henry spluttered, facing me angrily across the kitchen table. "Surely he's not staying the night."

"Yes, he is. He won't get in your way. He'll be off first thing in the morning."

"But, *Mother*!" Henry's face was contorted with rage and embarrassment. "Where the devil's he going to sleep?"

"With me. In my bed. He's - you know . . . We're . . . He's sleeping with me."

"Oh, fucking hell!" He was on the verge of tears. "He can't do that. It's not fair on Claire. She's only a kid. Think of it from her point of view. It's down right immoral."

I looked at my darling son in astonishment.

"How about you and Belinda then, love? It's no different. You're at it in the attic. We're at it down here."

"Sorry, but it's not the same at all. You're married, for one thing."

"*Married*! Come on, I'm no more married than you are, boy. I went to great lengths to get *un*-married. Five years ago and more."

My stars! Such outrage! Such self-righteousness. And to think of the times I'd turned a blind eye on his affairs. That's one of the troubles with motherhood. They don't see you as human any more. Only as *mother*.

"It's disgusting, Mum! Bloody disgusting!" And he slammed off to bed.

"Poor old Henry," said Walter, bringing me back to the Saracen's Head and the damson tart. "He didn't take very kindly to *me* at the beginning either."

I'd forgotten how bolshi the kid had been. He'd behaved like a devil the first time Walter came to see us.

"I expect he felt threatened. Thought I'd steal you away. Leave him motherless. Quite understandable."

Walter had come up to take me to the theatre. We were all having supper beforehand.

"I don't want anything to eat," said Henry rudely.

"Come on, love - it's fishcakes. Your favourite."

"I'll take mine through and watch telly."

"No you won't. Come and eat with the rest of us."

Sulkily he came to the table. He brought the paper with him and propped it up in front of him preparing to ignore us all."

"Oh, Henry . . . !"

"I don't want to talk to *him*. I don't see why I have to be charming to your posh friend."

"Come on! Be civilised, can't you ."

"*Be civilised*," he mimicked hysterically. "*Come on, be civilised.*"

Christ! Now what? Surely we weren't going to have another show down. And in front of Walter.

"Come on, old chap," he said, quietly taking control. "We all have to make a bit of an effort when there are visitors around."

"It took him a long time to forgive you for coming to my rescue, Walter."

"I could hardly sit there and watch him defying you. He was goading me into action."

"And then bitterly resented your firm father act."

"I seem especially good at putting people's backs up," he said later. "It was the same with Victoria's young composer. If only he'd made it with his damn guitar! If only we could have been wrong about the fellow."

Chapter Twenty-Five

"Henry's usually pretty civilised," I explained to Walter as we set of for the Little Theatre's production of *Macbeth*. "But now and again there's an outburst like that." An outburst of defiance. And quite honestly I didn't know how to cope with him then.

"I don't envy you," he said. "Girls aren't easy. And boys can be devils. It's no joke for a woman bringing kids up on her own."

There was a time when I seriously wondered whether I could handle Henry.

Immediately after our divorce I started work in a Solicitor's office, training to be a probate clerk.

"This could be a splendid opportunity for you," Andrew Sinclair, the senior partner, told me. "Probate work is traditionally a male preserve, but knowing your background, I've persuaded my staff to give you a try,"

There was a three month trial period after which, if I'd proved satisfactory from their point of view, I would be expected to sign a contract committing myself to a two year training and at least five years service with the firm.

"I can't do it," I said to Stella. "It's so bloody boring. The male clerks won't let me into their individual territories. They really resent me." All I was allowed to do was type little notes to clients and fill in various official forms.

"But you've only just started. You've got to give it more of a chance. Things are always boring to start with."

I knew I couldn't stick it out. Having just struggled free of the bonds of marriage, I was hungry for life. I couldn't devote the rest of my working days to the dead. And they were all dead, our clients. In the Probate Department everyone is dead.

In any case, a full time job was killing me. I was being shredded up by the pressures of coping with house and garden, children and chores. On top of those relentless hours of under-employment and boredom on the top floor of Messers Starsky & Hutchinson.

And it was then that Henry was at his most difficult.

I remember staggering home from work, usually laden with groceries that I'd lugged up from town. In no state to cope with the welcome that awaited me.

"Oh, here she is. At last. Come on, Ma, when will the supper be ready? I've got to go out at seven. It's my table-tennis night, in case you've forgotten. Come on!"

"Shut up, Henry. Leave Mum alone. You're always bloody well grumbling, you are."

"Oh, yeh! Mummy's little darling, eh! You're such a creep, Claire. You make me sick."

They start to fight, punching and kicking. Claire is soon screaming as he overpowers her and twists her arm behind her back.

No point in trying to mediate. They're both bigger than I am. Wearily I start the supper.

Pop music blares through from the sittingroom. *We don't need no education . . .* Throbbing aggressively through the house.

Potatoes on. Mince to brown. Down the garden for greens. Rush, rush, rush. No time for a cup of tea or a breather. Rush, rush, bloody-rush.

"Can we have the news, please? Switch the record-player off, one of you."

Delighted to have a legitimate opportunity to irritate him, she switches it off.

"You bloody little cow!" he shrieks. "Now look what you've done. You did it on purpose. She's scratched my fucking record, Ma. She's ruined it."

Another fight begins. Worse than ever.

I get on with supper, shouting to them half-heartedly to stop it. But no one can hear anyway above the noise of battle. I go through and take the record off the turntable. And hold it above my head.

"Stop it!" I yell, trying to swallow the tears. Tears of exhaustion and hopelessness. "Stop it at once or I'll smash the record."

Henry leaves his sister alone and turns on me instead.

"Oh, my God! Not crying are we? Women are all the same. All you can do when you know you're beaten is burst into bloody tears."

Ignoring his language, allowing for the ruined record and having no choice anyway, I return to the stove.

"Set the table, Claire. And, Henry, you feed Cilla." We still had Cilla, our dear soppy old mongrel, mostly spaniel. Bruno had gone.

"No, I won't," he says coldly and deliberately, beginning to sound like his father. "I won't do anything else in this house. You can't make me. Come on, try and make me Ma!"

I strain the spuds and give them to her to mash.

"Don't listen to him, Mum," she tries to comfort me. "He's a typical male chauvinist."

"Oh, yes - there's Mummy's little darling, then. You're a right bloody sucker. My record's scratched. My best record. It cost four quid. Well she's going to pay for it, Ma. Got it? Oh, no - here we go again. More bloody tears. No wonder Dad divorced you . . . "

That does it. That really makes me wild.

"Don't you dare talk to me like that," I tell him. I divorced *him* as you very well know. And you know why. Perhaps I'm crying because I'm ill. Anyone would be ill living with you. You're turning into a selfish uncivilised pig. Feed Cilla . . . "

"No, I'm not feeding her. I'm not taking her for walks. You all seem to forget how busy I am. It is my O Level year, in case it's slipped your memory. I'm not doing anything else round here, not till my exams are over. So there!"

"We've all done O Levels in our time. You're never too busy to watch telly, I notice. Never too busy for your table-tennis."

"Christ, Ma! Be reasonable! A chap's entitled to some relaxation."

"Well, I've had enough of this. Either you start behaving like a civilised member of the family or . . . "

"Or?"

"Or there will be trouble."

"Trouble. Oh, my stars, now I'm for it," he mocks, sitting down at the table, his knife and fork poised to attack his meal. "Go on, Mother. Scare me."

And then it came to me, all in a flash.

"This isn't an empty threat. I'm telling you straight that unless there's a change of attitude round here you will be looking for a job at the end of the term. Not a holiday job. A permanent one. No Sixth Form College. No University. An ordinary hum-drum job . . . "

"But what about my education, Ma? My career?"

"Bugger your education, boy. You've had too much bloody education already as far as I can see and a fat lot of good it's done you. You're getting more like your father everyday."

"But, Ma . . . "

"You can find a job, pay for your keep, and study for your A's in your spare time. Lots of people do it that way. Maybe you'll get into college later on when you can support yourself. And maybe you'll appreciate it more after a few years in an office or on a building site."

"Surely you wouldn't . . . you don't mean it. Come on, Ma - you're joking."

"Why wouldn't I? Why should I allow you to terrorise me and Claire just because you're bigger and stronger than either of us. One more outburst from you and I shall write to the school and tell them you'll be leaving as soon as you've finished your exams. And I'll tell them why. You can always go and live with your father if you can't live here amicably. If I appealed to the courts, told them I couldn't cope with you, they'd send you up to live with him anyway."

There's a stunned silence. Then he starts to dish out Cilla's *Pal* for her, stirring in a measure of *Winalot* with great concentration. We have a subdued but civilised meal. They wash up together while I load the washing machine. No protests. No disputes. It's a bloody miracle.

"Oh, come on, Ma," Henry protests loudly now, "you're making it up! Would I ever have behaved like that?"

"Huh!" says Claire. "I remember it quite clearly. If anything it was worse than that. I used to run away when you and Mum got going. I got on my bike once, and whizzed over to Christchurch Road, and sat on the park gate there weeping."

"Oh, lovey," I said guiltily. "I'm sorry. They were dreadful days. I suppose we were all scared of how we'd survive without Dad. You went silent. I went weepy. And Henry..."

"And Henry went mad!"

"But it was OK after that big showdown, wasn't it? I can't remember any more trouble, apart from the night the poor old Admiral came to supper."

"Admiral?"

"Mum's old Admiral..."

"He means Walter, love."

"And now *this*," said Clair, bringing us back to last night's outburst against my lovely young Rupert.

"Oh, *him*. You deserved an outburst over him."

"Come on, love. He's nice. He's sweet. Don't let the old Oedipus complex rear it's ugly head. It's so darned childish."

"I'm not being childish. You're besotted with him, Ma. You think it's glamourous having a snazzy young dentist hanging around. Can't you see that he's using you."

"Henry . . . " Claire tried to stem his wrath.

"You know what he is, this Toy Boy of yours, he's shit, Ma, shit! You'll see it for yourself one of these days."

"My God!" I said to Walter later. "He was really wound up about it. Must have Oedipal undertones, don't you think? I've never seen Henry so upset. And that's saying something!"

"Hm! Henry's no idiot. In fact he's turning into quite a respectable fellow. All credit to you for that. I shouldn't get too serious about your young Romeo, not if you can help it."

Chapter Twenty-Six

"How did this Andrew Sinclair chap come to know so much about you?" asked Walter. "I never understood how you came to get that Probate job."

"His wife Suzanne was a friend of mine." I got to know her years ago when we moved down here from Norfolk. I used to go to the Young Wives Group she held in her kitchen on Tuesday afternoons. "After the kerfuffle at the Kremlin ..."

"The Kremlin?"

"County Hall. Well, I needed someone to act for me then, and never having had a solicitor of my own, I fell back on Andrew."

The kerfuffle at the Kremlin! My stars!

After my first taste of office life (with Trenchards) I applied for a job at County Hall.

"I feel I'm ready for something a bit more demanding," I explained to kind Mr Grimshaw. "It's not that I haven't enjoyed my time with you, but I don't honestly want to spend the rest of my days checking off invoices and filing them."

"We could find you something more responsible within the company," he said. "I'd be sorry to lose you."

But I was ready for a change and Local Government sounded just the thing. Worthwhile. Demanding. Responsible.

"I'd like you to start in the Student Grants Department," said the Important Young Executive who interviewed me. "Your qualifications are good, even though you haven't much in the way of experience."

Funny, the mileage I got out of my Teaching Certificate, when in fact I was probably the worst teacher ever to emerge from the sacred portals of Beckett Park Training College in all its long history.

"That's partly why I married so young and so silly," I told Walter once. "To extricate myself from teaching."

Not consciously, mind. But in those days you had to commit yourself to so many years. Had to sign something when you started your course. They don't do it now. They couldn't do it now, not with all this unemployment. But *then* pregnancy and death were the only loopholes.

We decided, Pete and I, to look for jobs mid-way, more or less, between his family in the Nottinghamshire Coalfield and mine down in Bristol. Rugby was where we ended up. In grotty digs. Separate, of course, and grim.

You'd share a flat nowadays. But not then, in the mid-fifties. Might have saved ourselves quite a lot of misery if we'd lived together that year in Rugby. I mean, I'd have had more sense than to marry him. But never mind.

Pete was one of the brainy set at college, and probably a good teacher as well. He was offered the first job he applied for, teaching English and History in a Boys' Secondary Modern School. I was interviewed for a post in a nearby Girls' School.

"Are you sure you're cut out to teach secondary children?" they asked me doubtfully. "Some of our girls can be very difficult."

"Oh, yes. That's the age group I trained for."

"Hm!"

It must have been blatantly obvious to the worthy panel of School Governors that I could scarcely cope with the interview, let alone the demanding job at the end of it.

"I believe you are specially anxious to teach in Rugby," said the man from the Local Education Authority. "Your fiancé has been offered a job at the Alderman Quiller Boys, hasn't he?"

They were trying to be helpful.

"Perhaps you'd like to wait outside a moment," said the Chairman of the Governors, ushering me into the corridor where a line of chairs was set out for candidates.

A bell rang. Two or three mistresses hurried by, confident, authoritative. Real teachers. What the hell was I doing, aspiring to join their ranks? Pregnancy was unquestionably the brighter option.

Hoards of girls in blue and white striped frocks surged past on their way to the next lesson - French, Biology, Music, RE.

"You going to be our new teacher, Miss?" one small blonde creature asked me, nudging her mates and starting a chain of sniggers.

"What's your subject, then, Miss?" asked another of them.

"Our last Maths teacher only stayed a few weeks. We drove her potty in no time."

"French is my subject," I told them, knowing as I said it that it was a mistake.

"Don't let yourself be drawn into personal chit-chat," they had told us at college. "Never let your pupils become familiar with you."

How right they were.

"Ooh la la!" the girls twittered now. "Mercy buckets."

"Cor!" said the blonde ringleader, starting to finger my frightful college blazer (in green, navy and silver stripes, like something out of *Brideshead Revisited*), "Where d'you find a gaudy thing like this . . . " And after an all-but imperceptible pause, " . . . Miss."

"Shouldn't you be on the way to the netball courts, Gloria?" asked the Head Mistress icily, before ushering me back into her study.

"We've decided you do not have the necessary maturity for a job in this school," she told me, to my utter relief, once I was seated in front of the selection panel again. "As you have probably realised, we have some pretty tough nuts to deal with."

"But I so wanted to find a job near my boyfriend," I choked.

"We've thought of that," they told me kindly. "There's a Church of England Primary School at Abbots Barton, a quiet little village a few miles out of town. They're looking for a teacher for their Lower Juniors. We think this might be more suitable for you until you've gained some experience."

"But I trained to teach older children, secondary children," I protested feebly.

They exchanged meaningful glances, silently deploring the abysmal standards the Teacher Training Colleges were producing generally, and Beckett Park in particular.

Six months later I was to be hauled up before the man from the Local Education Authority.

"I can only say we are very disappointed in you, young woman. You've had more than enough time to settle in and learn the ropes. Mr Ashworth tells me he finds you totally incompetent. What have you got to say for yourself?"

"I think it's the needlework he's complaining about."

As the only woman on the staff of that two-teacher school, Tuesday and Thursday afternoons I took all the girls, all nineteen of them, for needlework while the Headmaster taught the boys craft and woodwork.

It was murder, needlework! Murder!

"Please, Miss . . ."

"Please, Miss . . ."

Dear God, what a shambles! In the first term alone we got through a whole year's supply of coloured felts, checked gingham and bright hanks of four-ply wool. Very few of the end products were fit to be taken home by the children.

"Me Mam says she's not paying for my egg-cosy, Miss. She says it's a mess."

"I can't get my hand into my gloves, Miss. The fingers are all tight and funny."

"She's been and knitted five fingers as well as the thumb, Miss."

"Mary Park can't count. Mary Park can't count."

"I didn't train to teach needlework."

"It's not the needlework. That is, it's not *only* the needlework. It's your performance as a whole, I'm afraid. I find it hard to believe that you were actually awarded a Teaching Certificate. Look at this, for instance."

He held up a disgusting dog-eared register, splattered with ink. "Well?"

"I'm sorry about that. There was an accident with the ink bottle. It could have happened to anyone."

"But it didn't, did it. Another example of your complete lack of control. This register is a legal document. The permanent property of the authority. And in this case, a permanent record of your inefficiency."

He tossed the offending article onto his desk and picked up a file.

"I see from your application form that before going to college you spent two years in domestic service."

I nodded dumbly. On leaving school I'd had a year as a kitchen maid at Eton College. From there I'd gone out to the Au Pair job in Switzerland.

"It would have been a blessing to all concerned if you'd *stayed* in domestic service."

"Which is pretty well what you did do, isn't it, lass?" said Walter sympathetically. "A life time of domestic service. Unpaid and unappreciated by the sound of it."

"Funny how things pop up from the past," I said. "I bust my Achilles tendon once. At Keep Fit, would you believe. They had to slit my leg open, fish around for the two ends and tie them together again. I was on crutches for weeks. Made life very difficult."

On crutches the simplest task becomes impossible. If you make yourself a cup of tea, for instance, you can't carry it across to the table, you've got to stand there and drink it beside the kettle balancing on one leg.

Before the operation I had to sign this form. Next of kin, religion, occupation . . .

"And you're just a housewife, aren't you, dear?" the Sister prompted me condescendingly.

Never mind the Just-a-Housewife stuff, I wanted to shriek at her. I'd like to see you coping with all the responsibilities on my plate, Sister . . . *dear*!

"Yes," I answered meekly. "Only a housewife."

"I think we'll have a drop of brandy with our coffee tonight, shall we?" said Walter, bringing the silver tray through to the sittingroom. "I have to confess that I'm quite enjoying being a housewife myself, but then it's still a bit of a novelty to me. There's a lot to be said for retirement. You must take a pot of my grapefruit marmalade home with you, by the way. I'm rather pleased with the way it's turned out. My own recipe, too. More coffee?"

We sat comfortably together in the firelight. It reminded me of my first visit, so long ago.

"It's five years now," he said suddenly, as if reading my thoughts. "I can scarcely believe you are the same girl . . ."

"*Girl*! Come on, I'm catching up with you, love. Rapidly."

"I'm not talking about age. You were so, so battered, my dear. And look at you now. Selling your paintings, organising conferences, lecturing. And now this. Before long, you'll be too proud to bother with an old codger like me."

"Oh, Walter!"

The local TV station had been running a series of discussions after the tea-time news. A panel of viewers. Different every week. I watched several Thursday evenings, and then I phoned the BBC.

"Look!" I said indignantly. "There's no point in having a discussion on air unless it's a good one. We have livelier debates over the breakfast table any day of the week. Where do you dig up such boring viewers? Not one of them has so far expressed an original idea or a positive opinion about anything. We'd be better off watching the adverts on the other side. No-one wants to watch a panel of puppets propped on a fence mouthing cliches, for heaven's sake!"

I tend to get carried away.

"I'm only manning the phone, taking messages," said a timid little voice when I paused for breath. "But I'll tell them what you said."

Later that evening the producer rang me back.

"What's all this stuff and nonsense about my programme, eh?"

"Well, it's true. They're flaming Zombies. Get us a panel of viewers who are not afraid to commit themselves. Liven it up a bit, man!"

"Right!" he said grimly. "Get yourself down here by ten o'clock next Thursday morning. We pre-record it. The subject under discussion will be bureaucracy. You'll get a £10 fee and we'll refund your train fare."

Bureaucracy! I'd plenty to say about bureaucracy, thank you.

"Oh, yes," said Walter, throwing another log on the fire. "You were going to tell me about your life in the Kremlin. I can't say I see you as a natural born civil servant, but I might be wrong."

Chapter Twenty-Seven

And of course Walter was dead right. I was not cut out for Local Government Service. No way!

They started me off in the Student Awards Section, processing Grant Applications through the computer. There was a lot to learn, and for the first few months we were wonderfully busy. Between the end of November and March, however, with our ten thousand students safely settled into their various colleges, things were slack.

"Hey! What's going on in here?" asked the Chief Assessor nervously, catching us in the middle of a Mastermind Tournament. "You're paid to work, you know. Put this rubbish away before one of the public catches you at it, frittering your time away, at the expense of the rate-payers."

"But there's nothing to do," I told him. "We seem to have been twiddling our thumbs for weeks."

"Ridiculous!" he said. "Have the cupboards all been cleared out? Is the filing up to date? There's plenty to do, I'm sure, if you look for it."

"But we've done it all. Everything. We're all suffering from underemployment in here, Brian. Can't you find us something to do before we go mad, eh?"

"Why can't you keep your bloody mouth shut," Daphne exploded when he had shuffled off to think the problem through. "They *will* find us work now, won't they, you idiot!"

"We're under pressure for most of the year," added Debbie sulkily. "We need our recuperation time. You'll learn. Come April, we'll be swamped with applications. From this year's 'A Level' candidates."

I was in the dog house. They excluded me from the cosy chats and drawn-out coffee breaks that now replaced

Mastermind and Scrabble. I was left alone to man the phones while the others disappeared into the attic store with ice-creams and bags of crisps.

"Please find me something to do?" I begged Brian again, catching him off guard with the Daily Telegraph spread out on his otherwise empty desk. "I'm going crazy doing nothing."

"I don't suppose you've ever had a soul-destroying desk job, have you?" I asked Walter. "It's sheer misery."

After a while you don't have to force yourself to work slowly, as they were suggesting, to spin the work out to fill the seven-and-a-half hours ahead. Before long it's all you can jolly well do to keep your eyes open and stop yourself falling off your damn chair. Under-employment really is agonising.

"Look," said Brian conspiratorially, now he'd got me on my own, "don't start stirring things up. You're new to the system. You've a lot to learn. As long as you appear to be busy, I shalln't ask any questions. Bring a book to read. Letters to write. Not knitting, but anything that *might* be work - OK? As long as you keep a low profile we'll all be happy."

"It's a scandal," I told him, full of righteous indignation. "Ten of us with bugger-all to do. I'd be more use staying at home and cleaning the windows." And I pranced off to see the Section Head in his sanctuary.

He was certainly concerned about the lack of work, but more concerned to shut me up than to keep me busy.

"We have several departments that are snowed under at this time of year," he explained. "I'm moving you into the Telephone Accounts Section for a few weeks."

Good. Just what I had hoped would happen.

"I want you to go through all these," the T.A.S. Office Supervisor told me, indicating a whole wall of racking, solid with lever-arch files. "The dog-eared corners must be straightened out on every invoice, got it?"

"That should keep her quiet for a while," I heard her mutter to her assistant.

I spent the morning conscientiously smoothing out creases. Before she went to lunch the Supervisor strolled over.

"Good," she said, seeing that I'd already worked through three shelves of files. "That batch can go down to the dungeon this afternoon. I'll ask one of the porters to bring a trolley."

"What's the dungeon?" I asked the elderly woman at the next desk.

"The basement strongroom. They'll be stored away down there for the statutory three years, and then destroyed."

"Destroyed!"

"Shredded. It's very unlikely that any of them will ever be referred to again."

I stormed back to the Section Head.

"Do you know what they've given me to do in there?"

"Yes, I know." He was thoroughly tired of me and my complaints.

"But it's utterly futile. The invoices are all destined for the shredder. It doesn't matter a hoot about the dog-ears. They are all going to be reduced to confetti."

"You insisted on something to keep you occupied," he told me wearily. "We found you just that. Now if you'll excuse me . . ."

I was so incensed I forgot about rank and protocol.

"If that's the best you can find me to do I'm going home to weed the garden. You might as well advertise for imbeciles to work here!"

"If you go home we will deduct a half-day from your annual leave," he told me coldly. "And tomorrow you will be sent back to get on with the task."

They were obviously determined to teach me a lesson.

"In that case, I shall stay home tomorrow and have a migraine," I said. And I did.

The following week, when I eventually 'recovered', they transferred me to the Salaries Section where there really was a lot to be done. And soon afterwards I was promoted to a Clerical 1c post in the Education Department, one step up the bureaucratic ladder.

"My dear girl," said Walter incredulously, "you must have been a real thorn in their flesh. Never mind promoting you, I wonder you weren't sacked!"

Chapter Twenty-Eight

"I was in the end. Well, not sacked exactly. They simply made it impossible for me to stay. What do they call it, Walter? There's a proper term for it. Industrial harassment? Constructive dismissal? Something like that."

I never really fitted into the bureaucratic mould. My clothes weren't right. My hair wasn't right. And my attitude, they told me, was downright impossible.

Somehow I managed to get away with wearing jeans to work. Long before this was universally accepted.

"I simply don't have anything else," I told Mr Edmunds, the Section Head, when he called me into his room to complain about my scruffiness.

"Hm!" sniffed Miss Masters, our sad little boss. "What are we coming to? It was a neat dark suit in my young days. Smart, business-like and anonymous. I don't know!"

"But you can't expect people to work properly if they're uncomfortable, can you?" We weren't actually dealing with the public, not face-to-face. What the hell!

"Hm!" she said with another little sniff. "I wonder you get away with it. And that hair!"

"Don't tell me you were wafting round the corridors of power with your plaits!" said Walter, giving one of them a friendly tug.

I'd only recently come to terms with my hair. It's not a bad colour, but straight and lank. Occasionally I've had it cut really nicely, properly styled and all, and then it would be tidy for six weeks perhaps. But I never had funds to keep it that way.

"Oh dear!" my mother would exclaim in despair whenever I got myself over to Bristol to visit them. "We really must do something about that hair."

Once she bullied me into having a perm. She and my three beautiful sisters. They persuaded me that with a halo of softly curling tresses my personality would blossom forth. But it didn't. I could never cope with curlers, and Amami Night became a nightmare as I struggled frantically to control my avant-garde Afro style.

"I'm not a curly person, Mum. Look what you've all gone and made me do - I look a right freak. How ever long will it take to grow out?"

I kept away from hairdressers after that.

"But a hair-do is such a tonic," they tell us. "Bucks you up no end. Good for the morale, a nice shampoo and set. Makes a new woman of you."

Personally I've always found it torture, sitting there surrounded by mirrors which somehow accentuate my drab and homely features. The more elegant the salon, the more glamorous the assistants, the more demoralising it becomes.

Perhaps there's a fortune to be made with a chain of beauty salons staffed by plain, dumpy middle-aged women with greasy hair and dandruff. A visit to them might indeed be a tonic. And come to think of it, I might qualify for a job with them myself!

"It's surprising how important hair is," I said to Rupert, curling the fine dark locks at the nape of his slender neck through my fingers. "I'm only just learning to live harmoniously with mine."

"I can just picture you in a neatly lacquered bee-hive," he said, rolling onto his back on the sheep-cropped turf and hand-cuffing himself to me with the nearest pigtail. "That would really turn me on."

It was soon after our magic had begun. I think, looking back, that he truly loved me then. That's something to hold on to.

"Tomorrow," he had told me, giving me one of his boa-constrictor hugs, "tomorrow is definitely the day for An Adventure. I'll pick you up at nine-thirty."

And here we were, naked and snug in a velvety hollow high up on Salisbury Plain.

"Hey! Look at this! Made for us, wouldn't you say!"

"It's the grave mound of a chieftain's lady," I told him, as we flopped down breathless from the climb. "It's a Saucer Barrow."

"Well, I certainly hope this little Neanderthal Princess won't object to us besporting ourselves on her tomb."

"It might cheer her up a bit. Break the monotony of centuries. We'll risk it, shall we."

We'd cruised along the early summer lanes with the roof open.

"Phaw!"

"Your genuine country aroma, kid. Pigsty pong to the initiated."

Further on, having driven through acres of orchards, he suddenly stopped the car. "How about that then! Calls for an action replay, I think." And he reversed back up the lane, tacking drunkenly between the banks of pink and white foam.

"Loveliest of trees," he sang, intoxicated by the sweetness of life, "the cherry now is hung with blossom along the bough . . ."

"Mary Webb came from Shropshire, you know."

"Precious Bane?"

"Uh-hu - her masterpiece."

"We'll go there one day, shall we? We'll go in Adam's boat."

"I'd like to get you," he burst out singing again, "on a slow boat to Shropshire . . ."

It was one of those silly days.

At lunchtime we found a pub with a pot of broth bubbling over the fire. Further on we discovered an Indian Festival in a marquee on a village green where we bought each other small mementos - a fierce painted dragon for him, a small tranquil Buddha for me.

"Come on, Swami," he chivvied, dragging us away from the dancing display. "If we get to Chithurst by five there'll be a cup of tea going."

Chithurst is a Buddhist monastery between Petersfield and Midhurst, right there in the Stockbroker Belt.

"I've brought a friend along with me," said Rupert, introducing me to the saffron-robed American brewing up a huge urn of tea in the kitchen.

"Welcome. Welcome," he said bowing solemnly over his joined palms. "Could you give me a hand with these mugs, please, both of you. We've got a lot of visitors with us this afternoon."

"Leave your shoes out here," Rupert whispered, slipping out of his own and adding them to the pile in the hall.

He was a regular visitor to Chithurst. He knew the ropes and most of the community now seated cross-legged on the floor in front of a gilded shrine waiting for their tea.

"They don't eat anything after mid-day," he had told me earlier. "That's one of their rules. And we take care not to stand above Somedo - he's the leader of the community. It's all symbolic," he added, sensing I was about to protest. "Like the Christian business of genuflecting to the altar. You know."

We shuffled in on our knees, bowing and nodding to those around us among whom were a dozen monks with saffron robes and shaved heads . . .

Heavens! I thought, shaken. There are women among them. Women with shaved heads. *Bare* shaved heads.

. . . and a few beautiful Asians with gentle smiling faces.

"They're mostly Boat People," Rupert told me afterwards. "Refugees from Vietnam. They travel miles to bring gifts to the Monastery. Food, lightbulbs, bedding, loo rolls, toothpaste. That's mainly how the place keeps going. You earn great merit from giving, the Buddhists believe. And especially from giving to the monks."

Somedo sat cross-legged on a low chair. He was an American too. He spoke quietly, simply, informally. Breaking into peals of contagious laughter, often at his own expense.

"But what makes you think I have the answer to the Secret of Life, young man," he answered one intense questioner. "I'm only here for the peace and quiet."

"I'm glad you took us over there," I said happily as we drove home. "What an extraordinary place. To find *here* and *now*! They don't actually go round the villages with their begging bowls , do they?"

"Yes, of course they do. How else would they survive? At first local people were hostile and suspicious, but they've learnt to accept them. They're simply striving to live harmlessly and selflessly. And with the utmost awareness. As Buddhists do. You can see how gentle and loving they are."

"But why the robes and the shaven heads? Can't you follow the path in jeans and jerseys? That's the bit I don't understand."

"It's the same in all religious communities, isn't it. You take on the *habit*, the uniform, and with it the rule, the discipline of the Order. It's like a public commitment."

"But *girls* with shaved heads - that's going a bit far."

"It's only the nuns, love - not your average Buddhist housewife."

"Well, it was a really groovy adventure, anyway," I said snuggling up to him in my big bed. "Goodnight, my love."

" 'Night!"

"I don't think I'm a Buddhist at heart," I decided after a moment's contemplation. "I'll take your harmonious life style. Your selfless awareness. That's fine. But not the full package, thank you. Not the shaved heads. I'm afraid I can't see the point of it all."

But he was fast asleep.

Chapter Twenty-Nine

"You've no-one but yourself to blame," Mr Edmunds told me the morning that the Staff Restructuring list went up on the notice board. "You've never made the slightest effort to conform."

"Oh, come on - look at the way I've worked."

"Yes, you're a hard worker. I'm not denying that. But you simply haven't fitted in. Look at your clothes. Your hair. Look at your attitude."

My attitude! I was only wanting to be allowed to do an honest day's work, for Christ's sake. Where's the harm in that?

"How smug that sounds," I admitted to Walter. "How self-righteous. No wonder they weeded me out. I must have been an absolute pain."

That's why it's so difficult for a middle-aged mum to find a job, starting work again once the kids are off her hands. A worthwhile job anyway. The employers know she'll be a menace, too jolly conscientious.

If up till then each day has been a test of strength, a survival course, a sophisticated 'Time and Motion' exercise, how can she suddenly re-programme herself to fit comfortably into the work-a-day world?

"Oh, no! Don't tell me there isn't a clean shirt this morning. Surely it isn't too much to ask of you. A clean shirt. I'm a reasonable man, but I sometimes wonder what you're doing with yourself all day long, woman?"

"Well," I might have answered, "let me see . . . "

I got you all off to school.

"Ma, where's my gym knickers? Miss Lewis'll kill me if I forget them again."

"Anyone seen my Latin book? I left it on the piano. Who's moved it. Mum? I can't go to school without it."

"We've got to take sixpence for Mary Elliot. She's in hospital with a bald head, Mummy. We're going to buy her a crayoning book and some sweeties."

"Leave me some money, Pete. I must go to Sainsbury's this morning."

"And I need sixpence."

"Come on, Claire. It's a quarter to, you're going to be late."

"I'm just picking some flowers for Miss."

"Oh, not the lupins love. It's a pity to pick them, there are so few."

. . . and tidied up, and cleaned the bedrooms, changing the girls' shirts. I did the washing including four of your sheets, dear. Hung it out on the line. Rushed down to the shops.

On the way home I bumped into poor old Margery and listened to a long sad story about her insensitive husband as I struggled up the road with the groceries.

I took the dogs for a walk, mowed the lawn, picked the gooseberries, wrote to my parents and to yours, met the little ones from school, comforted Henry over some injustice he had suffered, and Charlotte later over her running quarrel with Emma and Sue. I cleaned out the fridge while the mince was simmering, and made a fruit jelly for Claire's Brownie Party.

I organised the washing up, supervised the construction of a Blue Peter moon buggy from cereal packets and egg cartons, helped with some Geometry homework, read Claire and Henry a bed-time story, and the riot act to the others . . .

"Turn that telly off while you're doing your homework. Switch it off!"

. . . patched Tom's school trousers again, stitched a buckle on Claire's sandal. I made most of the gooseberries into jam, stirring it while I watched the Nine O'clock News on the portable set. I wrote a note about someone's dental appointment, filled in a form about someone else's outing to London. I made hot drinks all round, setting the breakfast table while the milk boiled. And wallowed briefly in a good hot bath with my Ovaltine before falling thankfully into bed.

"Come on, love. Don't be mean. Put that book away. I'm feeling really horny. You were too tired last night. You're always too bloody tired. Come on, just a quick one. That's it."

"There are plenty of shirts clean," I answered instead. "I'm sorry, I didn't get round to ironing them last night."

He gave a long-suffering sigh.

"I'll run one over for you now while you're eating your toast. Won't take a minute."

And we were into another day.

Just a housewife, eh? I remembered the supercilious tones of the Hospital Sister. Could any job be more demanding? And all for love, of course. Naturally you would expect to put more effort into a job they were paying you to do. Stands to reason.

"I've finished these forms," I said to Mr Edmunds. "What shall I do next?"

"Pop over and fetch us some ices, dear. It's such a sweltering afternoon."

We ate a lot of ice-cream in the Advisors Section. Winter and summer. Morning and afternoon. There was scarcely a session went by without one of us popping out for refreshments.

"Anyone want anything from the shop?"

"Bring us a Mars Bar..."

"Bring us a can of coke..."

"Bring me an apple..."

"Anything to relieve the boredom," I told the man from *The Observer* who came to check out the letter I had sent to the Editor "You should have seen what we got up to."

"Hold on," he said, getting out his notebook. "Start from the beginning."

I left my secure job with the Local Authority just before Christmas after several protests about the lack of work, I had written.

While teachers and ancillary staff in schools are being pared back to the bone, while classes get larger and more difficult to handle, while the equipment and facilities are reduced to the bare minimum, armies of under-employed administrative staff sit tight in their bureaucratic stronghold.

"I don't suppose this County is any worse than any other," I said to the reporter. "In fact, when I complained about having too little to do they laughed and told me it's the same everywhere in Local Government. That I'd get accustomed to it eventually."

"And did you?"

"No. And asking for work only made trouble. Look what happened to me in the end."

"Constructive Dismissal," he said, flicking to a clean page in his spiral-bound note pad. "That's the legal term for it. They obviously intended you to storm off. Not that I blame you, mind. You were certainly provoked. But they knew perfectly well how you'd re-act."

Trouble had been brewing all through that long hot summer. There was never a great deal to do in the Advisors Section, but at least with my modest promotion I was able to organise my own time to some extent, making sure I was as busy as circumstances permitted.

But not in August. With the schools closed and most of the Advisors on leave, August was a wicked month in our department.

"Perhaps I could take a month's unpaid leave," I suggested to Mr Edmunds early in July. "I don't think I can cope with six weeks of enforced idleness again." It was my third summer in Education.

"Oh, come along now," he said in his jovial way, "you mustn't take things so seriously, dear. Learn to play the system. Take me, for example. You won't hear me complaining about lack of work. I thoroughly enjoy my Augusts. I wouldn't dream of taking official leave during the school holidays. Such a waste. You know what I mean. It's as good as a holiday here at work, bar the sandcastles. How about running over to the shop for some ice-cream, eh? Come on, I'll treat you. Can't say fairer than that, eh?"

"I'm sorry," I persisted stubbornly. "I can't stand the thought of another August in this office. Pissing about here when I've a thousand things to do at home. If you gave me unpaid leave it would be saving the Council money. I refuse to be paid for twiddling my thumbs. If you can't understand I shall go and see the Chief."

"Now let's look at this calmly, shall we dear. Close the door. Sit down a minute. Let's start from the beginning again. What exactly is the problem?"

He knew very well what the problem was. It was partly his fault. There was a large proportion of youngsters in the Section, several of them straight from school. Discipline was very slack.

"Don't pick on me!" Carol would shout across the office if anyone dared suggest she should think about doing a little work. "Or I shalln't do anything, so there!"

"It's best not to upset these young girls," confided Archie, the veteran among us. "Much easier to turn a blind eye."

It wasn't easy.

Flexi-time had just been introduced. As long as you clocked up the stipulated number of hours each month you could work more or less to please yourself. Archie used to come in every morning at half-past-seven and sit reading his Daily Mail over a flask of tea and bacon sandwiches. And take a day off at the end of the month in lieu of all that extra time he'd put in.

Several people regularly stayed late, chatting, drinking tea, to avoid the rush hour or to make up a bit of time on the old flexi-clock.

Flexi-time was a very popular innovation.

In our office there was scarcely a day when every one was in by nine-thirty, the dead-line for clocking on. OK we all over sleep from time to time. But with our teenagers things had reached ridiculous proportions.

"Hi!" Carol would phone in at ten-fifteen perhaps or later. "Overslept again! Sorry! Won't be long."

"You'd better get a move on or it won't be worth bothering."

"Be reasonable. Got to have some breakfast, haven't I?" Don't want me wilting at my post. See you in an hour or so. By-ee!"

Re-arranging the furniture was a useful way of passing a dreary afternoon.

"Let's put all the desks in one block in the middle, right," Andrew our bright young junior might suggest. "Come on. Everyone lend a hand."

"I want to be by the window this time."

"No, that's my place. With my HNC I take precedence."

Rank was very important in that narrow world of ours. And rank depended on qualifications. Increments were paid for CSEs and O Levels, of course. And if they agreed to take a Day Release Course at Tech the youngsters were paid additional increments for ONC or HNC. So without too much effort they could be at the top of their salary scale by the time they were nineteen.

Carol and Wendy and Charlie Brown were all in this exalted position. They would sit round endlessly grousing because they were not getting the promotion they deserved.

"I'm not sorting the post any longer. Not with my qualifications."

No one insisted for fear of sulks and tantrums. One of the middle-aged married women would be asked to do it, me or Mollie or Esther. We knew our place, no matter how many qualifications we happened to have.

"You've really got it in for these kids," said the man from *The Observer*. "Sour grapes, is it?"

No. I didn't entirely blame them. Why bother when you could get away with this sort of lark. They always somehow managed to have their own way, to browbeat the rest of us.

They'd decide it was too cold to work, and there would be a big drama ending up with all of them sitting there in coats and scarves.

"You can't fill forms in with your gloves on, Wendy. Don't be daft."

Someone might have had a tiff with her boyfriend and three of them would disappear to comfort her in the loo.

"I tell you, it's more like a holiday camp than bloody Butlin's."

"You must have been unfortunate. That Section must have been an exception." He was taking a lot of notes in his spiral backed pad, that's for sure.

A week or two before I left I was asked to do some urgent calculations. For the Deputy Chief, no less.

"We must have the staff : pupil ratios for every year in every secondary school in the county," I was told. "It's in order to standardise the size of classes." Which was their way of saying paring down staffing figures to the absolute minimum. Teachers, mind. No schemes for cutting back on Headquarters staff. Only those out in the field. Out in the firing line.

"This is a priority exercise," they told me. "Drop everything else. You can borrow the calculator. Get the up-to-date figures from the Statistics Boys."

They were none of them busy, as far as I could tell. "We haven't had them through from Mr Francis," one of the Stats team told me. "Room Seven. You know, the Deputy Chief."

But the Deputy Chief's Secretary was engrossed in a Mills & Boon propped up on her typewriter. "Ask Jill," she suggested, weary with boredom. "His P.A. You know."

When I tracked her down, Jill was sitting at an enormous empty "P.A." category desk reading *Woman's Own*, but at least she had the grace to shove it under her blotter.

"They could easily dispense with hundreds of clerical staff," I bawled at Mr Edmunds the morning I left. "And no-one would even notice."

"It's very unwise to go round accusing people left, right and centre," said *The Observer* man, biting his little finger nervously. "After all, you're basing these accusations - and very serious they are too - on your comparatively limited time in one particular Section."

"You're right. Of course you are. There must be people in The Kremlin who *do* phone back, who *do* make sure documents get posted on time, who *do* try to provide a fast and efficient service to the public. Yes, there must be. It's just that I haven't come across them."

That's what they didn't like about my Resources Library. I was in charge of the County's collection of tapes and records, films and sheet music that we loaned out to schools. I'd set up a fast and efficient system for dispatching these resources. I was really rather proud of my library.

"And?"

It was so bloody fast and efficient that they actually asked me to devise what they called 'a Delaying Factor'! Said I was creating an embarrassing precedent. The schools were beginning to ask why other departments took so long to deal with queries.

He scratched his nose with his pencil. "Come on - you can't expect me to believe that!"

I couldn't believe it at first either. I thought they were joking. I said I couldn't leave orders lying around waiting for dispatch. Once I'd packed them up - films, tapes, music or whatever - I'd shoot down and put them on the van each evening ready for delivery around the schools next day. Simple.

"Jolly good. Thoroughly efficient. What was the problem?"

"A fortnight is a reasonable time to make them wait," I was told firmly. "We're giving you a special cupboard.

Simply to store Library parcels in. Here we are. For added efficiency, it can stand here beside your desk."

They'd labelled it for me. *Education Department : Resources Library DELAYING CUPBOARD*!!

"Supernumary!" I said, rushing in to see Mr Edmunds the morning the Staff Restructuring list went up. "Super- fucking- numerary!"

"I'm sorry," he told me, "but you've only yourself to blame."

"No wonder this country's in such a mess," I told him. "It's getting more and more like your flaming Roman Empire. Top heavy with idle bureaucrats. Under-employed administrators. I'm off! Back to the real world out there. And I'm going to write to the papers about this. It's a damn scandal."

"And did *The Observer* print the story?" asked Walter.

"No. No-one would risk it. Said they believed me OK but without corroboration . . . "

"Wouldn't anyone back you up?"

"No way. They were scared silly. For their promotion prospects. And their pensions. There was a conspiracy of silence."

"Well, I admire your courage, lass. But it's a wonder the Big Wigs didn't have you assassinated before you could make any more trouble."

The best bit was walking out. Not giving in my notice but walking right out. There and then.

"Next morning, Pete took me in before anyone was around. To get my bits and pieces. Clear my desk. And all across their stupid list, the Staff Restructuring list, in large purple letters I scribbled . . . "

"Yes?"

" . . . 'S H I T' I scribbled, and I felt a lot better after that."

Chapter Thirty

"It's always a blow to one's pride, rejection," said Rupert sagely.

"I know. But it was a bit much. I mean to say - *tea-girl*! That's what it boiled down to."

"In the West we're all too jolly concerned with our egos, love. It's like the Lord Buddha said . . . "

"But it was so unfair. And all because I asked for work." The injustice of it still choked me, then. Six or seven years later.

"Oh, come on, Swami - if you think about it, it was the best thing that could have happened. Say they'd promoted you. Or even left you where you were. Would you be here with me now?" He nibbled my throat greedily. "Would you have done any serious painting? Would you have divorced Pete?" He pulled the duvet up over our heads. "Would you have blossomed out at all?"

It is the rejection that hurts. The humiliation. Much the same as being ditched by your - your *dear acquaintance*, as Mary Webb would say.

I shrank from labelling it any more precisely than that, the thing between Rupert and me. I was acutely aware of the transient nature of our relationship. Our generation gap.

I fluffed his hair through my fingers, and snuggled down beside him.

"And for once we don't have to worry about the bedsprings, Swami!"

Yes, incredible as it sounds, we had the house to ourselves. The last of my brood had flown.

Claire had failed to get enough A Levels for a place at University. Her grades weren't good enough.

She was up early on the Thursday morning waiting for the postman. She brought the mail through to the kitchen where I was making the porridge.

"Well, open it then," said Henry, but not unkindly. He'd been through all this himself a couple of years back.

"Oh, hell!" she groaned shoving the fateful scrap of computer print-out across to me. "Bloody hell! That's it, then!"

She'd had five offers to do Geography with Anthropology. One from Liverpool, the others from Polys.

"Don't you despise the Polys," Henry had told us. After a year of misery on a Computer Science course at Bristol he had transferred to an Ecology course at Poly. And he was loving it. "They work you far harder at Poly, I can tell you. I do a regular nine hour day, with essays and all on top. By comparison University was a doddle."

"Well," he asked now, "what's the verdict?"

My heart sank as I read out the list. "Geography : B - that's good. Biology : C. Chemistry : D. That's it then, lovey."

For Claire and her shattered (or at least *postponed*) hopes. For myself too, and mine!

Quite frankly, I had been looking forward to getting the last of my fledglings airborne. But without three good A Levels . . .

"I shall be thankful when you've all gone," I'd yelled at them more than once, coming in from work tired and hungry to find the house full of pop music and smoke and their friends. And the breakfast dishes still in the sink. Chaos. "I've had enough. I'm sick of the lot of you."

"Oh, come on," they would chorus cheerfully. "You'll miss us, you know. You'll really miss us. The place won't be the same without us." And another *Adam and the Ants* record would start up at full blast.

No, it wouldn't be the same. That's precisely the point. It would be quiet and tidy and clean. There would be no aggro, no tantrums, and no soggy towels left on the sofa. Miss them! They must be joking. How could anyone miss the hassle, the wrangling over chores.

"Look, it's not my turn to wash up. I've done it three nights in a row. It's her turn, Ma. I'm not doing it."

"Claire's got her revision. It's only ten days till her first paper."

"Eleven days, thirteen hours and twenty-seven minutes actually."

"And I've made the supper three nights in a row, in case you hadn't noticed." (Three thousand nights in a row actually, but that's a mother's lot, I guess.) "Those who expect to eat must expect to help, Henry."

"It's not fair."

"Life's never fair, love. It's never ever fair."

"Oh, now what am I going to do?" Claire wailed. I was so looking forward to college. It isn't fair."

With a little persuasion and a copy of *The Lady* she found herself a job as a Mother's Help, setting off for Newcastle early in September.

"How are you doing, Ma?" she asked, phoning to tell me about two year old Edward, whose parents were running a country house hotel in a hamlet up in the Dales. "Are you lonely? Are you missing me? "

"It's funny on my own, but I'm beginning to get used to it."

Funny! I looked down at Rupert who was sitting on the floor doing his daily meditation before, you know... Being on my own was sheer bliss!

Peace and quiet. Responsibility for no-one but myself. Freedom to live on apples and cheese and goo-ey raisins. Freedom to play Radio Three to my heart's content. And paint solidly through the night if I felt like it. Freedom to entertain my friends without censure.

"Do you have any free time, love? Are you doing any revision?"

She had applied to resit the Chemistry and try for college again.

"Not much. I work pretty hard. It's tiring looking after Edward. I'm whacked by the time I get him to bed."

Her first taste of motherhood. It's OK but it goes on so damn long, so unremittingly. That's the trouble with motherhood.

"But I'm glad I got the job. It's really groovy."

"Send a card to Granny, won't you. And don't forget to write to your father. I do miss you. I'm glad you're enjoying it."

"Not long till Christmas. Then you'll have us both home. Must go now. Edward's got out of bed. By-ee!"

"She sounds happy enough," I said to Rupert when he returned from his trance. "Probably do her more good than going straight to college."

"She certainly needed some wider experience," he said with a sniff. "I'm sorry to have to say it, but your children really are incredibly boring."

"Oh, come on! They've got their faults, of course they have, but they're no more boring than you or I were at the same age. I bet."

"Sorry. Forgot about your blind spot. Forget it, Swami. Just forget it. I forgot that you are incapable of recognising the defects in your off-spring. We all have our problems, and this happens to be yours."

"But . . ."

"No, no. Better let it drop. There's no way you're going to admit that Henry's an uncouth moron, and Claire is immature and suburban. No. Don't let's argue. Just take my word for it."

"But you didn't, did you?" Walter was to ask later. "The arrogant young pup. I can't understand why you put up with him so long."

Arrogance? I suppose it was a kind of arrogance. Everyone else could see it except me. Talk about rose coloured spectacles . . .

"I never could understand what you saw in him," said Stella. "He's impossibly self-opinionated."

"He's alright," said Claire generously. "Though I must say I was pretty pissed off when he turned up on my last night at home. From then on he was going to have you all to himself. He'd no need to turn up that night."

"She was terribly hurt," Charlie told me over the phone a few days after Claire had gone north. "She phoned me in tears. Said she'd never forgive you . . ."

Oh, Gawd! I should have thrown him out. I am a pig, a thoughtless pig.

" . . . said she felt totally excluded. And on her last night at home. Her last night of childhood."

"That's what I mean," said Rupert at the very end. "Can't you see how pathetic it is for a great girl of eighteen to expect a big farewell drama just because she's going out into the world. It's so immature."

I don't care what you think, I ought to have said. My instinct tells me it should have been a family evening, even if the family has dwindled to the two of us. Claire and me.

Chapter Thirty-One

Looking back, I realise it was exactly then, when Claire went off into the big wide world and I had the house to myself at last, it was then that Rupert began to withdraw from me. It was as plain as plain, I realise now. But at the time I couldn't see it.

"Oh, come on, Mumsy, let's make it up," said Claire on the morning she was leaving. "I forgive you, you old idiot. It was mean of you, shutting yourself away with him when I'd thought we were going to have a friendly evening to ourselves, but don't let's waste any more time quarrelling about it."

I gave her a quick hug, and we began to enjoy the last-minute preparations together.

"I've packed my mac and now it's raining."

"Doesn't matter. I've ordered a taxi."

"Nearly forgot my McEnroe poster," she said, scraping the blue-tack off the wall. "Do you think they'll let me put my posters up, Ma?"

"Course they will. Did you get your tights and things out of the dryer?"

"All the partings," she said, kneeling on her case while I tried to fasten it. "It's difficult to remember how it used to be with everyone at home."

I could remember. But only when I made a deliberate effort.

"They're like the hankies a magician pulls out of his wand, aren't they?"

"What are, Claire?"

"You know - memories. You pull one out and there's another tied to it. A whole string of bright silk hankies."

She's right, I thought, sitting at the kitchen table with a pot of tea to myself after seeing her off. Listening to the silence.

"The train now standing at Platform One is the Inter-City Service for York, Darlington, Newcastle-on-Tyne . . . "

"Bye, Mum," she'd called as the train pulled away. "I'll phone you tonight. By-ee!"

"Miaow." Percy jumped onto the table, rubbing his nose against mine to remind me it was time for his dinner. "Miaow . . . "

"Off the table! Go on with you!" I opened a fresh tin for him. "You're looking a bit moth-eaten, old boy."

He's getting on a bit, I thought, remembering the summer he was born. Must have been before things began to disintegrate, I reckon.

We'd a photo of Norma, his proud mother, holding court on a piece of pink blanket on the lawn in the old house. On the first balmy day of May. Lilac and apple blossom. And Norma's joy in her kittens. One ginger, one tortoise-shell, and Percy, black and white and wicked. As different as a family of kids, but the differences more immediately obvious.

That was the day Miss Wiseman had come to visit us, the first day the kittens were out in the sunshine. To visit *Pete*, I should say.

"Miss Wiseman!" Claire had started to giggle. "You can't have a Miss Wise Man!"

And they'd all joined in.

"Mister Wise Man."

"Misses Wise Woman."

"Master Silly . . . "

"Master Silly Billy."

"Oh do stop it, all of you. What childish nonsense."

"They are children, Pete."

But he carried on reading his letter.

I happened to run into your mother in town recently, she had written in her spidery copper-plate, *and when she heard that we were planning a trip to the New Forest she gave me your address. You probably won't remember me, Peter, but I've never forgotten what a bright little lad you were in my class of, let me see, 1939. While we're in the area may we drop in and see you?*

"That's nice," I said. "Nice she remembers you."

"She would do," he said. "I was the first Scholarship success the school had ever had. She'd hardly forget me."

"She'll be able to see the kittens," said Henry proudly.

"She's scarcely coming all this way to see bloody kittens. It's me, she's coming to see, right. And I'd appreciate it if just this once you could all manage to keep quiet. And keep out of the way. If that's possible."

That included me, of course.

"You could bring a tray of tea through for us later on," he said, going to answer the door.

"How kind!" said one of the Miss Wisemans. "Drop-scones, what a treat!"

"How kind," said her sister, the teacher. "Aren't you going to join us, my dear?"

"I've a pile of ironing to finish. And anyway it's nice for you to have a quiet chat about old times. About Pete's school days and all."

"We've covered that ground quite satisfactorily," she said. "Couldn't we come and talk to you in the kitchen?"

"We'd love to see the garden," said her sister.

"You engineered that," Pete said when the two old ladies had gone, setting off for Bournemouth in their black Morris Minor.

He was furious. The afternoon hadn't turned out in the least as he'd expected.

"I didn't engineer anything. Don't be such an idiot. Naturally they wanted to meet the children. They are among your achievements, aren't they?"

It had just happened that everyone was around.

Charlotte was making herself a sun dress on the old Singer. Claire was busy kneading the dough for her special ginger biscuits. Out on the back path, surrounded by spanners, forks and oily rags, Henry was mending his bike.

"Oh, no - not the good forks, Henry!"

Up on the steep bank at the top of the garden Tom and his Maria were clearing the undergrowth with a couple of bill-hooks her father had lent us.

And on the faded pink blanket under the white lilac tree, was Norma, basking in maternal pride with her two-week old triplets.

An idyllic picture of family life, you might say.

"We have enjoyed our visit," the sisters chorused accepting a bunch of lilies-of-the-valley with delight, and a bag of warm gingerbread men. "You've a lot to be proud of, Peter."

"You'd set it up," he said again, when they had chugged out of sight.

But I hadn't. It had just happened that way. The children had each found something to do that would keep them out of their father's way. As instructed.

"Extraordinary!" my mother said when I described it to her once. "He must have been afraid they would steal his thunder, when they *were* his thunder! Poor Pete."

Yes, I thought now, pouring out the last of the tea and taking it upstairs to my bedroom. Poor Pete. He wasn't cut out for family life. He's probably happier on his own.

I'd meant to finish the picture on my easel. Three fishermen beside one of our sparkling chalk streams. I flopped down on my bed to squint at it critically as I sipped the tepid tea. I was pleased with what I'd done so far. I'd got the figures right, each intent on his line. Casting, winding-in, waiting. Like some rustic tableau.

They were portraits of three of the men in my life. Jim the writer, Henry the real-life fisherman, and my Rupert.

"Your figures are good," Eddie told me, looking at the folio of illustrations I had produced for Jim's book. "They've got something of Ardizzone in them. You manage to capture the essence of personality in a few deft strokes."

"He's right," Walter had agreed later. "They're good. You should people your landscapes. This one," and he picked out the painting I'd done on our trip to Sidmouth, "this one is incredibly poignant. The insignificance of the human figure against those red cliffs. Man against the forces of the universe and all that."

"That's *you*, Walter. That distant figure battling against the wind."

"Well, this can't be me," he said holding up the watercolour of a tumble-down farmstead with a dumpy red-faced farmer stomping across the yard to let the chickens out.

"It's Eldon. You know, my friend on the Island."

"He's not a farmer, is he?"

"He's a librarian. But you can't very well put a librarian into a winter landscape, can you?"

"Good heavens, lass. I can't keep track of all the fellows in your life."

"He's only a friend. These days he's only a friend. My promiscuous days are over, you'll be glad to hear."

It was Rupert I had to thank for that.

"It's not that I want you all to myself," he had told me the morning after our first ecstatic encounter. "It's not that I'm jealous or possessive. But *honestly*, what are you getting from either of them? Nothing but pain and aggro, as far as I can see."

And it was true.

Eldon had come into my life while I was working at the museum. He'd brought in a small bronze object which he hoped one of the archaeologists would be able to identify for him.

"We only deal with local finds," I said, seeing the address he was filling in on the official form.

"It is local. My mother found it in her garden here years back. It's only just come into my possession. She never bothered to do anything with it."

"You'd better hang on a minute," I suggested when he'd given me all the relevant information. Where the artefact was found. When. How. "You can't go out in this."

An electric storm had suddenly broken. By the time it eased off we had decided to go and have lunch together.

"I'll be back next Thursday," he said. "To pick up the archaeologist's report. Could I take you out for a pub meal that evening, perhaps?"

And that's how it started, my affair with old Eldon. He was married, of course. All my friends were married men. Except the last one.

"But we've had separate rooms, separate lives, for years," he told me sadly. "Philippa hasn't had anything to do with me since she went into the menopause."

Well, he'll be all right with me, then, I thought. I don't believe I'll have to go through all that misery.

After Claire was born, Doctor Olaf put me on the pill.

"Four's enough for anyone," he said, writing out the prescription. "Early days, I know, but this little white tablet looks like revolutionising things for many a down-trodden wife and mother. I'll need to monitor your reactions for the first few months. I'll call in again on the twenty-third. See how you're getting on."

"I can't keep on with them," I told him when he came to check up on me. "I've never stopped bleeding all month."

"Good God, girl! Why didn't you let me know?"

So he took me off the pill and for some reason from that day on I never had another period. I was thirty.

"I think we should send you to a specialist," another doctor told me a few years later, after we had moved down here.

But why? I was fine. Full of beans. Had never felt better. So I left it as it was.

"Well, you're damn lucky," Stella said glumly, covered in hot flushes and confusion as she approached her forty-fifth birthday.

"Bloody lucky," said my sisters, one after the other, as they too were overtaken by the inevitable. "Pity it didn't run in the family."

"Not only that, but you've never had to worry about getting *caught*," said Jo. "You could risk going off the rails a bit."

With Pete, after the first year or two, this had been my biggest problem. The actual semen.

"Put something on," I'd insist, even when I was pregnant. "It makes me utterly sick being pumped full of *that*. I feel like a bloody piss-pot. Yach!" And mopping myself dry I'd hobble off for another bath.

I suppose that alone shows what a mess our marriage had become.

"At least I don't present too much of a threat in that respect," said Eldon, making light of his little problem.

"It was only with Pete," I tried to explain. No trouble with anyone else.

Philippa used to go away a lot . . .

"Perhaps she's found herself a boyfriend, Eldon?"

"Who, Phil? She's not the type."

. . . and he'd ring me when the coast was clear.

"She's off to a Sales Conference on Tuesday. Can you come over? I'll meet you off the six o'clock boat. I can't wait. I'll send you your fare."

"Send you the fare!" Rupert screwed up his face in horror. "Yuck! Grizzly!"

For all his intuitive powers, Rupert never really appreciated quite how hard up I was. And poverty is so boring. But Eldon knew. He was always very generous, showering me with gifts - books, records, knickers and nighties.

"I'm sorry, but he sounds a bit kinky to me, Swami."

He certainly had his funny ways. But then he also had this problem. He'd lost his, well, you know - his *drive*, shall we say. His stamina. Probably to do with his wife losing interest in him. Or vice versa. Men do need to feel desirable. I suppose we all do if we're honest.

With Eldon, we used to have to go through all these preliminary antics. Warming up exercises. Licking and sucking and all that stuff.

"If you don't like it, why on earth did you put up with it?" Rupert had asked, incredulous. Long before our thing started.

I don't know. It's hard to explain. Out of kindness, I suppose. You let things happen at the beginning, don't you. You get carried along by the excitement, the novelty, the thrill of exploration. The charting of new territory. All that.

And later when things calm down a bit you find a pattern has developed. It's not easy to turn round at that stage and tell a fellow you don't much care for his funny games. You just can't do it. It would be too humiliating for him to discover his bedfellow was only playing along out of kindness, politeness.

Dear Kate, I wrote to my sister soon after she had flown out to Germany to join Tony whose firm had moved to Hanover.

I've been tremendously busy with the illustrations I've been asked to do for this children's book . . . hope you're getting over the homesickness by now . . . I'm feeling a little bereft myself at the minute . . .

Rupert had gone to Thailand for six weeks. He'd got a grant to study Thai dental practices. In fact, he was deeply into Buddhism by this time and had been dying to visit Asia. On any old pretext. To carry on his search for the meaning of life in a Buddhist environment.

I do miss him, I told Kate. His enthusiasms. His Zany humour. And his penetrating mind. I missed the bed thing too. He was great in bed. Not that he did anything special.

It was somehow so simple. So natural. So innocent. Just the way Mother Nature intended. Beautiful.

He'll probably tire of me soon enough. Might even come home with a ravishing little Thai bride, I realised. But not to worry, it had been good, so good, and nothing lasts forever.

You'll be pleased to hear that I've given up the promiscuous life altogether... Underneath my wildness had been a faithful constant monandrous woman. It was simply a matter of finding the right man.

All for now. Love to Tony and the kids. Back to the drawing board, as they say...

Brr-brr. Brr-brr. Brr-brr.

"Hi! Swami. Did Claire get her train safely? Enjoying your new unhampered life-style? Look, I know I said we'd go out for a drink this evening, but something's cropped up. I've got to go over to Southampton. Tell you about it later. The thing is, can I still come and eat at your place? Yes, beforehand. I haven't managed to get near a shop today. I'm down to my last crust."

"Of course you can. I was expecting to feed you tonight, wasn't I? I've got mushrooms in and rice and things."

"And a pudding, I hope. One of your luscious bread-puddings, eh?"

"Oh, get away with you. I'm doing my best to get this canvas finished." I was supposed to be hanging eight pictures in the Petersfield Exhibition. I had to have them ready by the following Monday. "I've got to paint to eat, don't forget."

"Oh, go on - *please*! You know how I love your bread-pudding. I'll see you at six. And I'll have to zoom off as soon as we've eaten."

Not to worry, my love, I thought. Now I'm on my own, we've all the time in the world, you and I. Haven't we?

Chapter Thirty-Two

All the time in the world. What an idiot I must have been. I should have seen then what was coming. As soon as Claire had gone up north and I was by myself.

Rupert still came to see me, it's true. We were still bedfellows when it took his fancy. But the pattern had changed.

"He was using you," Jo was to say indignantly. "It's perfectly obvious he was using you."

No, I don't think he was. It was just that he was suddenly terribly busy. Tied up with other things.

"And did he ever invite you along with him?"

"No, but . . ."

But he had once.

"We're hoping to start a Tai Chi class, locally," he told me with excitement. "I'm putting some posters round the town. Why not come along to them?"

How lovely, I thought. He's including me in his Oriental Studies.

He brought Lee Wan, the Tai Chi Master, to supper with me the night of the first class.

"I won't have time to feed him myself. We'll be coming straight up to you from the Southampton class."

After we'd eaten, we went down to the Community Centre in Rupert's car together. There wasn't much of a turn out, but enough to cover the rent.

"Tonight was demonstration only," Lee Wan explained, as we put our shoes on again. "Two-pounds-fifty each from next week. OK?"

Heaven knows how I was going to scrape that together from my meagre budget. But it would be worth it, to spend an evening with Rupert, and share in a small way his passion for the Buddhist path.

"See you at Tai Chi, then," I said naively when he phoned on Friday afternoon to tell me that he was tied up all weekend.

"You weren't listening, Swami. You weren't listening again. I won't actually be attending the local sessions. I already go to Southampton class on Sunday afternoon, don't I? I only came along last week to get him launched. In any case, Madam Butterfly expects me round there for supper on Sunday nights nowadays."

Madam Butterfly was his name for a Japanese Law student he'd met at their Tuesday Aikido class.

"You'll have to meet her one of these days," he'd said. "I really enjoy my evenings with her. She gives me the full works. Welcomes me with a steaming bath, hot towels, perfumed oils." Quite something. In a pre-war semi in Eastleigh. "And she produces all kinds of exotic dishes. With due Japanese ceremony. Sitting at my feet. Shuffling in and out on her knees. I love it."

"I don't know how to put this," I began anxiously next time he was wallowing in my boring bath suds. "But if it's Madam B that you really fancy, I'm quite happy to, er - abdicate. She sounds altogether more suitable for you."

"Oh, come on, Swami!" he protested, holding out a hand for the shampoo. "Surely you're not going to turn possessive on me, are you? For God's sake don't start playing all those boring suburban games. Do I find her more desirable than you? Is Jenny falling in love with me? Am I excited by Miranda's incredible awareness? Jealousy is such an ugly emotion."

"I was only trying to tell you . . . " To tell him that I knew perfectly well that someone younger, more suitable, someone of his own generation was bound to turn up eventually. Probably a Buddhist to boot. And when she appears, I was wanting to tell him, you don't need to feel I'm standing in the light.

"Never mind about that. We'll miss *Shogun*." And he gathered up his clothes and padded through to dry by the sittingroom fire. "Bring us some coffee when you've finished washing up."

"Oh, you got dressed again. I thought perhaps you were staying tonight."

"I can't. You know I can't. Not now I'm round at my mother's."

The builders were working on Puddle Down Cottage. And once they'd finished, Rupert decided he had vermin in the roof. He was still with his mother at Christmas.

"We don't want Mumsie asking awkward questions, now do we, she's difficult enough as it is. Now I'm living there, she won't ever go off to bed until Jenny's safely tucked up."

Jenny was a young nurse, one of his mother's lodgers.

"She's a nice enough kid," he told me.

"And pretty . . ."

"And pretty, yes. But . . ." and he'd rattle off a list of her inhibitions. Her psychological handicaps. Her neuroses.

"I believe you fancy her, for all that. You talk about her enough."

"Oh, no! Not that nasty old jealousy popping up again, Swami."

There was a letter from Jessica on my desk one evening when he called round.

"Whose writing is this?" he asked, scrutinising it closely. "Ah, Jessica, eh! Good job I steered clear of *her*. She's got some enormous personality problems. I can see it in her writing. I suspected as much, though I was tempted at one time."

"He's the one with the bloody problems," Jess was to say afterwards, when I told her. "Bloody cheek! You're better off without him, love. He's a sod. For all his Buddhist pretensions, he's an ego-centric sod."

I remembered the first time Jess met Rupert. It was the evening she heard from Adrian that he'd found himself another girlfriend. We were trying to drown her sorrow in my black coffee laced with the dregs of the brandy this Adrian had given her for her birthday.

"Beware of fellows who give you bottles of brandy," she said bitterly." Subconsciously, they are preparing to abandon you. Right?"

When Rupert turned up, we were laughing over it, but she was badly wounded.

"There was Ian as well," she had groaned. "I can't take much more of this. It's scarcely worth the hassle, is it. I'm really happier between times. Pleasing myself. None of this heart ache. I think I'll settle down and enjoy my spinsterhood. Right?"

"You won't. You know you won't. There'll be somebody else breaking your heart before long. It's inevitable."

Ian had had to decide between Jess and the dishy Spanish girl he'd been living with for two years.

"I do love you, Jess," he'd told her, weeping into his lager in a London pub. "It's just that I need time to sort myself out. I can't handle things at the moment, darling. I was going to suggest . . . "

"Yes?"

" . . . that we kind of put it on ice for six months. By then I'll come clean with Isabella. How would you feel about that?"

"Christ!" Jess exploded to me. "Put it on bloody ice! He was too damn cowardly to tell me straight."

"Have you heard from him since?"

"Not another word. Marvellous, isn't it. Men!"

"Might as well enjoy his brandy, anyway. Come on, there's still some coffee in the pot."

"I thought she'd never go," Rupert said when she left. "I don't want to have to share you with any of these boring negative characters."

"She isn't boring. And she isn't negative. She's had a big shock today. Her lovely boyfriend's ditched her. Just like that. They were supposed to be going to Sweden next week, and all."

"Can't say I blame him, ditching her. She's so darned possessive. I know her type. It's one of the less attractive Cancer characteristics."

"But you're Cancer as well . . . "

"It's the *rising* sign that counts. I'm sorry, but Jess is another of your lame ducks."

"She isn't! She's one of my best friends. She just happens to be feeling sad today. Lame duck, indeed!"

"OK - we'll leave Jess out of it. But what about all the others, eh? Maggie. Brenda. Louise. Rhona. It's your own fault for encouraging them, of course."

"I don't encourage them . . . "

Rhona was a natural pessimist. She came over every so often to share her problems with me.

"It's the usual old thing," she'd say, lying on the sofa in tears. Speaking to the far wall, the ceiling, rather than meet my eye. "Sometimes I think I'll go mad."

"Oh, come on, Rhona love - don't let him upset you so. He's never worth it."

"We lie there," she sobbed, "night after night we lie there. In complete silence. In total darkness. And I have to, er - you know, wank him off! For his part, he does nothing, mind. Just lies there like a god-king. While I work on him. And if ever I make a sound, groan may be before changing hands, he throws a fit."

"That's ruined it, hasn't it. When it was just coming to the boil. You stupid cow. Why can't you keep your gob shut. Next time try to remember to concentrate on the job in hand. In *bloody silence*. No, it's too late now. You've managed to ruin it again. Damn you."

"He must need treatment, Rhona. He can't be normal."

"Won't see a doctor. Says I'm the one who needs treatment. Course, you know what he's doing . . . "

"What?"

"He's off in some fantasy world of his own. With a dream girl, isn't he. If I speak or groan or the curtain blows to remind him where he really is, then the illusion's shattered."

"Oh, surely not. Not your Mike!"

"I feel a Nothing. He's wiped me out."

"Tell her," said Rupert, the budding Buddhist philosopher, "tell her you've enough problems of your own."

"But my problems are all behind me. Bar the cash. There's been plenty of times I've needed a shoulder to cry on. It's little enough to ask of a friend."

"Ah! Now we're getting to the root of it, Swami. I think you rather enjoy being comforter and confidant to all these inadequate women. We've all got our weaknesses, and this is obviously one of yours. You're flattered, aren't you, by their dependence on you? Now for once be honest."

Perhaps he was right. There might be an element of self-gratification in playing Mother Confessor. I hadn't thought of it that way, but . . .

"Poor old Madge . . ."

With her eight children and her drunken Irish husband.

"He'd come in drunk every pay-day," she'd told me. "If I resisted him he'd wake the kids and take it out on them. He'd spew his beer back as often as not. Beer and pee in the bed, and everything else. When he'd had a few he lost all control. I've had to burn no end of mattresses over the years. Double mattresses that he'd messed up. The WVS have helped me out a time or two. And the Sally Army. He's no better than an animal is Bert."

Poor Madge. She was taken off to Park Prewett eventually. A total wreck. When she came out she refused to go back to him. But his name was on the rent book so that left her homeless. They took her into a Church Refuge for a few weeks, until she found herself a boyfriend through an ad in the evening paper.

Smart divorcee looking for friendship . . .

"Friendship!" she told me, gripping her coffee mug tight to disguise the shakes. "That's a laugh - friendship!"

All she had found was sexual abuse. *More* sexual abuse. Of one kind or another.

"Hello! Is that you? Madge here, Madge. You've got to help me. I've no one else to turn to . . . "

She'd moved in with this latest fellow.

"He seemed so nice, seemed like a real gent. But he's locked me in here. Not been out since I arrived . . . weeks now . . . I'm his prisoner." She sounded terrified. She was risking a phone call while he was in the loo. "Are you still there? He makes me do all these funny things . . . puts it in my mouth . . . my MOUTH! I was only looking for a roof over my head. And a little affection."

There was one crisis after another with Madge. I rang the Samaritans for her once. And the Welfare people.

"But she was bringing it all on herself," Rupert pointed out with exaggerated patience. "As fast as she's rescued from one dreadful situation she gets herself into another. You shouldn't waste any more sympathy on her. That's what I mean, it feeds your own ego. Doing a Mother Teresa and all that."

In the end, she put her head in the gas oven, poor soul. Not even her own oven, mind.

"You can't blame yourself," he said, when I got back from her pathetic funeral. "If someone intends to commit suicide she'll do it eventually. You did what you could. If you seriously think you could have prevented things turning out this way, you're suffering from enormous self-delusion."

"But sometimes it's no more than a sympathetic ear people need. You do yourself, love."

I remembered the hours we'd spent analysing his own difficult relationship with his mother.

"My mother's different. She's my responsibility. A problem I've got to learn to live with. I can't shrug her off . . ."

"I know . . . "

"I'm not suggesting you should be utterly callous with your pathetic friends. Be firm. Be positive. Don't encourage them to wallow in their misery."

He's so right, I thought again. I must be firmer. It's some weakness in me that attracts them. These War Wounded. Casualties of the Sex War, mostly. I do admire Rupert's clear sightedness. His powers of analysis. His gift for winkling out their weaknesses. Their delusions.

"But how about his own?" Walter was to ask afterwards. "It sounds to me as if he had quite a few problems himself."

"He is incredibly intuitive," I was to explain.

"I happen to have a sharp nose for these things, Swami." That's how he put it.

We went to a party at Jessica's once. A good party. Super food. Fresh strawberries, buckets of them. Lovely warm interesting people.

"What a ghastly crowd!" Rupert had exclaimed, dragging me away long before the end. "All their preposterous affectations. Their ego games. What a grizzly gathering."

"I thought they were great," I said, apologetically, thinking I must be terribly dense. Never to notice people's glaring deficiencies.

"That's another of your shortcomings, I'm afraid. You don't have much sense of discrimination. It boils down to a lack of intuition."

Oh dear - not much I could do about *that*, I thought.

"Meditation might help," he suggested kindly. "Might increase your awareness. Eradicate some of your *dis*harmonies."

"Did you try it? Did you try meditation?" Walter asked, coming over a few days after Christmas. To see what was wrong.

I hadn't actually got round to it then. And now, of course, it was too damn late.

Chapter Thirty-Three

"I hope you don't include me among your lame ducks," said Walter, having a quick warm by the fire, before leaving for home.

"Oh, Walter - I should say *I'm* one of *yours*! That's more like it."

"Put this under your Christmas tree, lass," he said bringing out a lumpy parcel from a carrier bag.

"I'm not bothering with a tree this year. Claire's probably not coming back till the new year. And Henry's sure to be spending much of the time over at Belinda's."

"You won't be on your own, will you . . . ?"

"No, no - my young Romeo will be here. And he won't worry about a tree. Buddhists don't keep Christmas, do they."

Actually he seemed to have become obsessed with Budhism.

"You must not mistake the finger pointing at the moon for the moon itself," he had often warned me, quoting the Buddha. But now . . .

He was like someone I once shared a country walk with. She kept her nose in the map the entire day. Not seeing the countryside. Only seeing it reduced to small coloured lines and squiggles by the Ordnance Survey.

. . . like someone determined to explain how to play chess, say. Or Scrabble. Or flipping Ludo!

"Now then, before you leave base . . . "

"What do you mean, *base*?"

"Before you leave the starting point you must throw a six."

"Oh, come on. Let's just start playing. We'll pick it up as we go along."

"No, no. Best to get the rules clearly understood before we go any further."

"But we'll never get started at this rate."

"*Now*, suppose I'm red, right, and you're blue . . . "

There's no need to agonise. It'll be as clear as a our Hampshire chalk streams, once we get into it. But they all do it, whatever path up the mountain they take (as the Buddha probably said). Worrying away at it. Tormenting themselves with doubts and difficulties.

I mean, there's Jo gone potty at the other extreme.

She met this bloke. A lovely man. Incredibly intelligent and well-read, but totally immersed in some weird Christian sect. Not the Salt Lake City lot, but something similar.

"It makes perfect sense," she told me, bringing over an extraordinary assortment of groceries one day and dumping them on the kitchen table. "Be a dear - take this lot off my hands. We're supposed to destroy them but it seems a dreadful waste."

"Destroy them?" I looked at the packets and jars in amazement. Yeast, Marmite, baking powder, gravy browning. "*Why?*"

"The Passover. You know, unleavened bread and all that. No yeast, no raising agents allowed in the house for the next ten days. That's why."

"But it isn't the Jewish faith you've adopted, is it?"

"No, but we are doing our best to live by the Word of God as revealed in the Bible."

"But, Jo! Surely you don't believe, literally believe in every darned word of it? Come on!"

She began to get agitated at that. These days we always seemed to be arguing. And always about this religion of hers.

"I'm afraid I do, yes. Every word. Just as it was written. If only you'd make an effort and study it seriously you might begin to understand."

We argued a lot about Adam and Evolution.

"What about the archaeological evidence, then, Jo?"

"You're very naive about some things. They're all fakes. We're being conned every day of our lives. Conned by the agents of the Devil."

"But dinosaurs, Jo . . . ?"

"Another con. No dinosaurs mentioned in Genesis. No dinosaurs."

"But who'd take the trouble to con us? And why?"

"It's the Forces of Evil, I'm afraid. I keep trying to warn you. The End Time cometh, my friend. We haven't got long. In his wrath at the way we've ignored his laws, the Lord God is preparing to wipe mankind from the face of the earth. Apart from His True Children."

"Your lot?"

"I've told you. A place of refuge is already being built for us. On a secret site chosen by the Lord himself. When the time comes we will be given a sign . . . "

"A sign!"

". . . when the holocaust is about to break."

"But, Jo - people have been foretelling the *end* of the world since the *beginning*. Look at Noah."

"Just read your Bible before you sneer. It's all in Revelations. The bomb. The Falklands business. Maggie Thatcher. It's all foretold. Microchips. Space Travel. Everything."

"Sorry, Jo, but I have this ludicrous faith in mankind. If you insist on bringing the Good Lord into it, then it's through you and me he'll work his purpose out. Through common sense, compassion and love. It's all so simple. So bloody obvious."

"It's all very well talking like that. That's the Devil speaking, you realise. He's only too happy for us to sail along in blissful ignorance. You're playing straight into his hands. We've become lax, all of us. Lax, self-indulgent, weak, wicked."

"Wicked!"

"I'll lend you some of my Bible Study notes. And, no. No coffee for me. This is a Fast Day for us, but I am allowed a sip of hot water."

I hadn't taken the Church, any church, too seriously for years.

"But the Church gets in the way of its own message," I'd protested loudly whenever the subject came up.

I liked singing hymns mind, especially at Harvest Time. And Easter.

All is safely gathered in . . .

Brings tears to your eyes, doesn't it. I always have Songs of Praise on TV on Sunday evening. A good sing. A good weep.

"Oh, no!" the kids used to groan. "Do you have to?" as I joined in heartily. No-one to protest nowadays. I can sing my head off.

. . . ere the winter storms begin . . .

So many interesting faces in the Songs of Praise congregation. I sketch them some Sundays. A fleeting impression. It's damn good practice. Capturing the essence of the face in a few quick pencil strokes. Such a plug, the programme, for decency and loving kindness. Not to mention the grand old hymns themselves.

"We don't sing," said Jo primly. "We're too busy preparing for the End Time. The world is sick. We're all steeped in wickedness."

"But I don't know one single person with any real wickedness in them." Blind and lost and foolish, but not wicked.

"It's not for us to judge," she said, skating neatly off the thin ice. "When the end comes . . . "

The End Time! That's another kind of arrogance, assuming the climax, the denouement, must happen now. In her lifetime. *Now* out of all the ages, past, present and future. Such self-aggrandisement. Such self-delusion.

"Are you an atheist then?" asked my sister Peg, anxious for my immortal soul.

"I'm a believer in life with all its mysteries. Here and now, I believe in. Here and now and love."

"What about the supernatural then? Where does that fir in?"

"Christ! If I could answer that I'd be a bloody genius."

Peg had just described a dream she'd had about visiting me in Railway Terrace. It was soon after the divorce. Before she'd visited us in our humble little Victorian terrace.

"I saw it in such vivid detail," she told me. "I even knew how to find my way here. Everything's right. The garden, the lay-out of the rooms, decorations, everything. And it was five years ago that I had this dream. When for all I knew you were happily married to Pete. That's the funny part. Nothing had happened to put the idea into my head."

"You're not the only one, Peg."

There'd been Alan. This ghastly bloke who'd picked my name out of the *Link* file. He'd had premonitions galore. About our predestined relationship, his were.

Dear Alan (I wrote in desperation),
Please understand me when I say that I don't find you the least attractive, and that I have no intention of getting involved with you. As for going on holiday together, you must be out of your mind . . .

The next Sunday his neighbour rang me. His *neighbour*!

"Look," she pleaded, "don't be so hard on Alan. He's such a kind fellow and dreadfully lonely since his wife left him . . ."

His wife, Sylvia, a Corporation Bus Driver, had run off with an older woman.

"That's not my problem." Rupert would definitely have approved of my firmness.

"How if we all come over to your place. Me and Hubby and Alan. We'll bring something nice for our teas. I'm sure we can make you appreciate what a decent fellow he is. All he needs is the right little woman."

"Hey! Hang on, I don't even like the man." But it was no good, she'd rung off.

Half-an-hour later they rolled up with two large Tupperware containers full of Sunday tea.

"He'd be no trouble," they assured me, over ham and tomatoes.

"He's such a kind chap, is Alan," they warbled over the tinned peaches and Carnation Milk.

"You'd like his old Dad."

"For Christ's sake!" I screeched eventually, stuffing the remains of their Lyons Chocolate Gateau back in its wrapping. "He may be a paragon of virtue, but I do not know him. I do not want to know him. He is absolutely nothing to me. Please take him away, and take your revolting tea with you."

But she would not admit defeat. "Oh, try to see it from his point of view, dearie."

"Don't *dearie* me, thank you! I'm not looking for a lover. And certainly not for a husband. I've spent a great deal of time getting rid of the last one. Alan must make do with his Bus Driver. Please take him away."

"Oh, at least have a little walk with him, love. Just the two of you by yourselves. You owe him that. We'll be quite happy watching the Quiz Show till you come back," she wheedled, totally insensitive to anything but her plan for getting Alan's life sorted out.

"Come on then, Alan!" At least I might be able to talk some sense into him away from his frightful protagonists. Whistling for the dog to come with us, I slammed out of the house.

"One thing, you never told me how it ended in your premonition," I said, having finally got the message through to him.

"Just like this," he said with resignation. "I knew what was coming. It ended with us sitting here on the park bench, you and me and the old dog. You tearing me to shreds. Exactly like this. My premonitions are always reliable."

Chapter Thirty-Four

"There certainly are more things in heaven and earth, Horatio," I said to Peggy, in our mutual state of sozzled philosophising. "I guess I'm a Don't Know. That's as far as I'm prepared to go."

I remember what put me off the jolly old C of E and made me positively ashamed of it.

It was the summer I was in Manchester Fever Hospital, with the jaundice. Bad epidemic that year. Two or three deaths in Matlock alone. Pete got it first. Brought it home from school. Then when he recovered it was my turn. They sent me to Monsaldale as there was no-one to look after me at home.

"Do you remember going to stay with Granny? In Nottingham?" I asked Charlie when we were going through the box of photos, sharing them out. Those for Pete, these for us. That was about the most poignant moment of the divorce, dividing up the photographs. Splitting the years between us. "You and Tommy were with her for weeks," I said, passing her a snap of a small girl swinging on a garden gate, with one curly pigtail down her back. "Remember?"

I remembered the journey to Manchester, by ambulance. The only time I'd ever been in one.

"There was dark glass in the ambulance windows," I told Rupert during one of our great discussions on the significance of the individual. "It was weird. Like being invisible or dead. Seeing life going merrily by without you. Not noticed through the blind windows of the ambulance. Not missed. Funny."

"You're beginning to think like a Buddhist," he said. "You must have been listening to me after all."

At Monsaldale, we were each in a sealed glass cubicle. Before coming in to wash or feed us or deliver bed-pans, the nurses had to don special protective clothing that hung in the airlock between, say, me and my infection and the outside world.

"Barrier nursing," said Walter.

There were some terrible cases in our ward. A baby, I remember, whose mother had had syphilis. The poor little thing was covered in weeping sores which were deadly contagious, they said.

"We can only handle her with rubber gloves on," one of the student nurses told me. "Poor mite. She'll never be any better."

"No, that's not entirely true," the Ward Sister said later. "Sometimes with a girl these things clear up at puberty. So there's just a chance. If she survives that long."

I think of that child now and again. A lifetime without any human contact. Her only experience of the world through the glass walls of her cage, and the well-protected hands that fed her and washed her and tended her inherited sores.

She'll be ten or eleven now, I thought, as the years went by. She'll be fourteen or so. Perhaps it's cleared up. Perhaps they'll have discovered a cure by now.

Talk about the sins of the fathers! God knows what ever I had to complain about.

On Easter Saturday the Padre came round the ward to ask which of us would like to take Communion next morning. I was a regular church-goer in those days. I was on St Wilfred's Church Council, actually.

First thing Easter morning the nurses tidied us up to receive the Bread and Wine. They put pretty little embroidered cloths over our lockers and brought each of us a small jug of flowers, primroses and forget-me-nots.

In the cubicle across the aisle from mine was a woman with dysentery. This was what most of the patients were suffering from. Most of them were from the inner city slums.

Gradually over the weeks I learned a bit about this woman. She was thirty-two. Thin and haggard. Sullen, hard and care-worn. Not only from the disease, but from bearing and coping with her twelve children. *Twelve* children! At her age! And they were all black. She wasn't but the children were. At that time, way back in the late Fifties, they were the first coloured family I'd ever seen.

One or another of the older ones would visit her occasionally, sometimes with a string of toddlers dragging along behind. They weren't allowed inside her cubicle, obviously, because of the infection. They could only stand in the ward and shout and mime things to her through the glass.

"Joey got the strap off our Dad again, Mammy."

"Mrs Willis made us a hot dinner last night but Billy sicked his up."

"The Welfare Lady comed and told our Dad the place was a mess . . ."

"A reet bloody mess, she said."

"When you coming home, Mam?"

A pathetic coffee-coloured band. With running noses and wet knickers. If it was fine they were allowed to stand on the grass outside the window of their mother's cubicle, a young nurse with them to make sure they kept well back.

The father of all this brood only came in once, as far as I know. He shouted and bawled till they fetched the Sister.

"Look, man!" he bellowed, banging his huge ebony forehead with his huge ebony fist. "She's got to come home, see. How'm I supposed to cope with all them kids, huh? Somebody answer me that one!"

Well, Easter morning she was lying there in a clean nightie, washed and brushed for the Padre. A jug of flowers on her dainty tablecloth. Just like all the rest of us. Awaiting the blessed sacrament.

"She is confirmed, of course?" someone must have inquired.

And of course she wasn't. Who would have organised a thing like that in the back streets of her youth!

"And would you believe it," I was to tell Rupert all these years later, "Would you believe it, they wouldn't allow her to share in the Communion. They took her flowers away, and whispered angrily together with the Padre. As if she'd been discovered in some petty crime. I was sick with shame. Where's the Christianity in that, eh? Even at the Lord's Table she was discriminated against. For her poverty and her ignorance."

"Rules is rules, I suppose. The poor man probably felt he had no choice."

That's not what Jesus would have said, I thought. She wept all morning, that poor soul. Until they gave her a jab to make her sleep. Wept with her face to the one solid wall in her glass cage.

It was twenty years later, the next time I found myself in Manchester. A few weeks before our divorce went through.

"We're sending you on a Job Jolt course," the woman at the Department of Employment told me when I signed onto their Professional and Executive Register soon after walking out of the Kremlin. "It's at Manchester University. Just for a month. All expenses paid, of course. It should help you to sort yourself out. Job-wise."

"How can you contemplate going just now?" my mother said, aghast.

"It's now or never, Mum. Once Pete's gone up to his new headship there'll be no possibility of getting away on my own. Since they're good enough to offer me the chance, I'm taking it."

"And was it any help?" asked Walter. "Did it jolt you onto a new path?"

I suppose it gave me time to think.

It had been a strange month. A month in limbo. The University had found digs for me out at Cheadle Hulme. With a Miss Jane Grey who was plump and jolly and well into her seventies.

"I'm afraid it's rather a pokey room," she said helping me up with my luggage. "But you're more than welcome to come and sit and watch telly with me. There's always a nice fire in the front room."

"Can I have a bath, please, Jane?"

"Yes, there's hot water Sunday and Thursday nights."

You only realise how lucky you are to have your own place when you *don't* have it. I felt confined, trapped in the box room. Smelly and depressed by the restrictions on baths.

"And the course?" Walter asked.

The course was disappointing. I'd heard about Job Jolt through an article in *The Guardian*. About how stimulating it was. How demanding. Probing into your subconscious to discover *why* you were unhappy, unsuccessful, unemployed, a square peg in your last job. What might suit you better.

We had aptitude tests, self-analysis sessions, mock interviews that were recorded on video.

"Look how nervously you were sitting . . ."

"You must endeavour to answer the interviewer's questions, not wander off on some rigmarole of your own."

"He was deliberately ignoring you. Part of the test, you see. Why did you carry on speaking when he had his head under the desk? He was testing your cool. You'll have to have another interview tomorrow. That one was hopeless."

I treated myself to a nice big sketch pad, and when things got too infantile I drifted quietly across to the Museum. The Egyptian section was good, and so was the Natural History collection. There was some marvellous Eskimo stuff too. Whale-bone knives delicately etched with hunting scenes : dog teams, seals, igloos. Very small and detailed and beautiful.

"Where have you been all morning?" the pompous Course Director asked me. "You've missed the talk on filling in application forms. And the lady advising us how to dress for an interview. You'll only get out of this opportunity the state has offered you as much as you're prepared to put into it. Think about it, please."

In class I started to do thumbnail portraits of my fellow students. The skyline in Manchester is dramatic. I did a series of sketches which together formed a panoramic roofscape of the city, stretching from the Cheshire Plain to the west across to the foothills of the Pennines. That was something!

What the hell am I doing up here, I said to myself, dismally squeezing onto the half-past-five bus to Cheadle. Back home Henry and Claire would already be in from school and settling down with apples and bowls of cereal to watch, let me see - Thursday - *Blue Peter* by the fire.

In the dark and the drizzle of that November night, we had gone way past my stop before I discovered I was on the wrong bus.

"This isn't the one, Duck. Should have got the 13 *A*."

"Where on earth have you been?" my landlady said crossly. "Your supper's spoilt but it's your own fault. You could have phoned to let me know you were going to be late."

"I got on the wrong bus. I was totally lost."

"Lost! You knew to ask for the Red Lion."

"When they put me off the bus, I honestly didn't know which direction I should be making for," I was to tell Walter. "I was all disorientated."

Even now, I find myself there in the night sometimes. Lost and confused in the wilds of Cheshire. I knocked on a couple of doors, but no-one answered. In the end I managed to hitch a lift. I was in such a state the driver thought I was drunk. It was a nightmare.

One way and another, I was glad to leave Manchester and get home.

"Tom's gone," said Henry. "He's taken his stuff and gone to live with Maria. Did you bring us anything, Mum?"

There was one clear week before we moved house to start life in Railway Terrace.

"You take whatever you want," Pete said, generous in the end. "I'll be quite happy with whatever's left. The main thing is that the kids shouldn't suffer too badly."

"That was noble of him," said Walter. "There was no acrimony, then?"

No. Once everything was settled and he'd found himself this plum headship up north, I think we each tried to be kind and affectionate till the last. It was pretty civilised as divorces go.

In spite of the fact that the kids had been nagging me to tell Pete that I'd seen a solicitor, when the letter came suing him for divorce it was different.

"It's going to mean selling the house and moving," I announced at lunchtime when their father had stopped weeping.

"Selling the house!" Henry was horrified.

"Selling the house!" They all were.

"Oh, no! This is our home. You can't expect us to leave it, Mum."

"I'm not flaming moving. No way. I have to be near the river, don't I, for my fishing."

It was when the Estate Agent came round to value it that I began to weaken.

"A lovely place you've got here, Madam. A real family home. We'll have no trouble selling it for you, I know that. Five bedrooms . . . a playroom . . . so spacious! Such character! And the garden, well the garden must be unique!"

"You're not serious about selling it, Mum?" said Tom, pale and drawn at the prospect.

"But it's part of the divorce package, love."

"Well then, I don't reckon you *can* divorce him. You've got to look at it from our point of view. It won't be so bad. You're being pretty selfish, Mum."

"But you've said yourself you don't know how I've put up with him all these years, Tom. You've said it over and over."

"But I didn't realise it would mean selling the house. You just can't do it to us all, Ma!"

"Give me one more chance, darling," Pete pleaded that afternoon as we walked along beside the river together on our way home from Sainsbury's. "I'll make a big effort. You won't know me. It's not too late. We could still try to make it work. Please?"

We rested the shopping on the wall and talked it over while a family of swans sailed majestically by, a cob, a hen, and four large grey cignets.

"OK," I agreed reluctantly, thinking of our stone-walled garden in the spring. "We'll stick it out for another year or two. Just till the kids are through school."

"We'll remember today," he said, gathering the baskets up again, and steering me along the path (in that infuriatingly possessive way of his) with a firm hold on my elbow. "August the tenth - the day I called your bluff, eh? I always knew you weren't serious. Thank goodness you came to your senses in time."

Chapter Thirty-Five

And now it was my turn to be rejected.

"No matter how awful anything is," Charlotte had said to me years before, "you do recover in the end. That's the important thing to remember, Mum."

Poor kid - that was a lesson she had learnt very early.

"Oh, lovie," I said giving her a last hug before she disappeared into the Departure Lounge at Heathrow for the start of her Australian adventure. "I'm sorry you had to go through all that. It's good of Robert and Liz to have you out there. That should help you get over it."

"No matter how awful anything is . . . " she said then. "And she certainly was a beautiful baby, my little Georgina."

At sixteen after a stormy passage through Secondary Modern School we discovered that Charlie was pregnant. Six months pregnant. There was nothing to be done about it.

"It was that bloody school," I explained once to Jo. "She was the last of the Eleven-Plus Failures." Pernicious system it was, that. They abolished it the very next year. Fancy writing off eighty percent of our children before they reach their teens. Wicked!

"But she's as bright as a button," her class teacher told me when the results were announced. "She's an obvious candidate for the High School. I can't understand why she's been turned down."

"I could not in all honesty recommend her," Pete eventually admitted. "She is bright, I grant you. Her IQ is excellent. Higher than Tom's actually . . . "

"Well then, why didn't she get through?"

"But she doesn't read."

"Doesn't read?"

"She's clearly not an academic. Bright but not quite in the category the High School are looking for."

"But you don't know that Jackie Beavis is a reader at home. Or Felicity either."

"I refuse to discuss it further. I am her Headmaster, remember. I am the professional. I have to deal with Charlotte as I would with any other border-line case."

"It's a pity any of them went to Westwood," my father said later on when everything was coming out into the open. "None of you went to my school, I made sure of that."

"They all used to pick on me," Charlie remembers today, but not bitterly. "All the teachers up at Florence Nightingale's."

"As for you, Charlotte," they used to say, whenever there was any trouble. "You should know better, with your Dad a headmaster . . . "

"Poor old darling . . . "

"Don't worry about it. I survived, didn't I? And I guess Dad was right, you know. I wasn't academic, not like our Tom . . ."

"And me!"

"And you, Henry. I was the dumb one . . . "

"The dumb blonde, eh - Sis!"

"I just pissed about. All my own fault."

She'd got in with a terrible rough lot.

"You can't go to school in those dreadful shoes, Charlotte. God knows where you got them. Put your Clarke's sandals on. Go and change at once. And hurry up or you'll miss the bus!"

"No. I wouldn't be seen dead in them. Clarke's bloody sandals! I told you I wouldn't wear them when you bought them. Everyone wears *these*. So there!" And off she tottered defiantly, this twelve year old rebel, in her 'Granny lace-ups' with four inch heels, the *in* thing at the time.

"You were a right little tear-away by the sound of it, Chalie," said Henry with new respect. "I'd forgotten."

I hadn't. Her common friends . . .

"They weren't common, Ma."

. . . smoking, drinking, shop-lifting . . .

"Not to mention your actual *sex*," she prompted.

"Wicked gal!" said Henry, putting on a Headmistress voice. "You wicked, wicked gal!"

"I wouldn't mind a baby myself," said Claire dreamily. "Un-married mothers don't have to worry about their A Levels, do they?"

"The big question there," said Henry with a snort, "is where are you going to find it a father?"

"Oh, shut up, you. I've got my fans. Danny loves me for one. Yes he does. It's just that he's too shy to mention it."

"It's all right joking," Charlotte said quietly, starting on the washing up. "But it was the hardest thing I'll ever have to face, parting with my little Georgie. I knew it was right, mind. I knew I wasn't being pressurised. But that didn't make it any easier. At the time I really thought I'd never recover."

I remembered that now as I lay on my bed. Rigid with grief. Weak with pain.

"Look, Swami," he'd said that morning (that very morning), sitting up in bed (this very bed) eating his bowl of Shreddies, "I'm afraid you're taking all this rather more seriously than I'd intended."

It was a week before Christmas. And the first time he had stayed the night since Claire went off to Newcastle in September.

"I don't want my mother to cotton on," he'd told me on the odd occasion I'd mentioned it. "You know how neurotic she is about sex."

"Neurotic! It wasn't his mother that was neurotic," Charlie was to say later.

He had taken me to a concert at the Cathedral the night before, me and Madam Butterfly.

"I've got tickets for the Monteverdi Vespers," he'd said.

"Oh, Rupert, that will be lovely."

"Um, well, Moshi's coming too. In fact I'm taking her out to supper first. We'll call for you at seven-thirty."

We hardly ever spent an evening together now. He was always busy these days.

"Hunting!" Henry was to say angrily.

He generally found time to come round for a meal two or three times a week. That was nice.

"But didn't he realise how hard up you were?" Walter was to ask.

It didn't matter. I wasn't actually starving.

"Hm! Delicious! I do love your pancakes, Swami. I'll just have one more then I've got to be off. Promised I'd run Madam B over to meet Fred and Louise this evening. Might pop back here afterwards. OK?"

He'd often do that now. Knock me up at eleven, eleven-thirty. Come bouncing in to tell me where he'd been. Who he'd met. That was nice too. But the zest had gone out of it. I can see it now.

"My sex drive is very low at the moment," he explained. "I think I'm entering a more spiritual phase of life,"

"It doesn't matter love. There's more to it than sex."

"Anyway, your bed's so bloody uncomfortable. It's not good for my back."

Oh, Lord! I thought blindly. How can I ever raise the money for a new one. A nice firm one like Claire's. Solid pine with wooden slats instead of springs. He'd be comfortable on that. Next time I sell a picture, perhaps.

"Mum! How could you be so dense?" Charlie was to ask. "It was glaringly obvious, wasn't it? I mean, you can make love on a beanbag, in a flaming hammock, if your heart's in it."

Poor young man. For months he must have been trying to tell me it was over.

"It's been a good year, lovey . . ." I'd said (I now remembered with shame), the night before my birthday. We had flopped down on my bed after supper. For once he was able to stay a little. The curtains were open, the room quite light from the street lamp opposite. ". . . the best year of my life."

We'd lain together like this so often. Listening to his records . . .

"Let's play that over again, shall we? This time, follow the voice of the cello. Aaah . . . Schubert really was a genius. A genius with strings. Now, pick out the viola's line - got it." And he'd sing along ecstatically, conducting heartily from the bed.

Sometimes playing the Frog Game . . .

"The secret of happiness, ladies and gentleman, is embodied in the frog . . . "

"Croak-croak-croak."

"To the initiated, a parallel can be drawn between the infinite potential of the human spirit and . . . "

"And the frog."

"Thank you, Madam Chairman. Now as I was saying . . ."

We'd go on like that for hours, when he was in his Frog mood. Rolling about, wrestling, getting sillier and sillier.

"There's only one way to make you see the error of your ways, my good woman . . . " And he'd start to undress me.

Indulging in our great philosophical debates.

"Debates!" Claire was to say afterwards. "He seemed to be doing most of the talking, Ma, from what I could hear from my room."

"That's right," Henry was to agree. "Yes, love. No, love. That's about as much as you ever seemed to contribute."

"We could hear quite a lot from downstairs, you know, Mum."

I wasn't always so reticent. There was the time I came up with my great metaphor for the theory of re-incarnation.

"I've got it!" I cried with one of those flashes of inspiration. "It's like an engine. A steam engine. Each wheel is equivalent to a lifetime. Right? Each one different. Separate. With an identity of its own. It's own particular role to play. Yet all part of the same engine. Eureka!"

"Hey!" he said in astonishment. "That's amazing! Exactly how Jung expresses it."

"I must have read it somewhere, then." Though I knew I'd never read Jung.

"That's really smart," he said, making the tenderest love to me. "Really perceptive. You're obviously picking up a lot of my insight into these things."

That was when he began to call me Swami.

"Swami?"

"Teacher. Wise One. My most honoured Guru!"

"Get away with you, you idiot!"

"Your wish is my command, O Rinpoche. I prostrate myself in wonder at your lotus feet. Anymore chocs?"

Yes, it had been a good year. The best year of my life.

"We're missing *Not the Nine O'Clock News*," he said, jumping off the bed. "How about some coffee, eh? I can't stay late tonight."

"Your bloody Rupert watching the telly!" Claire was to screech in disbelief.

I was surprised as well. Before I had the house to myself he had constantly scoffed at the kids.

"They're morons, Swami. Both of them. It's no use denying it. All they ever seem to be doing is watching the damn telly. Don't they have any other interests?"

"Oh, come on! You do exaggerate."

But the minute Claire and Henry left us to our own devises it was a different story.

"Dallas - good, Dallas! I'll just stay and watch it before I go to the pub. OK?"

"Rupert! It's crap, absolute mindless crap."

"No, no - there's a lot more to it than meets the eye. I've been watching it at Mumsie's lately. It's good sound psychological stuff."

"You don't mean to tell us you sat through rubbish like that with him, Mum?" Henry was to say. "*You*, that's so jolly supercilious about Coronation Street, let alone Dallas!"

But I'm afraid I did. I sat there besotted, watching bloody Dallas with him.

"But *why*?" Walter was to ask afterwards. "I'd have thought you'd have more sense. What ever came over you, lass?"

Heaven only knows. That's what love does for you. Love. It softens your brain.

"One thing I liked about our relationship was its lightness," he tried to explain now, chasing the last Shreddie round the bowl. "None of that gruesome till-death-us-do-part stuff."

I remembered a discussion we'd had. Not so long ago. Talking about relationships, attachments, possessiveness, jealousy.

"With our lovely casual set-up . . . " I began.

"Casual?" he said, surprised. "I wouldn't have called it casual."

"Not casual. Easy. That's what I mean, easy."

"Well, that all seems to have changed somehow," he said now, putting his cereal bowl on the floor and snuggling back into bed. "No need to get into a state."

"Don't worry about it," I managed to say. "Let's just be friends. That's OK by me."

I'd known something like this was coming. As soon as we'd found our seats in the Cathedral the evening before, the three of us, he'd passed me this envelope.

"Open it, Swami! It's an early Christmas card. I thought of you the moment I saw it. It's perfect for you. Come on, open it. It'll kill you!"

I didn't hear much of Monteverdi's masterpiece.

"There you are, Mum," Henry was to say later, relieved to discover that it was over. "I told you he was shit. I told you when it started."

"I'm staggered at you," said Jo afterwards. "Casual sexual relationships are inspired by the Devil. Why couldn't you see it for yourself?"

Because I was flattered perhaps. Because he was young and bright and beautiful.

"Phaw!" he'd exclaim, watching his own reflection in the kitchen window as he went through the Tai Chi cycle while I made the supper. So vibrant from the exercise. So incredibly aware. "Phaw!"

"I couldn't stand him," my mother was to say, thankful to hear that this highly unsuitable affair had finished. "He hadn't a kind word to say for anyone. And as for the way he wolfed your birthday chocolates . . . "

"Well?" he whispered, leaning across the Japanese beauty sitting between us as the orchestra tuned up. "Isn't it the perfect card?"

It was a rural scene, a picture of a cow, a cow wearing sunglasses. Reflected in each dark lens was a highly excited bull. 'Udderly in love' was the hilarious caption. He'd drawn pigtails on the cow. Just in case I hadn't got the message.

"That must be how he'd come to see me," I told Walter, when he came to take me out for a meal on New Year's Eve. "As a randy old cow." The humiliation choked me.

"Oh, don't get all hurt and difficult on me," Rupert said now, pulling the duvet up to our chins. "I don't mean I'm tired of you exactly. But it's obvious I'll meet someone my own age, someone more suitable eventually. That's what I'm worrying about. How it will hurt you in the end."

And with that, as if relieved to have got the tricky matter off his chest, to have extricated himself comparatively painlessly from his predicament, with that he jumped on me for a final fling!

Chapter Thirty-Six

Charlie had been right, of course. By Christmas Eve I had almost recovered.

All week I'd stayed home, hiding away like an injured animal, licking my wounds.

"Miaow!" Percy protested when I dished up yet another dried dinner for him. Out of a packet. "Miaow! I've had enough of that stuff. Why don't you fetch me a nice tin of Kit-e-Kat? Miaow!"

I must pull myself together, I thought. I must go down to the bank and the shops. There will be nothing open again before Tuesday.

"OK - OK Percy." I got my dufflecoat on and Claire's wellies. It had been snowing in the night.

"Hello, Mum. Everything all right?" Claire had said, phoning earlier in the week. "It's really deep up here. Snowploughs out. Toboggans. You should just see it. Are you sure you don't mind my not coming home for Christmas?"

"Course not, love. It would be a shame to miss all the fun and games up there . . . "

"It would. It's going to be terrific. Big parties every night. And we're fully booked from Christmas Eve. Seventy guests. That's just the residents. There's so much going on . . . "

"What fun, love . . . "

"The granny's coming to look after Edward so that I can help in the dining room. We're going to be so busy. But I should come home, Ma. It's selfish of me not to. You'll be on your own and everything."

"No," I lied, stroking Percy. "I won't be on my own."

"Oh, right - I'd forgotten about the Toy Boy. I'll be home on the third. By-ee!"

I found I couldn't do anything. I couldn't eat. I couldn't read. I couldn't watch telly.

"He wasn't worth it, my lass," Walter was to say in the New Year. "I wish you'd phoned me."

I couldn't cry. I couldn't even paint.

I lay on my bed a lot, a fierce pain in my heart and my scalp tingling so that I scarcely dared get up and look in the mirror in case my hair should have turned white. Or indeed have fallen out leaving my plaits on the pillow like a wig.

Post came. Christmas post. Cards and parcels from my loving family and friends. I left it all piled on the sittingroom floor. There was no word from Rupert.

"Was Rupert his middle name?" Walter was to ask. "I remember you once told me he was really called Thomas."

"She recognises something of Rupert Brooke in me," my young dentist would explain to people, chuffed. "Something of the poet's delicacy. His sensitivity. The same fine profile."

"Was that it?" asked Charlie, amazed.

"Actually, I called him after Rupert Bear. Remember that scarf he always wore? Yellow and brown checks?"

In the middle of the night I wrote him a long pain-full letter.

How could you be so cruel? Why didn't you tell me sooner? They were right after all - you were just using me. Oh, Rupert...

But in the morning I tore it up.

Come on, Swami, I told myself firmly. Haven't you learnt anything from this? Nothing is permanent. It was good while it lasted.

I started again.

Dear Rupert,
I'm sorry I've been so blind. I'm an idiot (but not a randy cow, thankyou), and an ageing idiot at that. Hope I haven't caused

you too much embarrassment with my ludicrous assumptions. Perhaps we can still. be friends. Affectionately . . .

P.S. The Buddha was right. Our pain does come from our attachments.

After I'd posted it, I felt better. I felt clean again. Free.

"You sure you'll be all right, Ma?" Henry repeated rather guiltily, phoning the night before he set off for a fortnight's skiing in Norway with Belinda and a party from college. "I feel bad about going away at Christmas."

"Don't be daft, lovey. I'll be fine. And anyway, I'm not going to be on my own. We'll have a family celebration when you and Claire get home."

"Oh, Mum," Charlie had said, phoning from work, "as we came to you last Christmas, we've promised Tony's Dad we'll go over there this year. I didn't realised the kids would both be away."

I was tempted to tell Charlie, but I knew it would only upset her. Spoil their Christmas. Bring her rushing down the M1 to comfort me.

"I'm not going to be on my own, love. And anyway, you don't all have to feel responsible for keeping me company for ever and ever. I'll be fine."

I was glad I'd ventured out at last. There was a brass band playing on the steps of the Town Hall and carol singers in the Shopping Precinct.

Good King Wenceslas looked out . . .

It was impossible not to step jauntily along in time to the music.

"Hello!"

"Hello!"

"Happy Christmas!"

I loaded my shopping trolley with tangerines and the most expensive cat food.

"Chrysanthemums, lady? Fresh cut this morning."

Oh, to hell with it. Why not? Only myself to please now. "Some white ones please, and a yellow bunch too. Lovely. Thank you. Happy Christmas."

"They're instead of a tree," I explained to Percy as I spooned him out a generous portion of supper. "And don't you go knocking them over, mind." I couldn't remember when I'd ever treated myself to a bunch of flowers before.

I stoked up the sittingroom fire and brought in enough logs and coal for a siege.

"Come on, Percy," I called, as he dug himself a hole in the snow. "I'm going to barricade us in, right? Hurry up, or I'll miss the Carols from King's."

This is nice, I thought, settling down with a tray in the firelight. No turkey to stuff. No sprouts to prepare. No mince-pies or Christmas pud. There's a lot to be said for pleasing yourself.

I began to open the post that had been piling up for days. Cards. A book token. Two Marks & Spencer tokens. More cards. Oh, Gawd - the bank statement. Overdrawn as usual. They could have waited till after Christmas to tell me. A long letter from Saudi Arabia. Poor Kate would be feeling lost out there at this time of year. So far from home.

The phone rang. Rupert . . . ?

It was Jim. "Hi! Why haven't you been in touch? Have you heard from Penguin? Have you seen our reviews? We've made it, kid! It's going to be a best seller."

I rummaged through the rest of the mail till I found the envelope from the publisher.

We are delighted to tell you that in addition to being chosen as Children's Book of the Year by The Guardian, 'Flora's Holiday' has been short-listed for the Hans Christian Anderson award . . . reprinting early in the New Year . . . negotiating with our branch in New York . . . our cheque is enclosed for £932 royalties up to December 31st . . .

Wow! We'd made it! Jim's book had made it. His story and my pictures. Wow!

The phone rang again. Stella.

"We're thinking of going to Midnight Mass. Out at Chilcombe. Wondered if you'd like to come with us? You know how quaint it is out there. Come over for a drink beforehand. I could pick you up in an hour or so."

"That's very kind of you, but I'm so cosy here, Stella, I don't think I can bear to move. I might watch the service on telly. Thank you for thinking of me. Happy Christmas."

Among the many parcels was one that looked remarkably like a bottle. Oh blow it, I thought. Why wait till tomorrow. I'll open it now.

I wept a little into my sweet sherry during the service from York Minster. For Christmases past and loved ones far away. But not much. You can't sing while you're crying.

Angels from the realms of glory . . .

I love that one. I got quite carried away by the 'Glorias'.

"Come on, Percy - we'll open another parcel."

I opened them all in the end. Well that's what they do on the Continent, isn't it? We opened our presents on Christmas Eve the year I was in Switzerland.

"Anyway, we've only got ourselves to please now, haven't we, Percy?" He sighed and stretched seductively on the hearthrug beside me.

I poured another glass of sherry and spread my gifts out around me.

From Claire there was a big thick hard-backed note-book, three hundred pages of fine lined A4. Brilliant! The sort we both used as Diaries. Could even write a novel in it.

Henry had got me a record. "Not my cup of tea," he'd written on the label, "but I know you always go into raptures when this fellow's stuff comes on the radio."

It was John Dowland. The lovely haunting songs of John Dowland.

There was a knobbly little parcel that Rupert had left on his last fateful visit. A tin badge with a rainbow on it that he'd picked up at one of the New Age festivals, no doubt. And a rubber frog. "A grizzly Christmas to one and all," he'd written.

The parcel from Walter was very heavy, and it clinked mysteriously. Oh, my dear friend, I thought when I'd got the wrapping off. Oh, Walter!

It was a Solitaire board. Carved from mahogany. Heavy and dark with a rich pattern in the wood. He'd made it himself, I knew. There was his benchmark on it, his double-arched bridge. With it was a hessian bag of glass marbles.

"They must be Victorian," Peg was to say with envy when she came over with her girls on Boxing Day. "Look at the swirls of colour in them. They are probably quite valuable. Wherever could he have found them?"

"Ah!" he was to tell me when I phoned him. "I was a great one for marbles in my youth. And as it happens, so was my Grandfather before me. I'd got a feeling you would appreciate them."

There was bubble bath from Charlie, and a box of *petits fours*. And a book.

"At last I've found myself a copy of *Precious Bane*," she'd written on a card inside it. "You've probably forgotten, but this is the copy you gave me when I went out to Australia. I was going to give you the new edition, but decided you'd rather have this one back. I know how hard it was for you to pass it on to me. I've taken good care of it, and now send it back with much love."

I'll leave the family parcels till they get home, I thought, surveying my spoils. How lucky I am. How very lucky.

I opened the *petits fours* (umm, delicious!) and put another log on the fire. Percy stretched luxuriously and settled back to sleep.

I picked up Mary Webb's masterpiece. This was quite the nicest present Charlotte could have sent me. It was the copy my mother had given me when I went to college. The 1928 edition published by Jonathan Cape. My father had bought it for her in their student days. Since passing it on to Charlie, I'd never found another *Precious Bane*, though now I came to think about it, I had read somewhere that Virago had brought out a new edition recently.

I flicked through it with delight. Here were old friends. Prue Sarn and her brother Gideon. Mister Beguildy and Jancis. And Kester Woodseaves, the weaver. Here was warmship and tossy balls of paigle, or cowslip as we would call them. And the brooding waters of Sarn Mere.

As soon as I could write . . .

Years ago, in my college days I expect, I had underlined the passage on page 14.

As soon as I could write, I made a little book with a calico cover, and every Sunday I wrote in it any merry time or good fortune we had had in the week, and so kept them. And if times had been troublous and bitter for me, I wrote that down too, and was eased.

I set Walter's bright marbles out on the polished Solitaire board and started to play. But it was no good, I always ended up with not one but five or six marbles scattered all over the place. I could never get one on its own in the centre hole.

I turned the John Dowland record over and poured myself another glass of sherry.

Then, as the Christmas bells rang out across the town, I took up the thick notebook Claire had given me, and opening it at the first page I wrote in bold capital letters :

SOLITAIRE

Chapter One

And underneath, neatly and firmly,

"I suppose you could say it started ...

Joy Peach
Whitby
January 1995